SIX SORC

Book O1.

THE TRIPLETS

By

Nicole M Davis

The Triplets

by Nicole M Davis

First Printing: 2017

ISBN-13: 978-1981522231

ISBN-10: 1981522239

To contact the author or for more information, visit:

nicole-m-davis.com

For every

quiet child
loner kid
freak
outcast
dreamer
and
fool.

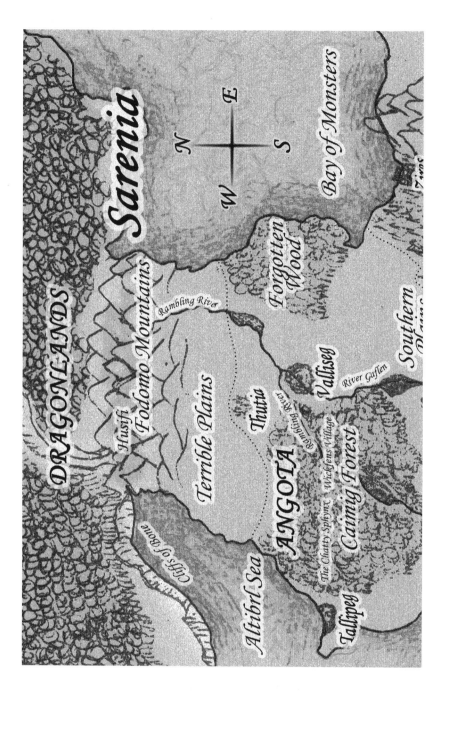

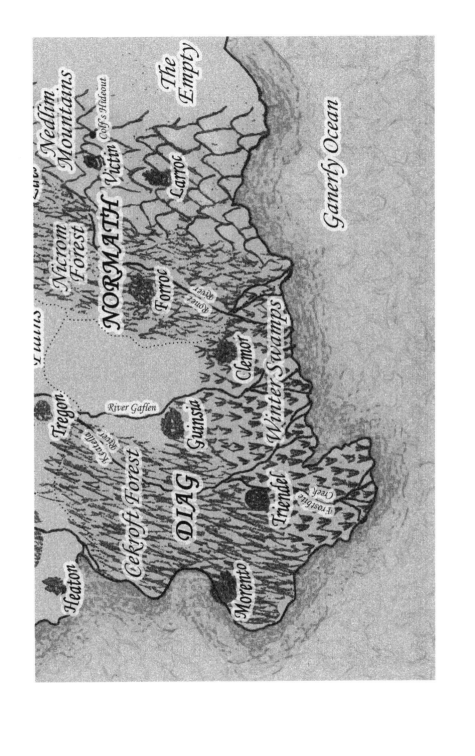

CONTENTS

A Note on Languages:

The native people of Sarenia speak Sarenian, which is a blend of mostly late-modern English, some early-modern English, some other languages, and lots of made up words. You'll hear what it sounds like at first from the characters who have trouble understanding it, but as they get used to it the accents and colloquialisms will fade out of the writing. Sarah is a special case: because she can instantly understand and translate any language she hears, any foreign languages or dialects in her sections will be translated to American English. Any time Sarah is using her powers to translate, the dialogue will be in italics.

Prologue

GRETTA

67th day of Summer
Year 1452

Basement of a house
Ontori, Denadia

retta Thomas looks up from the pile of papers on her desk when the door creaks open. Darkness creeps in through the single high window, kept at bay by the stack of candles at the corner of the desk. Distant sounds of yelling and singing echo through the night air, far away from Gretta's cellar. Four streets away, the festival of Larosri is in full swing. So who would rather spend their time in Gretta's cellar than out on the colorful, spectacular streets of the Ontori market on festival night? Besides Gretta herself, of course.

A gloved hand and the toe of a boot emerge from behind the door, followed by a familiar face beneath a pair of dark sunglasses and slicked back hair.

Gretta sets her pen down, a smile tugging at the corner of her mouth. "Mr. Lee."

He smiles back at her, though it seems forced, and dips his head. "Gretta."

"Is there a reason you've come by so late? And on festival night, at that?" she folds her hands together on top of the desk, covering the papers spread across it.

He forces another smile and moves to sit in the chair across from her. "I came to ask for a favor." He takes the sunglasses off so he can stare at her with deep brown eyes —haunted eyes, too old for his face.

Gretta unfolds her hands and picks up the papers, shuffling them into a neat stack. "What sort of favor?"

He hesitates, thumbing one of the hinges on the sunglasses.

Gretta glances pointedly down at them, "Those aren't meant to be worn at night. You shouldn't even have them out in plain sight. This is Denadia, not America. Sunglasses aren't supposed to exist here."

He grins, and this time it's real. "Is anyone going to notice at the Ontori market?"

Gretta snorts. "You have a point. But enough of that— what did you need?"

Mr. Lee digs through the inside pockets of his jacket and produces three envelopes. Gretta can make out the tangled lines of Mr. Lee's handwriting through the thin paper.

"I need these Cursed," says Mr. Lee, leaning back in the chair and crossing his arms in front of his chest.

Gretta raises an eyebrow. "Cursed how?"

Mr. Lee lets out a long breath. "You're not going to like this."

"Colf's making you bring the boys back, isn't he?" The

2

corner of his mouth tips downward into a slight frown. So that's why he's here: Colf must have convinced him to try and fix things. It's not going to do any good, not in Gretta's opinion anyway, but Colf tends to get what he wants and people tend to get hurt if he doesn't. "Okay," she says, "You're right, I don't like it. But you don't have to argue; I'll help you. I understand."

Mr. Lee stares back at her, face impassive, no doubt schooling away his surprise. Gretta swallows down a laugh. "I know what he did to my daughter—that was a long time ago. You're here on the night of Larosri's festival, one of three nights when the veil between the worlds is the thinnest. I have to assume you want those letters Cursed to bring someone—or three someones, in your case—from one world to the next." Gretta stops and closes her eyes for a minute as a combination of guilt, sadness, and mild panic wells up in her chest. "My plan to stay away didn't help much, did it?" *And not just that plan—all of it was for nothing.*

At least she's always had her daughter's best interests at heart, which is more than she can say for Colf. Gretta splays her fingers flat on the desk, feeling the smooth grain of the old wood. "And I would rather *you* did it in place of Colf and his gang of misfits. At least you know what you're doing." *At least you actually care about those boys.*

Mr. Lee's face continues to be unreadable. "Not all of them are like that, you know."

The corner of Gretta's mouth quirks. "Not Cremon, right?"

"Or his brother."

3

Gretta decides she won't scoff, and bites her tongue to keep from doing so. "Let's agree to disagree on that count. But you have letters that need Cursing, and I have to get to bed some time tonight. I'll need your help for these, correct?"

Mr. Lee nods. "It *is* a Vanishing Curse."

Gretta gets to her feet, stretching out the kinks in her back. "Right. Let's get this over with, then."

PART 1

ACROSS WORLDS

Chapter One

TYLER

October 28th
2016

Aurora, Colorado

Tyler Martin holds a book open between the fingers of his right hand as his feet crunch across the gravel. Tall picket fences loom on either side, shielding the houses and their occupants from view of the alley. The pages of the book are rough and worn under the pads of his fingers. He's walking home today so he can read. There would have been too much noise on the bus, and right now he needs to lose himself in someone else's life.

The reason is tucked just inside the cover of the book. A note—a slip of lined paper, the inky silhouettes of words bleeding through it's envelope. He found it on the top shelf of his locker this afternoon, just beneath the ribbed slats that let in the air. He recognized the handwriting before he could open the letter, so he hadn't dared to read it.

Even now, the sickly sweet mix of anxiety and anticipation tugs at him, dragging his mind out of the book and back to the here and now. He tries to swallow it down —pushing it behind Hamlet's cold detachment and the pleading of Rosencrantz and Guildenstern. But the book can only do so much. His eyes glide over the words without taking them in, his thoughts drifting back to the note.

Mr. Lee gave Tyler this book. In fact, Mr. Lee gave Tyler an entire collection of Shakespeare plays. But *Hamlet* has always been Tyler's favorite, the one book he tucks under his pillow every night because he can't sleep unless it's there. The others are gone—stolen, lost, and burned—but *Hamlet* remains.

The note is the first he's heard from Mr. Lee in seven years. Before he left, he was the only real friend Tyler had ever had. The note—now tucked carefully into the inside cover of *Hamlet*—isn't welcome, not anymore.

Tyler's fingertips scrape across the cover as the book is pulled from his grasp.

"Well, well, well," Rick Andrews snaps the book shut and claps the cover against the palm of his hand, "What have we here?" The syllables drip like poison from his mouth, past the smirk decorating his *stupid* face.

Tyler's feet are stuck to the ground. He doesn't dare look away from the book. Andrews could take it, throw it, stomp on it—Tyler can't let that happen. "Give it back, Andrews," he snarls.

"Oh-ho!" Andrews crows, glancing over at his pack of friends just behind him, "Tough guy, huh? That's funny," he looks up at the sky, scratches the side of his head, "Wasn't it just last week I found something of yours?" He looks at the book and then back up at Tyler, frowning, "Was it this book, Zack?"

"Yeah, you know, I think it was."

"Yeah, that's right. I tried to return it, didn't I? And what does *he*—" Andrews sticks his *grubby, disgusting* finger into Tyler's face "—do when I try to give it back?"

"He tried to punch you, didn't he?"

Andrews smirks again, waving his hand with the book around like the *stupid lunatic* he is. The others laugh.

"Though," Andrews says with a frown, once his cronies stop laughing, "It's not like it would have hurt much, since you're a talking twig." *Try for something original, Andrews. You used that one last week.* His friends laugh again, like a gaggle of incompetent hyenas eager to please the lion so he'll leave them a scrap or two. Tyler doesn't care. Andrews will throw the book over the fence and into one of the yards if Tyler isn't careful. The book—and the note.

A new kind of panic seizes Tyler's buzzing veins. *He's going to lose the letter.* Or, even worse, Andrews might read it.

Andrews and his friends are talking, laughing again. The bully's face is turned to the side. Tyler lunges forward, reaching for it. Andrews jerks it out of the way and a fist collides with Tyler's jaw.

He staggers backwards, cupping the side of his face. Laughter echoes around him, pounding through his skull. *The book.* Where's the book?

There—dangling in the loose grip of Andrews' right hand. Tyler lunges. Andrews grabs his wrist, and purely on instinct, Tyler swings his other hand at Andrews' face. Andrews lifts his arm up to block the blow, and Tyler's open palm collides with a smack just below Andrews' elbow.

A scream rips through the air as Andrews stumbles backwards, the book tumbling from his fingers to hit the ground with a quiet thud. Tyler lurches toward it, but doesn't pick it up. Why did Andrews cry out like that? Tyler couldn't have hit him *that* hard, could he?

He looks up. Andrews is standing a few yards away, flanked by his posse, cradling his arm against his chest.

"What did you do, you freak!" he yells. Andrews' gaze is fixed on Tyler's hands. Tyler looks down, and jumps backwards, stretching his arms out as far away from the rest of him as possible. Thick, ruby-red tendrils snake out from the centers of his palms to the tips of his fingers. Smoke drifts up from the red lines and dissipates into the cold October air. As Tyler watches, his palms burst into flame.

He jerks backwards, feet scrabbling for purchase against the loose gravel, but loses his footing and falls onto his back. He rolls sideways and scrambles to his feet, losing sight of his hands for a second. When he looks at them again, they're not red. Breath escapes his lips in gasping puffs, mixing with the smoke still drifting out of his palms. But there's no more fire.

Andrews and his posse are gone. Tyler grabs the book and stuffs it inside of his jacket, out of the wind and away from grasping hands. His knees are shaking so hard he can barely stand. He swallows, trying to disperse the panic crawling up his throat.

He turns around and sprints down the alley.

Chapter Two

ALEX

October 28th
2016

Hughes Academy High School
Denver, Colorado

lex Scott sits at his desk in his world history class, tapping the eraser of his pencil against the fake wood. He usually pays attention in this class. History is stories, and buried in the dates and names and other trivia are people— just regular people—doing extraordinary things. Alex often wonders if he'll ever do something significant enough that people will remember it hundreds of years in the future. He knows the odds of that are so low they barely count at all, but he likes to pretend sometimes that he could be capable of changing the world for the better.

But today his thoughts aren't with the lesson Mrs. Hampton is giving. His stomach has been twisting itself into tighter and tighter knots since this morning, and by now it's getting kind of hard to breathe.

Today, Alex's mother is coming home. Or she's supposed to be. The past three times she's promised to come back and try to talk things out with Alex's dad, she hasn't shown up. Each time she'd canceled, she'd had a different excuse. The first time she'd called his dad, Alex had snuck down the stairs and stood in the hallway to listen. When she explained that Alex's sister Lilly needed her and she couldn't leave the older girl by herself right now, it stung Alex more than he'd like to admit. It felt like she was putting her older daughter over her younger son. An older daughter who also refused to talk to Alex.

Though maybe he deserved that from both of them.

Alex isn't sure if he wants to see her again—he might manage to screw things up even more. But the anxiety is killing him and he wants to get it over with.

The bell rings, jolting Alex out of his thoughts so sharply that he jumps, hitting his knee against the bottom of the desk and losing his grip on the pencil. It lands under the desk. He bends down and retrieves it, feeling sick. It takes him several minutes longer than usual to pack his notes up into his backpack. The wane smile he gives Mrs. Hampton as he walks out the door takes about as much effort as rolling a boulder up a steep hill. She looks like she's going to ask, "Are you okay, Alex?" like she does sometimes when he doesn't participate in class, so he walks faster and forces another smile. He doesn't want to talk to her. Not today. Alex *hates* it when people worry about him. If he's honest with himself, he doesn't think he deserves it.

Once he's out of the building, Alex looks up at the clear sky and lifts a hand to shield his face from the bright sunlight. It's supposed to rain today, but it doesn't look like it will. Clear skies are supposed to be good, sure, but Alex likes the rain. And anyway, good for who? The plants would appreciate the rain. It's all just a matter of perspective.

He taps his fingers against the side of his leg as he walks, unable to keep them still. He should stop at the store before he gets home. His dad asked this morning if Alex would pick up a few things before his mom showed up. If she shows up at all. At least it'll give him a chance to try and settle his nerves.

The chime on the door rings as he enters the market. The cashier gives him a nod from the counter: Alex nods and tries to smile back, but it comes out more like a grimace. As he heads for the refrigerated aisle to pick out some milk and eggs, a familiar smell drifts through the air from somewhere to his left. It's coming from a table stacked with pies: cherry, lemon, and apple too. Alex frowns and walks over, picking up one of the apple ones.

Memories of his mother and older sister, crowding up the kitchen and laughing, flood his mind. He's nine again, his hands covered in flour and butter, trying to stir the lumpy dough with a large wooden spoon. His mother tosses together apples and cinnamon and Lilly does the dishes in the sink behind them. Alex's dad walks in the room, eyes shining and happier than Alex has seen him in a long time, a tiny, crying bundle cradled in his arms—

Alex shakes his head, stopping the memory there. He can't think about that yet, at least not until he sees his mother. If he sees her. But just in case, he adds the pie to his basket. He pays for the food, packs it into his backpack, and heads out the door.

Red and blue lights flash down the sidewalk on the way

home, an orange-and-white striped barricade fencing off the walkway. There's a different way he can go, but—oh, it's not *that hard.* He won't look at it.

But when he turns the corner before the playground, he can't help but stare. The equipment is shiny, new, and reminds him that it's been a few years since he walked home this way. He walks at the edge of the grass and cranes his neck to glimpse the basketball court. *It* hasn't changed—the tarmac's still cracking, the paint on the rackets rubbing off. Alex even imagines a tiny pink bow, stranded in the middle of the faded tarmac, glinting softly in the sunlight.

And suddenly he can't look anymore. He can't go this way again. Never, never again. He hunches his shoulders, pulling his backpack higher by the straps, and sprints down the rest of the street.

His foot snags on a crack and Alex barely has time to fling his hands out in front of his body to break his fall. His knees smart from scrapes and the palms of his hands sting. A car skids somewhere far away from the playground, cutting into the relative quiet. He curls into a ball, hugging his knees to his chest. Something crinkles in the pocket of his jacket. It's an envelope. Alex pulls it out, running a shaky finger across the seal at the top. *Alex Scott* is written in neat cursive across the front. Desperate for something to distract him from his memories of the playground, Alex runs a fingernail through the top of the envelope, ripping it open. He crosses his legs on the sidewalk and lets the paper fall open into his lap.

Hello Alex,

My name is Mr. Lee. I don't know if you remember, but we knew each other once, when you were very young. I'm going to assume that your parents have told you that you are adopted. I knew your birth parents. As of now, I do not know their fate.

Alex's fingers curl around the edges of the paper. Who is this Mr. Lee? His birth parents? Yes, Alex knows he's adopted, just like his older sister Lilly. She's his biological sister; his parents adopted them both through an agency when they were very young. Alex knows his birth parents didn't want him, and he can't say he's surprised. He isn't going to lie and say it doesn't bother him, but he hasn't thought about his birth parents since he was little. He never knew them, and he isn't sure he would ever want to meet them. He has no memory of this Mr. Lee.

But I do know the fate of someone who was close to them, someone who blames himself for what he did to you and five other children like you. However much he believes that there is no way to right this wrong, a friend of his insists that he attempt to set things right, even if doing so would cause you more harm than good.

Please understand that I am sorry, excruciatingly so, for what is about to happen to you. I just need you to understand that I wanted no part in this: my hand has been forced.

Sincerely,
Mr. Lee

For what is about to happen to me? That's pretty ominous. And maybe a little threatening. Alex swallows, glancing back at the park and across the street, making sure no one is watching him. He starts to get up...but he can't. Nausea roils up from the bottom of his stomach all the way to his throat. He shuts his eyes tightly, trying to block out the too-bright light. His ears are ringing. The sidewalk falls out from beneath him, and he's dumped into endless space.

Chapter Three

DARN

October 28th
2016

Harrison Residence
Denver, CO

arn Harrison (well, Max Harrison really, but he hasn't gone by Max since he was eight) has the upper half of his body buried in the closet. Shirts and sweaters dangle down against his back as he leans over a set of drawers, groping helplessly in the crack between it and the wall. His nose is smashed against the top of the dresser. It's uncomfortable. He can't stop a whine from escaping his throat as he opens and closes his fingers around nothing.

"Darn!" His cousin, Trish, calls from downstairs, "Are you in costume yet? We're going to be late!"

"I can't reach it!" It was just there, on top of the dresser, and now he can't reach...

"We're going to be late!" He can hear the sour twist of Trish's mouth in her voice, "We should have left already!"

Darn slumps into a boneless heap on top of the dresser. He blows a strand of hair out of his face and groans as he gets up and backs out of the closet. He'll have to pull the dresser out. He grabs each corner from the back, wrapping his fingers around the polished wood, and wrenches it forward. Sure enough, there's the costume, puddled on the floor against the wall. He slips out of his regular clothes and squirms his way into the black fabric.

He throws on an extra-long black t-shirt with triangles cut out of the bottom over the morph suit, then fastens a thick black belt around his waist to hold it in place. There's supposed to be a hat. Where's the hat? Darn swears.

"We're already late, in case you didn't catch that the first time I said it!" Trish yells, "I'm leaving without you! Now!"

"Shit, shit, shit. I'll be there in one second!" Darn twists around to reach the zipper down his back and tugs it up to the base of his neck. He can see fine with the suit zipped over his head, but Trish is paranoid and won't let him drive that way. Darn runs into the bathroom to glance in the mirror, just to make sure it looks okay. He looks sort of like what he's supposed to be…maybe. As long as Peter Pan's shadow is a seventeen-year-old kid with bright orange hair and freckles. It should be more obvious once he has it zipped over his head with the hat on. The hat. Trish makes a frustrated noise so loud Darn can hear it upstairs. He winces. He'll just have to leave the hat.

He dashes down the hallway and slides down the banister of the stairway, hoping to catch Trish at least before she's in the car. She can't leave without him—it's his car and he's driving—but he doesn't want to tick her off any more than he already has. Mad Trish is no fun.

She stands in the hallway, dark hair pulled back in a bun under her fancy green Peter Pan hat with the usual pair of

enormous glasses perched on her nose. She's all dressed up
—probably has been for several hours—in green tights and
a long green t-shirt that matches Darn's black one. She's also
not yelling at Darn. Or moving much. Her attention is fixed
on the newspaper in her hand.

Darn half-walks, half-trips to where she's standing so he
can peer over her shoulder. Her hands are clamped,
knuckles white, around the edges of an article that takes up
half the front page.

THREE GIRLS VANISH WITHOUT A TRACE LAST
JUNE: FAMILIES RENEWING SEARCH EFFORTS

A picture is printed across the top. The three missing
girls stare back out of it. On the left, a short, bronze-
skinned girl with dark freckles and corkscrew curls wears a
smirk and walks a bright red bicycle. On her right, a pretty
black girl with pigtails and a shy smile clutches a book to her
chest. On the far left, a third girl grins so wide it nearly
splits her pale face, her blond hair messy and tangled. The
caption reads: *Anna Thomas (left), Sarah Miller (middle), and
Kaylor Williams (right), all missing since 21st June, 2015.*

Somehow they seem familiar, like Darn knows them
from somewhere or has met them before, but he can't
remember where.

"That girl," Trish points down at the girl with the smile
and the messy hair, "Kaylor. She was in one of my classes,
in middle school."

"Huh," Darn says. Where does he know them from? He

grabs one side of the paper to hold it still so he can read it.

The three friends, who've known each other since they were eleven, never made it home from school on one sweltering June day last summer. Anna Thomas's father, Evan, is convinced his daughter may have left him a trail—

"Darn," Trish drops her end of the paper and tugs once on his sleeve, "We really need to leave."

Darn reluctantly folds the newspaper and sets it down on the table, following Trish out the door. *Anna Thomas. Sarah Miller. Kaylor Williams.* But it's not the names that seem familiar—it's the picture. Darn stops in his tracks to grind his teeth. There's something about that article—those girls —that unsettles him. He turns around and walks back to the table to grab it. He'll be able to look at it once they get to the party.

But it's not the newspaper that catches his eye. Tucked half-under the paper is a plain white envelope, with Max Harrison written on the front. Max, not Darn, so it's not from a friend. There's no return address. Darn picks the envelope out, running the pads of his fingers over the ink. He doesn't recognize the handwriting.

"Darn!" Trish calls from outside.

The party isn't half bad, but the envelope is scratching

against the inside of Darn's pocket. He clutches the glass of punch with a vice-like grip, trying to will the sheen of sweat across his forehead back inside his skin. It doesn't work. So instead, he wipes his brow off with the sleeve of the morph suit, which only works slightly better. Trish is off talking to some of her friends. Darn nods along as the girl in front of him—Jenny something?—chatters on about some movie she saw the other week. Normally, he'd be chattering along with her, probably flirting, certainly drinking, and not worried about Trish or a newspaper or a strange letter in his pocket. But the whole thing is eating at him so much he can't focus. So he smiles at Jenny, excuses himself, and escapes to the bathroom.

He shuts the door and locks it, then pulls the envelope out of his pocket. The writing is visible through the paper of the envelope, but jumbled with folds and not clear enough to make out. Darn slips a finger through the top and tears it open.

Hello Max,

Or should I call you Darn? I hear that's what your friends call you. You'll have to tell me why some day.

It's frustrating, that people always expect an explanation for his nickname. He didn't name *himself* that. He just— doesn't respond to Max, he never has, and one day someone broke a plate and yelled 'Darn it!' and he looked up. Trish started calling him 'Darn it' until it shortened into 'Darn'.

His parents and even some of his teachers have started using the nickname because Max just *isn't him* and he can't *stand* to answer to it. He's tried to go by Dan before by pretending his middle name is Daniel, but that didn't feel right either. For whatever reason, *Darn* is special; it's *his* in a way that Max and Dan never could be.

So he puts up with the taunts and tells the story again and again no matter how much it bothers him to repeat it.

I don't know if you remember, but we knew each other once, when you were very young. I'm going to assume that your parents have told you that you are adopted. I know your birth parents. your father is an associate of mine. As for your mother, I think it would be better to ask your father about her. There are some things I'm not certain either of them would want me to divulge.

But that's not the point of this letter. I also know someone who was close to your parents, particularly your mother, someone who blames himself for what he did to you and five other children like you. However much he believes that there is no way to right this wrong, a friend of his insists that he attempt to set things right, even if doing so would cause you more harm than good.

Please understand that I am sorry, excruciatingly so, for what is about to happen to you. I just need you to understand that I wanted no part in this: my hand has been forced.

Sincerely,
Mr. Lee

What the hell? Who is this guy? For one thing, Darn's not

adopted. He looks *just like* his parents. *Please understand that I am sorry, excruciatingly so, for what is about to happen to you?* That's creepy. That's *really* creepy.

Darn turns around and grabs the doorknob to unlock it, but trips instead. His head hits the door with a thud. The air is heavy as bricks, crushing his lungs and eyes and ears and stomach, forcing him to curl up into a tight ball. The floor drops out from beneath him, and he plunges into a free fall.

Chapter Four

TYLER

October 28th
2016

Aurora, Colorado

The alley dumps out onto a sidewalk, next to a street buzzing with cars and cyclists. Tyler grabs a gray beanie out of his backpack with shaking hands and pulls it down past his ears, covering his bright blond hair. His foster mother, Emily, offered to buy him a pair of dark sunglasses when she took him shopping last weekend. He should have let her get them. He's tall, he's blond, he's blue-eyed, and that makes people notice him. Tyler wishes they wouldn't.

He starts down the street toward his foster home, hunching his shoulders and ducking his head.

He holds his hands out in front of him as he walks, breath billowing out into the cold air. They aren't smoking anymore. They're not red. Did he imagine all of that?

There was something—an inexplicable clicking in the back of his head—that's the only way he can think to describe it. Like flint striking steel, or the click of a lighter as it ignites. He *has* always been fascinated with fire: he lit one of his old foster homes on fire when he was six. He'd been playing with a set of birthday candles from the drawer next to the kitchen sink, trying to find out what they would and wouldn't burn. Come to think of it, he can't remember how he lit the candles in the first place. A lighter? Matches? Either he's forgotten what he used, or he hadn't needed anything.

Tyler takes a deep breath, trying to slow his stuttering heart, and balls his hands into fists, tucking them into his armpits.

But curiosity soon gets the better of him. He sticks his hands out in front of his face, palms up, and concentrates so hard his eyes are forced shut. He cracks open one eyelid, only for a second, as if the fire is shy and might run if he sees it. But his hands are empty. He lets them fall back to his sides. A dog barks in the yard across the street. He's almost home—almost to his foster home.

He goes in through the back door. Emily is probably still at work. Brian, the foster father, is still out volunteering at the soup kitchen, or the homeless shelter, or someplace equally charitable. Which is good for him, but Tyler can't imagine being that selfless. Maybe that sort of thing only comes to people who've always had food and loved ones and a roof over their heads. People who have so much comfort and happiness in their lives that they can afford to give some of it away to strangers.

At least Brian and Emily trust Tyler enough to let him in the house by himself. A few sets of foster parents haven't. He has vivid memories of sitting out on porches or doorsteps in the cold rain, pulling his jacket over his head so he could read without getting his book wet.

Tyler climbs up the stairs and into his room, dumping his school backpack onto the bed. He collapses next to it, hooking an arm through the strap and pulling it up to his chest. He's about to unzip it and look for *Hamlet* when he remembers the book is still in his coat pocket. He sits up and digs it out, tugging the letter from behind the cover. His heart is pounding in his ears. His veins are on fire. Ha—on fire. He chuckles. *God, that wasn't even funny.* He's a wreck.

The envelope rips in a jagged line beneath his trembling fingers. He unfolds the paper, smoothing the creases almost reverently across his lap.

Tyler,

Let me start by saying that I'm sorry. I never meant to leave you all alone like that. I know any excuse I have is going to fall on deaf ears, so I won't bother giving you any. Just know that it had nothing to do with you, and that I did not want to break contact with you.

There is something you need to know. I knew your parents. Even better, I think I know how you can find them. Unfortunately, I cannot write that information here. We'll have to meet in person.

Tyler, when you finish reading this, you are going to be disoriented, confused, and more than likely scared out of your mind. Just remember this—there are five others like you. Their names are Sarah Miller, Kaylor Williams, Anna Thomas, Alex Scott, and Darn Harrison. Find them. You can't do this alone, no matter how much you might want to.

your friend, always,
Mr. Lee

Mr. Lee knew my parents? Why didn't he say anything? Is that why he found Tyler scared, hungry, and alone, on the streets of Denver when he was four? Did Mr. Lee take Tyler away from his parents? Did Tyler's parents *give* him to Mr. Lee? And if so, why?

And Tyler's parents—*I think I know how you can find them.* It says so right there, in the letter. Tyler's parents could be alive. Tyler's parents *exist.*

Around the time he turned seven, Tyler decided he needed to find his birth parents. He asked endless questions of the agents from social services and Mr. Lee, scoured the internet for information about himself and his genealogy, even dug through all the old records at the library looking for someone with the last name "Martin" who might have lived in the area at the time when he was abandoned. He'd found nothing, and later gave up on his search when one of the agents told him he'd picked the name "Tyler Martin" from a list shortly after he was found, because he couldn't remember the one his parents had given him and they needed to call him something.

And, all along, Mr. Lee knew. He *knew*, and he told Tyler nothing. Tyler can't decide if he hates Mr. Lee more for abandoning him or for lying to him about this.

He's going to throw up. In fact, he's also incredibly dizzy. Invisible, heavy coils wind around his chest, choking his breath out through his nose. Tyler gasps, clawing at the air around his torso, but nothing's there. His eyes are forced shut as the bed slides out from beneath him. He falls to the floor, but doesn't stop. Crushing blackness crowds in around him, dragging him down, down, down.

It's dark but for the light of the stars. There are many; more than Tyler's seen before in his entire life. He remembers being told that the city lights cancel out that of the stars, but he'd never imagined just how much. They're so dense in places, they look almost like clouds.

He's not in Colorado anymore.

A laugh explodes out of his mouth. He claps a hand over it to keep them in, but it doesn't help. *You're not in Kansas anymore, Dorothy.* He collapses onto the grass, clutching the backpack to his chest, his face buried in the scratchy fabric, gasping through his breathless laughter. *Mr. Lee, you're a fiend. What have you done?* He stops, sitting up and wiping his mouth. The rough paper is still clasped between his fingers. He brings it up to his face and sniffs it. It doesn't smell off. So that rules out chloroform.

Did he drift off to sleep after he read the letter? But it doesn't feel like a dream. For a start, he's keenly aware of the cold breeze dancing past his face, the strands of long grass pricking through the material of his socks. You're not supposed to feel things like that in dreams.

Something rustles in the dense tangle of trees and brush to Tyler's left. A whisper—barely louder than the quiet murmur of the wind—snakes its way across the surface of his mind. Tyler turns toward the noise, body stiff and ready to move. Another noise, to his right. The whisper skims through his thoughts again, and this time he catches a word:

"...*daylight*..."

Tyler gets to his feet and slings the backpack onto his back, staring deep into the tangle of woods, trying to see past the shadows of undergrowth.

"...*should not be awake!*"

Tyler almost jumps out of his skin. Where is that voice coming from? It doesn't seem to be from any particular direction—and something in his gut says he's not hearing it aloud. Tyler takes a step backward, hardly daring breath. What is this thing, and what does it want with him?

"...*not welcome here.*"

The brush in front of him moves. Something's coming toward him.

"...*is for creatures of darkness.*"

The voice is growing louder. Tyler takes a few more steps backwards, still wondering what the hell's after him. Or if he's just going crazy.

"*You should be sleeping...of darkness. You are not...night is for those...*"

The murmur grows into a whirlwind, chasing his own thoughts around in circles through his head. A single voice rises above the wind, in an icy moment of clarity:

"The day is for creatures of daylight.
The night is for those of darkness.
You are not of the darkness.
You are not welcome here."

He has to get out of here.

Stray branches and leaves tear at Tyler's hair and clothes as he runs through the forest, ripping and scratching against the skin of his face. The beanie's lost somewhere along the way. The creature—or monster—whatever it is, still echoes through his thoughts, pounding at his temples, whipping round the edges and past the corners of his mind. A branch tugs at Tyler's sleeve. He doesn't slow down, barely caring when it rips the sleeve in half.

After what feels like an hour of running, the voice finally starts to soften and drain away. Tyler's muscles ache, his arms and legs sting from hundreds of tiny scratches, his lungs burn as he gasps for air, and his heart feels like it might explode at any second. He chances a glance over his shoulder.

Something rough snags his foot. Tyler's hands fly out in front of his body for balance, but it doesn't do him any good. The ground rushes up to meet him as twigs and branches scratch his face, his forearms flying forward just in time to stop him from hitting the ground. The backpack thuds into the dirt next to him. Something hisses past his ear—more voices, but softer this time, and higher, outside of Tyler's head.

Tiny—fingers?—brush past his cheek, and something

like leaves. Tyler whips his head around to stare into the face of a tiny person, pale against the darkness of the forest, no bigger than the palm of his hand. It's floating in the air, right in front of his nose, with tiny, bat-like wings beating behind its back. It glares back at him before letting out a low hiss and disappearing into the night.

Fern fronds stroke the sides of his head, coaxing it down onto a pillow of moss. More fairies dart about overhead, whispering in harsh voices. Exhaustion steals over him like a thick blanket, chasing away any reservations he might have about sleeping in the forest and replacing them with a bone-deep weariness. His eyelids already drooping, Tyler lays his head down on the forest mulch and lets them close.

Chapter Five

ALEX

67th day of Summer
Year 1452

Altibrl Sea

lex doesn't fall forever. Instead, he plunges out of the darkness and hits a flat surface of water with a smack. It bubbles up and into his nose, through his mouth, stinging his eyes and making him gag. He flails forward, tipping himself upright and swimming to the surface. Water streams out of his mouth and nose as he hits the air. He coughs, getting the last of it out of his lungs. Once his eyes are clear and he's got his breath back, he looks around. The surrounding water is a clear, startling blue, even against the sparkle of stars in the night sky above him. A brilliant full moon glints off the surface, illuminating miles of water around him. It's nothing like the sharp, chemical sting of the pool water where his sister Lilly taught him to swim. It smells salty and a bit like fish.

He treads water for a few minutes, trying to get over the shock of getting dumped in the middle of an ocean—that's what it must be, because of the smell—and figure out where he is, exactly. Something splashes in the water nearby, trying to stay afloat. A head and a pair of shoulders breach the surface, barely recognizable in the bright moonlight. Alex starts to swim over, and that's when he realizes that he's still wearing his backpack. He shrugs it off. There are a couple of notebooks, textbooks, and pencils in it, most of which are probably ruined by now—and the pie. But that doesn't matter, it can't. Alex propels himself closer to the struggling person.

The person gets his head above the water and tries to lunge over to Alex. His head drifts back under, his arms flailing just above the surface. Alex grabs one of the boy's wrists, pulling his arm up and over Alex's shoulders. His head breaks the surface and he sucks in a huge breath, blinking water out of his eyes.

"T-try and tr-tread water," Alex says as the boy's weight pulls him down, "Kick in c-circles, m-move your h-hands in circles."

After a few minutes, they get the hang of it, and manage to keep both their heads above the water. Alex tries to turn the boy loose, since it'd be easier for each of them to swim on their own, but he won't let go of Alex. He tightens his grip when Alex tries to nudge him off. So Alex gives up and tries to look for land while the boy clings to him. Fifty or so yards to the west, beneath the light of the moon, there's a prominent chunk of rock. Alex turns them toward it, trying to kick and move his arms in something resembling a swim stroke.

It takes them longer than it would have if they'd been swimming separately, but they get there. For a minute, Alex worries that his arms are too tired to lift himself out of the water, much less pull them both up onto the rocks.

"Y-you have to let go now," he lifts the boy's arm up and away from his shoulders. He doesn't protest this time.

Alex leaves him in the water while he clambers up the rocks, then reaches down to pull him up and out. Little rivers run down rivulets in the stone, leaving dark trails to the sea. Once they've found a level spot on the rocks, out of the waves' reach, Alex sits on the cold stone and tries to catch his breath. The boy sits next to him. They're both soaked to the bone, and Alex shivers along when the boy's teeth start to chatter.

"Thank you," the boy croaks, and Alex almost jumps out of his skin. That voice...he's heard it somewhere before, but he can't place it. It unnerves him though, like it's connected to a memory he'd rather not revisit.

"I'm Darn." That's an odd name, yet it tickles the back of Alex's mind. The boy—Darn; where has Alex heard that name before?—holds a hand out for Alex to shake, "I think —I probably would have drowned if you hadn't found me."

Alex blinks back at him, meeting the wide eyes and the cautious smile, and even in the dark he recognizes the boy's face.

"A-alex," he takes the offered hand, "You—I was o-only returning the f-favor."

"You—what?" Darn arches his brows, his nose wrinkling, "What do you mean, ret—" he stops short, his forehead wrinkling too. Then his face splits into a wide grin. "Hey—I do know you! You're the guy Trish and I found—

Alex! Hey, you look great, I'm glad you're all right."

Alex swallows, his face starting to burn. *That* is a dark memory. He never thought he'd see Darn—or the girl who'd been with him, Trish—again. He'd kind of hoped he wouldn't. Darn found him after he'd…done something very, very stupid. Darn and Trish more or less saved his life: he had a concussion and several broken bones when they heard him hit the bushes beneath his dad's apartment. Alex doesn't like to think about what could have happened if they hadn't walked by. Still, it's nice to have someone he knows—sort of—around, here on these rocks, in this strange place.

And that, more than anything, convinces Alex that this is all going on in his head. Maybe he's finally gone off the deep end.

"Where are we, anyway?" Darn asks, "I can't remember how I got here."

"I d-don't know," Alex mutters, hating the way his voice drags and jilts, the way it has for as long as he can remember, "I was…walking d-down the sidewalk, and th-then I just…collapsed. And f-fell in…water."

It's strange—too strange. Like something out of a dream, and yet not like that at all. The rock's solid and rough beneath the pads of his fingers, the waves crash and the breeze bites at his skin. It's too vivid, too full of whisper-thin sensations and details to be a dream world. But isn't that what he thought before, too? Isn't that exactly the kind of thinking that got his little sister killed? But wait— there was something else, too.

"I—I was r-reading a letter." *I am sorry, excruciatingly so, for what is about to happen to you*, it had said. He must have lost the letter in the ocean. Who was it that gave it to him? What was the name signed at the end? He glances over at Darn. He's staring back at Alex, but Alex can no longer make out the details of his face in the fading light. Nervous under Darn's stare, he turns back to the ocean.

"I got a letter, too," says Darn.

Alex looks back at him, startled. "W-what did it say?"

Darn shrugs. "Something about how I'm supposedly adopted, some other creepy stuff about me. I think it was from—some guy, Mr. Lee?"

Alex swallows and nods, gut clenching. *Mr. Lee*. "Mine was f-from him, too."

"Huh," Darn picks a pebble out of the rocks and tosses it into the water, "I wonder if he's the reason we're here? Think he kidnapped us, dumped us in the ocean, and left us for dead?"

Alex shoves down the feelings that jolt through him at the mention of a kidnapping and nods. "U-unless it's n-not real," he mumbles. He stares at the water for a minute, trying to find the sidewalk or the neighborhood or even— he forces himself not to wince at the thought of the playground. But there's nothing: nothing but ocean.

A soft breeze floats over the rocks, but Alex doesn't doubt it'll get fiercer and colder the longer they sit here. Especially while they're still soaked to the bone. So he gets to his feet and offers Darn a hand.

"W-we need to find shelter," he explains. Darn takes his

hand and gets to his feet.

Past the rocks is a small section of beach, where they stumble upon a small, narrow cave that's barely tall enough for them to stand in. It's dark, so Alex approaches it cautiously, stepping across the sand as quietly as he can. He stops at the mouth of the cave, Darn at his heels, and hesitates for a second before he enters.

It's shallow, but out of the wind, and a little larger past the narrow entrance. Something moves along the wall, close to the top of the cave. Alex freezes, staring at the movement until it stops.

"It's probably just a bird," Darn's whisper echoes through the tiny space around them.

"Or a b-bat," Alex says. Either way, it's small enough that it shouldn't be able to hurt them.

They sit cross-legged across from each other, backs against the cave walls. The cold night air pricks Alex's skin, despite the absence of the wind. Darn wraps his arms around himself, rubbing his palms against his elbows. It's cold, they're wet, and they both could get sick if they're not careful. But what can they do? They sit in silence for a while, Alex trying to sort through his busy thoughts while Darn rubs his arms and glances back out at the sea.

Alex had been going to see his mother. He'd walked past the playground—*that* playground—and then he'd fallen onto the sidewalk. He'd tripped over something...he hadn't hit his head when he fell, had he? No, the letter. The creepy letter from a strange man, and maybe that had made him faint? But it's not a dream. Dreams feel—different.

But what if Darn's right—what if this Mr. Lee knocked them out and carried them away, only to dump them in the ocean later? Images flash through his mind of a little girl screaming, carried off in the arms of someone Alex couldn't recognize as he tore down the sidewalk after them, running hard until his legs were on fire, feeling so helpless and so desperate as he lost sight of the car speeding down the street. Guilt swamps him, rushing from the top of his head to the tips of his fingers until there's nothing left but shame, and *it was all Alex's fault.*

No. No no no no no no. Alex rocks back and forth, clutching his knees to his chest, forcing the thoughts back into their little black box in the back of his mind and locking it shut and *not thinking about it.* They're out here now. It's cold. Darn's stopped moving, and the shame turns quickly into panic. Alex leans forward, eyes fixed on Darn's chest. After the longest second of Alex's life it rises and then falls—he's still breathing. Alex leans back, scraping his shoulders against the rough stone, heart still pounding in his throat.

It takes him a few more minutes to think to look for firewood.

There isn't much out on the beach besides a few tufts of grass growing between the rocks. Alex picks those out and gathers three or four tiny, sandy pieces of driftwood. He gets back to the cave and sets it up, even though he knows the tiny pile of material won't last long. He has no idea how to light a fire without a lighter or a match, so he tries rubbing two sticks together, but that doesn't do anything.

He groans, drops the sticks back onto the pile, and tries to get comfortable against the stony side of the cave.

They'll head for shore tomorrow and hope it gets warmer. The air is cold, but not freezing: once the sun's out they should warm up quickly. But they have to make it until then. Also, water. The water they fell in is salty, and Alex is already getting thirsty.

There's nothing he can do about it now. He tries to settle in for the night, leaning against the smooth rock behind him and struggling to ignore the dampness of his clothes. But the lack of distractions gives his thoughts room to wander into other unpleasant places. Like the night when Darn found him.

He'd jumped from the fourth story window and ended up bruised and broken but whole in the bushes at the bottom. It was a stupid, *stupid* thing to do. But the guilt made him do it. It had crept up on him, all at once, and with much greater force than it had just now. There was a reason Alex had lost sight of his little sister—*not* lost sight, been distracted—and that's the other thing. Alex is *crazy*, and not in the harmless-almost-cool way other kids sometimes claim to be, but legitimately bonkers. And his older sister knows it. That's why she hasn't come back home. He's sure of it.

His mother knows, too, and his father, but his parents never believed him the way Lilly does. Maybe she finally convinced his mother. If his mother hadn't trusted Alex to look after Cassandra, if Alex had never tried to tell them about the ghosts, if he'd never tried to end his life by jumping out of the apartment window. They all would have been happier without him.

So what use is he? What good is he if he ruins the lives of everyone around him?

Feeling the guilt creep up on him again, Alex tries to steer his thoughts in another direction. He has to be alive for a reason: so what is that? Alex just saved Darn's life. Maybe he's here to save Darn, the way Darn saved him before.

That's what he'll do. Alex will watch Darn like a hawk, get them both out of this place alive and safe, and bring Darn home.

Chapter Six

TYLER

1st day of Tivar
Year 1452

Caimig Forest

Something scratches Tyler's cheek. Something that certainly isn't a blanket or a pillow, and therefore has no business being in his bed. Then again, the hard, lumpy surface beneath him doesn't feel much like a bed. A rock digs painfully into a soft spot between his shoulder blades. And why does everything smell like dirt?

A tiny stream of air billows past his ear.

Tyler jolts upright, his eyes snapping open. A small cloud of fairies flutter into the air, hissing angrily. Fern fronds rustle with the movement, the closed purple flowers wound through their leaves spilling little cascades of black seeds down into his lap. He picks up one of the seeds, holding it to his face and crushing it between his fingers. It smells sweet, and just a bit smoky. A sudden wave of dizziness roils through his head. He chucks the crushed seed away and wipes his fingers off on his pants, trying to get rid of the smell.

One of the fairies buzzes past his ear, grumbling angrily.

Somehow the fact that there are fairies flying in front of his face doesn't seem as strange as it should. Oh. Right. There was a letter, and—whatever the hell happened that brought him to this forest. And then the stars, that terrifying voice in his head, and the fairies.

What is Mr. Lee playing at?

Tyler's memories start when he was around five or six, and the first vivid one he has is of Mr. Lee. It's of a smile on Mr. Lee's face, a tousle of Tyler's hair and the answering warm feeling when he the stack of books into Tyler's small hands. "Keep those safe," Mr. Lee said, "Books can be your friends when you've got no one else." Tyler took that to heart, nodding along solemnly. Mr. Lee's expression turned sad then, distorted in a way Tyler's young mind didn't like.

"What's wrong?" he asked.

Mr. Lee smiled at him again, but there was something stretched and wrong about it this time. "I have to leave, Tyler. But I'll be back soon," the hand was back in Tyler's hair, a thumb stroking across his cheek, "Just keep those books safe for me, okay?"

Tyler nodded. "Okay."

Tyler's stomach grumbles. He closes his eyes for a second, trying to bring the memory back to the surface, but it doesn't come. Mr. Lee came back many times, at least once a month, until Tyler had turned seven, then three or four times a year until he'd turned ten. Then he disappeared, and Tyler waited and waited and waited, but he never returned. So Tyler cut his losses, held on to the books, and tried to forget the only person who'd ever really cared about him.

He crosses his legs and pulls his backpack into his lap. He's lucky it was hooked around his elbow when he read Mr. Lee's letter, and that he had the presence of mind to swing it onto his back last night. There's a water bottle in the side pocket, and a few granola bars. Tyler pulls them out.

Where is Mr. Lee, anyway? Hadn't he written to tell Tyler they needed to talk in person? The letter is still tucked into the pocket of his jacket—he pulls it out and looks over it again. *When you finish reading this, you are going to be disoriented, confused, and more than likely scared out of your mind.* Mr. Lee must have known about this—about the forest, and the fairies, and maybe even that creature that chased him last night. He takes another bite of the granola bar, setting the letter down on his lap and tracing the words with a finger. *Just remember this—there are five others like you. Their names are Sarah Miller, Kaylor Williams, Anna Thomas, Alex Scott, and Darn Harrison. Find them.* But how? Why? He groans, crushing the wrapper of the granola bar into a tiny silver ball. This is insane. Why is he here, and where is Mr.

Lee?

A sprinkle of cheerful sunlight flickers overhead as a bird streaks through the leaves, crowing loudly in the quiet of the forest. Maybe it has razor-sharp feathers and a poisonous tongue. Who knows? There were fairies this morning.

Cryptic messages from ex-friends and poisonous birds aside, Tyler needs to focus on getting out of this forest as soon as possible. He hasn't been out in the woods more than once or twice, when he lived with a family who liked going camping. But he's read all about this sort of thing. The first thing you're supposed to do is find water. He gets to his feet, brushing dirt and bits of crushed leaves off of his shirt and pants. His second objective is to find food. You're not supposed to eat the plants if you're not an expert, which means he might have to hunt for squirrels. He grimaces, hiking the backpack up higher on his shoulders. Third is shelter. Fortunately, the thick cover of trees overhead should be enough to protect him from large amounts of rain or snow, but it won't be enough to keep out the cold. He hesitates, and then scoops up a handful of the black seeds he's crushed earlier and shoves them into his pocket. If this plant put him to sleep last night, the seeds might be a good thing to have around. In case he meets someone he needs to knock out. Or maybe he can use them to make a trap for a squirrel.

But if he can find other people, he won't have to worry about eating squirrels. His best bet for that is a road. After a few minutes of wandering aimlessly through the trees, hoping to God he'll see someone or something that indicates the presence of any people at all, he finds a very small, very narrow trail. It looks more like a deer track, but it's not like he can see anything else here to follow. Luckily he hasn't run into anything nasty yet. Besides the shapeless monster that screamed at him in his head last night, of course. But that doesn't seem to be out and about now.

He could climb a tree…but none of these really look large enough to support his weight. This part of the forest obviously hasn't been around for very long, since most of the trees around him are aspens—at least, they look like aspens—and none of them have very thick trunks. They're large and dense enough, though, that they block the sunlight with a spider web of shadows.

The path opens up to a small clearing, and on the other side is an oak tree. Maybe he can climb that.

He soon finds out that he's much, much less than adept at climbing trees, as he can only manage to get a few feet off the ground. Once his hands are covered in scrapes and his shoe has fallen off twice, he finds that it's much easier trying to jump up and grab a higher branch than it is to wrap his arms around the trunk and try to dig his fingernails into the bark. He's never done this before, okay? He's used to hiding in his room, with his books, where the other kids can't pick on him. Or make fun of him for failing at climbing trees.

After several frustrating minutes, he does manage to get up the tree far enough that he can see over the top of the forest. There's a dark line—a small gap in the solid green blanket of leaves—and it isn't too far away. If it's not a road, it's probably a stream, and that's just as good. A stream might lead somewhere too, or will at least give him a source of water once the plastic bottle runs out. He climbs down and stumbles through the forest towards it.

It's a road. Or else a very wide, very straight path. People—or perhaps some other sort of intelligent creature, who knows—definitely had a hand in making this. Wheel and horse tracks litter the packed earth. Tyler sticks to the edge of the trail, following the direction of most of the horse tracks. He's delighted when he finds some shoe prints too, since this makes the whole thing seem a little less dangerous. Other people—lots of other people, judging by the number of tracks—have been this way. Tyler hikes his backpack higher on his back and keeps moving.

The sound of hoof beats and the clack of cart wheels sets Tyler's heart racing a few minutes later. Should he stop? Turn around and say hello? Or should he duck into the bushes on the side of the road and hide until they go past? He'd much rather go with the second option, but what if these people know where the next town is?

The cart gets closer. Tyler, heart pounding in his throat, ducks sideways into the bushes, crouching down low enough to make himself invisible. It's a horse-drawn carriage. Two men sit at the front, one of them gripping the reins. They're talking, but Tyler's too far away to make out what they're saying. From what he can see, the cart is full of closed barrels. They must be heading somewhere with those barrels, and Tyler's willing to bet people and safety are in that direction. If not, he can always ask the people on the cart for help. If he gets desperate.

He moves back onto the road once they've passed and follows the cart, sticking close to the trees.

He's finished the rest of the water bottle by the time there's a fork in the road. One way goes further into the trees, straight on ahead with no end in sight, and the other trails off towards a large gate. High stone walls and two painted statues of lion-like creatures flank the metal gate. He hikes the straps of his backpack further up on his back. The cart ahead of him turns toward the gate. He decides to follow. If there's a gate like that out in the middle of the forest, there might be a town or a settlement behind it. And that means shelter, food, and water.

Tyler jogs up to fall in line directly behind the cart, ducking his head low enough that the drivers or any guards at the gate won't be able to see him. Curse his blond hair and blue eyes. He misses the beanie already. This town, or house, or whatever, might not be inclined to welcome strangers. Once he's inside the walls he'll figure that out if need be. If he's not welcome he can slip away and hide in the stables or on the grounds. He really doesn't want to have to spend another night outside with strange voices that can worm their way into his head.

As he passes the life-size tiger statues, one of them looks straight at him and blinks. *It's alive.* Its four front teeth are huge—so huge they protrude a good four or five inches out of the cat's mouth. And even more peculiar, a single, twisted horn sticks out through the flesh of its nose. *Not a saber-toothed tiger then.* It blinks slowly at him, and then nestles its head back down on its fore paws, closing its bright yellow eyes. It's striped—or streaked, since the markings down its side aren't nearly solid or long enough to look like tiger stripes.

"He *bid* no bite ya, ya knowe."

Tyler jumps backwards, snapping his mouth shut. He's been staring, bug-eyed, at the cat while the cart ahead of him went on through the gate.

"He is *realid* quite gentle. A' *Gauekos* art *afeared* o' these. They art *bon* guards. D'ya want a come in?"

Tyler tears his eyes off the cat and looks back at the gate where a boy only a little younger than Tyler stands, propping it open. He's got dirt on his face and is dressed in odd, rough-looking clothes.

"I…um…yes?"

The boy grins, and Tyler follows him inside the gate.

"Y'art a traveler, art ya not? Ya must be, *si yast* na *begu* a *Naraco afore*. Where art ya from?"

He can kind of understand some of what the boy is saying, but he doesn't know all the words. He's fairly certain he called the cats "naracos". And then asked where Tyler is from.

"Somewhere…not here." Should he tell this boy where he's really from? Will he know how to help him? *Where the hell am I?* he wants to ask, but he doesn't want to draw attention to himself, and he's not completely certain the boy would understand him. So he keeps quiet and follows the boy inside.

Inside the gate there are still plenty of trees. Nestled among them is an L-shaped building made of wood and stone, three stories tall, its roof painted a brilliant green. There's a small roofed balcony built right into the corner, high off the ground. Just to the right is a stable of the same build and color as the L-shaped building. A wooden sign creaks on its pole a few yards ahead of the house: *The Chatty Sphinx* is painted in pale yellow letters on the wood.

"Oh," says the boy, "I guess *mayhap* it's *hail* a request. *Ach*, y'art *pragmatic dith* ya make it here *si* ya do not knowe a' zone." He goes on, rambling about the *fiost* and *Gauekos*, but Tyler doesn't understand much of it. "Ya do not happen a has't a *fara*, do ya?"

He shakes his head mutely. But the boy seems to be expecting an answer. Tyler will just have to ask what he meant. "A fara?"

The boy looks at him, puzzled, and then points toward the stables at one of the horses, "A *fara*. Do ya speak Sarenian?"

Tyler pauses, then shakes his head. "Maybe…a little. Not much."

The boy seems to understand. He considers this, standing a few seconds to scratch the side of his head, then says another strange word, pointing at the stables. Tyler shakes his head. The boy frowns, and tries a couple of different words, but gives up when Tyler doesn't recognize any of those.

"What do ya call it, then?" he asks, eyebrows drawn close together.

Tyler clears his throat, "A horse." He shakes his head, pointing at the stables, "And no, I don't have one."

The boy nods and motions for Tyler to follow him. "*Uiell*, let us *dol* under-roof." *Under-roof?* He must want to go inside the inn.

Tyler stops him with a hand on his arm. There's something he wants to try and ask first. "I…heard something, in the forest, last night. It—" he falters, gaze dropping to the ground. Can the boy understand him?

"In a'…**forest**? *Fi-ost*, ya mean? Ya did hear a voice?"

Tyler nods, swallowing.

The boy grins, shaking his head, "T'was a *Gaueko*," he says slowly and loudly, "they *deign* a mess with yar head. Y'art *pragmatic* ya *diget* hence. They art quite *afearing*."

"Oh."

"Ya *realid ar'n* from 'round here, art ya?" The boy shakes his head again, his eyes wide, "Y'art *pragmatic dith* ya find us."

Pragmatic. There's that word again. Tyler frowns. "I…you should know…I'm afraid I might not have money," he mimes rubbing a couple of coins together, "To pay for a room, that is."

"*Uiell*," says the boy, scrunching his eyebrows. He must have understood enough of what Tyler told him, because he continues, "Mine oncle need *na-temp* send *sofolk* out in a' *fi-ost* this *tard*, na matter *si* y'ave payed 'r no. Mayhap he shall let ya *dorm* in a' *stavels*." He motions for Tyler to wait, and then hurries off, disappearing into the main building. If Tyler understood that correctly, the boy went to go and ask his uncle to let Tyler sleep in the stables. Which is definitely better than the forest, even if he'll have to share the place with the horses.

He decides to look around while he waits for the boy to come back. As far as he can tell, the stone fence encases the inn, the stables, a small garden, and the oak trees immediately surrounding them. The garden doesn't look big enough to support one person, let alone an inn: he wonders if they have to import most of their food, and if it all comes in carriages like the one he tried to follow. He looks up at the sky. It's past noon.

Oh, how could he have been this stupid? He drops his backpack onto the ground in front of him and opens the front pocket, groping around in it for the cell phone Emily bought for him a couple of months ago. He holds the on button down, and nothing happens. The screen stays black. While he fiddles with it, though, the back covering slips off and lands in the dirt at his feet. Cursing, Tyler picks it up and is about to shove it back on when he sees the inside of the phone. The battery's a lumpy black mess, melted and fused to the components around it. No wonder he couldn't turn it on. He drops the phone and the case into his pocket, feeling a little dizzy.

The boy's back a few minutes later, leading a large, red-faced man who scratches at his thin gray mustache. The man meets Tyler's gaze with an intense one of his own and Tyler looks back at the ground, unable to meet his eyes.

"Mine nephew says ya can not afford a stay at a' inn the *sungone*," says the man, and Tyler forces himself to look up again, "I suppose ya knowe how a wash plates y sweep?" He mimes washing a plate and sweeping the floor with a broom. Tyler nods so the innkeeper knows he understands him. "I shall let ya *dorm* on a' rug in a' back room in front o' a' flame. Though *si* ya can not work, I am *afeared* ya'rt go-ag a *dorm* out in a' yard."

Tyler swallows. So if he washes some dishes and sweeps, he can sleep inside. "I can work."

The man steps over, clapping Tyler so firmly across the back he stumbles forward. "*Bon* lad."

Tyler nods. The innkeeper leads him back over to the building, opening the door and inviting him inside.

Chapter Seven

DARN

1st day of Tivar
Year 1452

Rocky outcropping
Altibrl Sea

That night, Darn doesn't get much sleep. Every time the blackness finally pulls him under, the sound of waves crashing on the rocks outside or the cold air and the shivers wake him up. He tries to pull the black t-shirt tighter around him, but it's still wet and cold. He should have worn a coat. At least the morph suit is almost dry. The rocks press against his back, a far cry from his soft mattress and pillows at home.

Home, where his parents are probably freaking out right now looking for him. Or not. Maybe the party isn't even over yet. And Trish—he wonders if she's even noticed his absence, or if she assumed he decided to walk Jenny home. It wouldn't be the first time Darn's left a party early without telling Trish.

He wraps his arms more tightly around himself and tries to curl into the rock. After what feels like hours of aching cold, his eyes slide closed and he's lost to the waking world.

"Hey," says a voice, floating somewhere above Darn's head, "H-hey, wake up."

It's cold. His clothes are stiff around him, the floor beneath him is hard as rock, and a slight breeze is nipping at his ears and the tip of his nose. He still doesn't want to get up.

"D-darn, you're going to freeze. It's m-much warmer out h-here in the sun."

Somewhere in the back of his mind, Darn's aware of what happened to him yesterday, but he doesn't really want to acknowledge it. He doesn't want to believe that he's out on a rock in the middle of some ocean, miles away from his parents and from Trish and from his house and even the city. But, if this voice—Alex, he remembers, the boy he found half-dead in the bushes maybe a year or so ago, back when the world still made sense—won't leave him alone to sleep, he'll have to do something about it.

"I'm up," he mumbles, "I'll be out there in a sec."

Alex's footsteps thwap away across the rocks. The other boy's up and walking around to stay warm. Being sensible. Darn guesses he should probably try and be sensible too.

His eyelids are heavier than they've ever been before in his life, but he manages to pry them open. There's a sandy little beach just outside, jammed between the cave and another large rock. The ocean laps at the pale sand, glinting prettily in the sunlight. Alex sits on a patch of weedy grass up from the beach, at the top of a small hill between the rocks.

Darn starts to get up, and smacks his head against the top of the cave with a loud crack. He winces and bites his lip. Well, now he's definitely awake.

Alex looks up, sees him, and smiles. So Darn walks over and sits down on the grass next to him.

How weird is it that Alex is here? The last time Darn saw him, he was lying in a hospital bed with thick bandages wrapped around his head, arm, and ribs. He'd been so much more helpless then: thin, drawn, and pale; like the life had been sucked out of him. Darn remembers sitting by his bed waiting, not wanting to leave him so alone and vulnerable, until Alex's dad burst in through the door. He'd left then, wanting to give them their privacy. And that was the last time he'd seen Alex. He doesn't know for certain why Alex was lying in those bushes that night, but he can guess. No one should ever feel that horrible, no one should have a life so bad that they want it to end.

Darn had meant to come back and try to help, to be a part of this boy's life if he'd wanted or needed it, but Darn's own life got in the way and he'd forgotten to look for Alex.

And yet here he is now, in—wherever the hell they are —and he's saved Darn's life.

"So…what now?" Darn asks, reaching down to rip out a clump of the short grass they're sitting on.

Alex shrugs. "I d-don't know."

They sit in silence for a minute, until Darn decides to

get up and look around. The ocean lapping at the beach is clear and blue—a little too blue in Darn's opinion. He's been down to the coast before, in Florida where some of his family lives, and the ocean hasn't ever been this brilliant shade of cerulean. The narrow peninsula of rock—broken up by hills of sandy grass and beaches—extends far out to sea, and they're almost at the very end of it. To the left, the mainland extends out a ways, and then turns in again, giving way to the brilliant water. To the right, it curves slightly outward, making a small sort of bay.

Darn's stomach growls loudly. It's been a long time since he ate last. He had lunch yesterday, but no dinner, and no breakfast this morning either.

"I'm hungry," he complains, leaning back until the grass tickles the base of his neck.

"Maybe we sh-should head towards the m-mainland," Alex says, craning his neck to peer out over the rocks.

That sounds like a good idea. "Let's do that."

So they get up and start to pick their way through the rocks, trying to stay as high up as possible so they can see where they're going. In case anything tries to sneak up on them. Darn feels uneasy out here, walking along the tops of the rocks, exposed to the sun and wind and whatever else.

"Where the hell are we?" He knows he isn't going to get a good answer—they've had this discussion a few times already last night, but Darn can't walk along in silence just worrying about it.

"On the c-coast, somewhere," says Alex.

"No shit, Sherlock."

Alex laughs, but plows on ahead, not even pausing to glance back at Darn.

"How the hell did we get here?" he wonders aloud.

"I d-don't know," says Alex, an edge of irritation leaking into his voice, "Magic."

"What about the letters? Are you saying those were magic?" Alex shakes his head, his lips pursed. That would be pretty odd, but they've got nothing else to go on. Or...

"What if we were on a ship, like a cruise ship or something, and it crashed and we both hit our heads really hard?"

Alex snorts. "No. My family d-doesn't have the k-kind of money—or time—to be g-going on cruises."

"We were kidnapped, then. And thrown in a boat, and taken away."

Alex stumbles and trips ahead of him, and Darn reaches forward and grabs his arm to keep him from falling down the rocks.

Alex lets out a shaky breath, staring down the slope with wide eyes.

"Th-thanks," he says.

"Don't mention it," says Darn.

They've walked for a good hour or so when the water starts to churn beneath them. They're on a narrow section of the peninsula, sandwiched between two vast swathes of the strange blue water. Darn pauses to stare down at it, but only catches ripples left behind by something large under the surface. The uneasy feeling in his stomach grows.

"Hey, how much longer do you think we've got to

walk?"

"I don't know. We're—m-maybe half way t-to the beach?"

There's the splash again. Darn stops, reaching for Alex's shoulder.

"Did you hear that?"

Alex nods.

The two of them look out over the water, listening to the waves sloshing against their bit of rock.

A dolphin launches itself out of the water—a dolphin with front legs—no, a horse—a horse with a fish tail? No—what?

"What the shit was that?" Darn asks, tightening his hold on Alex's shoulder.

"I…don't…know…" says Alex slowly.

"It was a dolphin, right? Just a dolphin," Darn stares down at the water, trying to peer through the eye-aching blue. Of course it was a dolphin, what else could it be? He's just woozy cause he's hungry, that's all. He forces out a laugh, "I'm seeing things, I think the sea air's getting to me, or something."

"I…I d-don't know, Darn," says Alex, "I don't think that was a d-dolphin."

"It was a dolphin," says Darn.

Except, then the ripples start again, and something very horse-like pokes its head out of the water to stare back up at them.

"It's not a dolphin," says Alex.

"It's not a dolphin," Darn agrees.

There's a horse swimming in the ocean, that's all. Just some really weird, really blue horse…

"I think they're c-called…hippocampuses," Alex says.

"No. It's a horse. It's just a horse." Darn says, voice rising.

"In the w-water," says Alex, "A-and it's blue."

Darn scrambles behind Alex as the horse—thing—snorts, tossing its head in the air. It stares at them for a few seconds, then seems to lose interest, and turns back to the water to swim away. As it goes, it ducks its head under the water and a tail—a dolphin's tail—breaks the surface of the ocean behind it.

"It's just a horse and its friend the dolphin," says Darn, his voice still unnaturally high, "They just like to swim close together, that's all."

Alex laughs at him. He's taking this a lot better than Darn is. Holy hell. But Alex's next words make Darn feel even worse.

"Th-that wasn't something…that's not a n-normal thing. W-where are we?"

Darn stares out over the ocean, still standing behind Alex, "I don't know," he says, "But I think I might be dead." Could that be it? That might be it.

Alex frowns. "I don't think so," he says, "I think it w-would be d-different…m-more peaceful, empty. N-not as r-real."

"I—" Darn starts, reaching up to run a hand through his hair, "How would you know, though? What if there was something in the paper of that letter? Some kind of

59

poison?"

They stand there in silence for a few minutes, until Darn hears something. Shouting—soft shouting, coming from far away. People. He looks back at Alex, and it seems the other boy's heard it too. His new friend's face is tilted toward the water, brow furrowed in concentration.

Darn puts his hand up to keep the sun out of his eyes and looks out over the water toward the noise. There's something heading straight for the rock they're on, something with large white sails that's floating, and if Darn squints he can see a giant swordfish figurehead taking up half the front.

"It's a ship," says Alex.

"We should do something. Make some noise, something. Maybe they'll help us."

But the people on board won't be able to see them yet, so they stand and watch. Darn squints forward into the sunlight, trying to make out the details on the ship as it approaches. *Annihilator* is scrawled in fancy white lettering across it's side, in stark contrast to the navy blue paint covering the rest of it. He can just make out tiny figures moving about the deck. One separates, moving toward the front, and there's something awfully familiar about her...a short girl in a knee-length flowery skirt with a head of delicate corkscrew curls, probably wearing a smirk.

The spitting image of one of those missing girls in the newspaper. The only thing missing is the bright red bicycle.

Chapter Eight

TYLER

1st day of Tivar
Year 1452

The Chatty Sphinx

Che innkeeper's name is Keripen, and the boy—his nephew, whose name is Agred—hands Tyler a new set of clothes. The dark brown shirt's a little big on him, and has string threaded through holes in the front instead of the buttons he's used to. The pants are pale green, fraying at the bottom, and at least six inches too short. The shoes are stiff leather and pinch at the toes. This is going to take some getting used to.

He starts working at a pair of buckets behind the kitchen, scrubbing the food crumbs and dust off a pile of dishes. While he works, he thinks. Where does he go from here? It's unlikely Keripen will let him stay for very long, and besides, he doesn't want to mooch. According to Agred, this place is between two cities, a day's travel or so from each. Maybe Tyler can find more permanent work in a city, earn some money, and etch out a life for himself there.

It's not like he had much of a life back in Aurora. He doesn't have family there, doesn't have friends, or work, or anything worth keeping. He hasn't graduated from high school yet, but does he really have to? If he still wants to teach English when he grows up, then yes, he does, but he might be stuck here and that might not be an option. Maybe things will be better here. He can wash dishes, after all, or he can write. Maybe he can be a scribe for someone, or be a tutor.

He can always fall back on flame-throwing, if he can manage to get a spark out of his fingers again. Tyler isn't sure which is stranger: hands that catch on fire, appearing in a strange forest in the middle of the night, or being chased around by a living nightmare. Not to mention the fairies or the giant cats. Or that letter from Mr. Lee. Maybe he should ask the innkeeper about some of that once he's finished with the dishes. Keripen might know something about people going back and forth, or maybe even where to find Mr. Lee, or Tyler's parents. Or those five other people Tyler's supposed to be looking for.

His mind buzzes with questions while he busies himself with the dishes. Where exactly is this place, and how did he get here? Is it a common thing to go from here to Colorado and back? Maybe Mr. Lee goes back and forth all the time. But if that were the case, wouldn't there be modern technology? Maybe everything melts when it's brought here, like his cell phone did. But then shouldn't they have come up with some technology on their own? Maybe this world isn't as old as earth is? Or maybe this is just an outside settlement—maybe the cities are more high-tech than here.

Once the dishes are all dry and stacked in the kitchen,

Keripen calls him into the dining room and hands him a broom to sweep with. People are starting to trickle through the front door in a steady stream, keeping Keripen occupied at the front desk. There are a few other workers at the inn that Tyler sees, but it seems that most of the management falls to Keripen and his nephew.

Tyler sweeps the hallway, lifting up the edges of the rugs to sweep the dirt out from under them. No one pays him much attention. His stomach starts to grumble as he glimpses Keripen's customers sitting around tables topped with plates of steaming food. Will Keripen be kind enough to give him any leftovers?

As the evening wears on, the inn's customers trickle out of the dining room, taking the noise and leaving a mess. Agred hands Tyler a towel and tells him to wipe down the tables, the benches, and the kitchen. When that's done, he's given a bowl of greenish-brown soup, or stew, or something. He takes the soup to one of the empty tables and scarfs it down. It takes him less than a minute to clean the bowl. The last of Keripen's customers have fled up the stairs to their private rooms or moved to the couches and plush rugs in the back room, leaving the dining room deserted. Tyler can hear quiet voices from the back room, but they aren't loud and there aren't many. He takes a moment to slump down in his seat and close his eyes. It's been a while since he's had to work so hard for so long.

There are too many things to think about, too many problems and too many questions. He's been going through them all day in his head and he still hasn't come up with a good answer for a single one.

His eyes drift open a slit and he catches sight of the fire, lit and burning brightly in the hearth a few tables away. He stands and walks over to crouch in front of it, reaching a hand out to feel some of the warmth.

It's pleasantly warm. He scoots closer, bringing his hand within inches of the flame, and then closer, and closer, until he's just shy of touching one of the white-hot slivers of ash at the center.

Someone grabs his elbow and wrenches it out of the fire. Tyler's concentration snaps like a twig. He twists around to find Keripen staring at him with a scowl on his face.

"D'not do that," the innkeeper whispers, "*Sofolk* may see ya." *Someone might see you.*

Tyler swallows and nods, scooting away from the fire to sit on the rug several feet from the hearth. Keripen stares him down, eyes searching for something in his face.

"Y'art a Flamestarter," he says. It's a statement, booking no room for disagreement. Tyler tries to digest that for a moment, but finds he has no idea what to think.

"I'm a what?"

"A Flamestarter," says Keripen, taking a seat on the rug across from Tyler, "Y'art a sorcerer, y that is not *sole-thig* ya want a flaunt in front o' any folk ya do not trust with yar life. Do ya understand?" *You're a sorcerer, and that is not something you want to flaunt in front of anyone you don't trust with your life.* Tyler still has to stop and think about what the innkeeper says when he talks, but it's starting to get a little easier. Keripen leans around him to look through the doors to the back room, and his face slackens with relief at what he sees there. "Y'art lucky *nane* was *look-ag* when ya did that." *You're lucky no one was looking when you did that.*

Tyler looks down at his hands, stretching his fingers out to check them for burns. There's nothing. The fire didn't touch him. "A Flamestarter?" he murmurs, looking back up at Keripen, "What does that mean?"

The innkeeper settles onto the rug. "'T means y'art a sorcerer," he says, still in a whisper, "ya can control fire, and it shall not harm ya when ya touch it." He stares hard at Tyler, settling his hands on his knees. "Where art ya from that ya do not know that? Gorthrofen, mayhap? Ya look Telegarathian."

Tyler looks down at the rug, trying to avoid the innkeeper's gaze. Should he tell him? Will he believe him? Despite the work Keripen's given him, and the food, Tyler still doesn't know he can trust him. Is there any way Keripen could use the information against him? He realizes with a jolt that he can't tell this man about Mr. Lee. He can't tell anyone. If it hadn't been important to keep his whereabouts and purpose secret from someone, Mr. Lee would have said a lot more in the letter. He would have told Tyler where to find him.

"Never mind that, then," Keripen's clothes rustle as he shifts his position on the rug. "At least *minse* me where y'art *go-ag*. You can stay here f'r a while *si* you *deign*; to figure out what you want to do."

"I—I'd like to go to the city, I think." It might be easier to find information in the city. It might be easier to hide there. Tyler needs a place to start looking for Mr. Lee, and the city would be as good a place as any. He studies the pattern on the carpet, tracing a green swirl with a finger.

"*Uiell*," Keripen huffs a long breath, "I can tell y'art not used to *viyage-ag* here, so do me a favor y attend 'til I can find *sofolk* a send you with?" *I can tell you're not used to travel, so do me a favor and wait until I can find someone to go with you.*

Tyler nods, and tears prick at the corners of his eyes. He reaches up and wipes them away roughly. Maybe he misunderstood. He's being stupid thinking this stranger might actually care about what happens to him. There must be something in it for the innkeeper. Tyler shouldn't let his guard down.

Keripen goes to bed, leaving Tyler sitting in front of the hearth and watching the fire. Tyler's so caught up in thought that he isn't sure how much time has passed when the door to the main dining room creaks open. He freezes in place, not daring move. The Naracos are outside, keeping the monsters that chased him last night at bay, but perhaps they've been killed? Maybe something got by them? Tyler's mouth goes dry as his heart beats a mile a minute. He drops to all fours and inches backwards until he's under one of the tables. He cranes his neck around one of it's legs, trying to see the door.

He's suddenly very glad that Keripen left all of the

candles lit, because he can see what's by the door, and it isn't a monster—it's a girl. She twists and shoves her way between the tables, links of the chain mail that covers her arms glinting in the firelight. Tyler tries to shrink into the shadows as she approaches and heads straight for the fire.

She crouches down next to him, so focused on the hearth that she doesn't even see him. She's wearing a purple shirt over the chain mail, with a bright red bird of prey design stitched to it's front. A sword, sheathed in leather, is strapped to a belt around her waist.

She turns her head and jumps, startled to find Tyler there watching her. But then her face melts into a smile, and she says, "I'm Kaylor. I'm a traveler, from Valliseg. Who are you?"

PART 2

INTO PLACE

Chapter Nine

SARAH

66th day of Summer
Year 1452

Northern Dragonlands

Sarah Miller crouches in a clump of large ferns, peering out from between the fronds into the forest beyond. A few yards in front of her, a lion's tail swishes through the grass. Well, not a lion's tail, exactly. Sure, it looks lionish, as do the paws and hindquarters attached to it. But when the creature lifts its head, it's clear that it isn't a lion at all. A long, sharp beak protrudes from beneath keen, intelligent eyes. Feathers ripple down its back as it shakes itself. Sarah gets to her feet, careful to make some soft noises but not sharp ones, enough to alert the griffin to her presence but not enough to scare it. As soon as she moves, its eyes are on her, tufted ears shooting upward to point at the sky. A spike of fear jolts down her spine at the movement, but she grinds her teeth and forces herself to ignore it. Instead, she smiles at the griffin as she extends her hand out, palm up and flat.

"Hey there, buddy," she murmurs, "*I'm not going to hurt you.*"

The griffin tilts his head at her and she bites the inside of her cheek. Was that right? Griffin language is full of sharp clicks and low growls, which can be difficult to replicate with a human tongue and vocal box. But Sarah's one of few people who can speak both dragon and human versions of Gaentuki, and compared to that, Griffin is a piece of cake.

But she still can't tell if he understood her. Maybe there are dialects, and she doesn't know the proper one for this region. He stares back at her, clacking his beak, and fear twists in Sarah's gut. She tries to squash it down. He won't attack as long as he doesn't see her as a threat. Griffins are easy to reason with—or so Sarah's heard. If this one would just *talk*.

She stares straight at him, right into his eyes, and takes a slow step forward. A rumble starts in the griffin's chest, and he bobs his head up and down. Sarah fights down a nervous laugh. Standing her ground against a griffin. Kaylor would be so proud of her.

He's two or so feet from her now. Sarah turns her hand sideways and moves it to the side of the griffin's face. His eyes snap to Sarah's hand, but he only flinches away a couple of inches, tiny feathers on his neck twitching. Sarah has to hold in another laugh: half out of amusement, half unease. *Don't be frightened, you'll only scare him.* She tries to quiet her squirming stomach as she moves her hand to stroke the griffin's neck.

A loud crash shakes through the forest around her. The griffin's beak snaps as he backpedals, letting out a screech and taking off into the forest. Sarah screams as an enormous pair of yellow claws dip out of the canopy and grab her around the waist.

"*Nellie!*" Sarah yells, grabbing at the talons and trying to pry them off, "*I almost had him! Nellie…*

"*You've got to stop fooling around, Sarah. We're not out here to pester angry griffins.*"

"*He wasn't* angry. *I'm not* stupid. *I just wanted to see if he could understand me. Put me down, Nellie!*"

"*No.*"

Sarah crosses her arms and glares at the talons clenched around her waist. "*Why not?*"

"*Because it's time to go home.*"

Sarah looks up, trying to study the face of the dragon carrying her. But Nellie's neck is too long, and Sarah can only see the underside of her chin. "*Who'd you offend this time?*" she asks.

Nellie huffs, the breath shaking her entire body as her wings pump against the wind. "*That's none of your business.*"

"*So you* did *get kicked out again! For someone who's supposed to be a diplomat, you sure are good at making other dragons angry.*"

"*But they're so uncivilized.*" The dragon lets out a thunderous sigh.

Sarah rolls her eyes. "*That is the problem right there,*" she pokes one of Nellie's talons, "*They're not really any better or worse than you are, just different. If you would just try to understand their way of life instead of criticizing it whenever you go to visit them, you wouldn't offend them so much, and you'd be able to convince them to agree to that treaty you're pushing so hard for.*"

Nellie turns her head to the side so she can shoot Sarah a brief, scathing look. *"You do have a point, but as long as they expect me to consume the remains of intelligent animals as a part of some ridiculous welcoming ritual, I refuse to cooperate."*

Sarah frowns. *"Were they eating griffins?"*

"Yes. And humans, too."

She swallows. She's been trying not to think about *that* aspect of wild dragon culture. The wild dragons know not to harm Sarah: Nellie had made that clear as soon as they'd arrived in the Dragonlands three days ago.

"What are we going to do about the food shortage, then?"

Nellie's tail swishes through the air, making her bob up and down. *"I don't know, young one. The Court might want us to push South. But that would mean fighting the Mad King, and that's not really something we want to do again."*

Sarah pats the side of Nellie's leg. *"We can't import it? Or…talk to the Mad King about it?"*

Nellie's chest rumbles in a growl. *"We have to hunt, Sarah. It's an important part of our culture. We need more land."*

They fly in silence for a few minutes, until Nellie's grip around her abdomen starts to bother Sarah.

"Um…Nellie? Can you let me go? I'd much rather sit in the saddle than hang down here…"

The dragon chuckles, the sound vibrating from the base of her neck to the tip of her tail. *"Of course, young one, I'm sorry. I forgot that you don't like to be carried."*

Nellie loosens the grip of her talons to let Sarah wiggle free. Like all Gaentuki dragons, Nellie wears a uniform: a padded harness decorated with the colors of her class and equipped with a saddle just behind her shoulder blades. The edges of multicolored streamers and strips of fabric Nellie has wrapped through or sewn to the straps whip and dance through the air as she flies, a particularly unruly strip hitting Sarah in the face as she climbs up the harness. Sarah bats it away with her left hand and scrunches up her nose, the fingers of her right hand gripping the edge of a polished, ornate buckle decorated with a pair of crossed scrolls and a book. Nellie, as a diplomat, belongs to the scholar class of Gaentuki society, one of the more esteemed classes found in the city of Husifi. Sarah, as Nellie's assistant and ward, has a shiny scholar pin too, fastened to her matching leather riding harness. She settles in to the saddle, attaching the leather straps hanging from her harness to the ones on Nellie's.

It doesn't take more than an hour or two for them to get to the city. Sarah leans over the side of Nellie's neck as the dragon glides over the mountains, peering down at the outlines of other dragons flying far below them. The enormous staircases up and down the sides of the canyon, the only part of Husifi not covered by overhanging rock shelves or tall trees, bustle with other dragons and people. It's four hours after noon—the city is coming to life again after the three hour break at midday. On most days, it gets so hot in Husifi that staying out and working past noon is as good as a death sentence.

Nellie soars into an enormous crevice packed with dwellings, people, dragons, and smoke. They glide over the tops of buildings until they reach a ground-level cave dug into the rock in one of the back corners. Other cave entrances dot the solid wall of rock around them, several with a dragon or two lounging at their fronts. Sarah leaps off Nellie's back just before the dragon lumbers through the entrance to their home. *"I'm hungry, I'm going to go get some food. You want to come?"* she asks, staring after Nellie.

"No, thank you. I ate before we left. I need a nap. My wings are killing me."

"Okay. Suit yourself."

Sarah forces herself to swallow her nerves as she makes her way down the cobblestones, passing through several quiet streets before she hits the market. She still isn't comfortable walking around the city by herself, even though she's been here for over a year. But that's kind of how she's always been, even when she was back in Colorado. The crowds and the noise make her nervous.

The smell of cooked meat permeates the air, wafting from the multitude of stone and wooden stalls set up and down the length of the street, making her mouth water. Despite her nerves, she can't help but smile a little as she takes in the bright colors and people around her.

Sometimes, she's convinced that she's still in a dream, that the life she lived before is going to nudge her back awake at any moment. That her mother will wander into her room and shake her shoulder gently, tell her that she's late for school and she needs to get up and out of bed. That she'll roll out from under the covers and back into the bleak little house in Aurora, and Nellie and the griffins and this market will be gone. Sure, she misses her parents and her two older siblings sometimes, but...he's been so busy this past year, she hasn't had time to dwell on it. Her life here is so much better, the rules vastly different than the ones her parents had in place for her back home. Here, she's free to do as she wants: no curfew, no restrictions, no pressure to be anything she doesn't want to be, no people telling her what to do or policing her every move. And there are dragons: dragons and griffins in the mountains and tree nymphs down at the bottom of the canyon, new wonders and adventures around every corner. She belongs here now, not there, and she doesn't want to go back.

A sign swings in the slight breeze not far from her, and Sarah picks up her pace, heading straight for it. The *Four-Eyed Griffin*. It's the inn where she stayed when she first got here, and where she first met Nellie. She also knows most of the people who work there, so she'll have someone to talk to.

She ducks her head into the inn and smiles at the man behind the counter—Jash. He waves back. It's full tonight—eight or so dragons have their heads stuck through the row of windows in the back wall, helping themselves to bowls full of meat as they grumble to each other with their mouths full. Three humans sit around one of the dragons, laughing and talking. All six of the other tables are full, and five or six people sit along the bar. A group of strangers—set apart by their light, sun-burnt skin and pale eyes—crowd into a back corner. The people of Husifi are all dark skinned, with straight black hair and dark eyes. Sarah has no problem blending in here, but these people certainly do.

Jash beckons her forward.

"*The usual?*" He asks. Sarah nods. Jash stares for a minute at the strangers, and then turns to her, "*Will you watch them for me while I tell Mira what you want?*" She frowns at him, but nods. She doesn't know how much help she'd really be if the pirates decide to try and rob the store or make a spectacle of themselves: Jash would be better off asking one of the dragons. Still, she guesses she can scream if anything happens, and then Jash can come and help.

While Jash heads into the back to tell the cook—Mira— what to make, Sarah turns around and looks at the door, all the while watching the strangers out the corner of her eye. Their voices have hushed into a whisper, and they're looking back at her: or rather, at her and then at something else across the room. One or two of them are staring. Sarah shifts her weight from her right leg to her left, crossing her arms protectively in front of her chest. She keeps her gaze fixed on the door.

She's relieved when Jash gets back with her food. She takes it and sits at the bar, right by where Jash will be for the rest of the night. He smiles warmly at her, grabbing a rag to wipe down part of the counter.

"*Thanks, Sarah,*" he whispers, "*I think they mean trouble.*"

She purses her lips. "*Well…they wouldn't try anything with the dragons around, would they?*"

Jash shakes his head and laughs. "*You can't ever really trust pirates, no matter how scary the dragons can be.*"

At that moment, one of the men, a smaller, younger one with a sharp nose and greasy-looking hair, leans against the bar right next to Sarah.

"*Another two pints of ale, please,*" he says, his speech already slurred.

While Jash turns to go and get the drinks, the pirate leans over to her.

"*There's a man just came in here,*" he says in Sarenian, under his breath, nodding toward the back of the inn. He reeks, and so does his breath. Sarah tries not to wrinkle her nose. "*He hasn't stopped watching you. Can't reckon why, unless he wants to bother you. Just thought I'd let you know.*"

She tenses up, getting ready to bolt. *Like this guy and his friends have been doing any different.* But still, it's good to have a head's up.

"*Thank you,*" she says back, just as quietly.

She glances over her shoulder after the pirate rejoins the others, and there *is* someone back there, in a small nook hidden from the front door. He looks out of place here, even worse than the pirates, with thick furs draped over his shoulders and dirty, pale skin. Invisible spiders crawl up the nape of her neck, forcing her nerves on alert while she tries to finish her dinner. She'll tell Jash about the stranger before she leaves. Maybe he'll be able to spare one of the staff to walk her home. But she'll eat first. She's still hungry, after all.

Chapter Ten

KAYLOR

66th day of Summer
Year 1452

Shaltac Castle
Valliseg

aylor Williams stares down at the maps spread before her, lit only by the faint glow of candlelight in the darkened room. These are her maps—she drew these. But the red and blue ink snaking over her carefully placed sketches and lines makes them into something new, something she isn't sure she's happy about helping to create.

Prince Casteor, son of King Shirot Tybold of Sarenia, stands across from her on the other side of the table, frowning and looking at his nails.

"What do you think?" he asks.

"I—" Kaylor starts, and then stops, letting out the rest of her breath. "I think this is ridiculous, my lord. Why *on earth* would you be drawing up battle plans against your own cities?"

Casteor glares at her. Kaylor holds his gaze for a second before she relents, "What about the cities, *my lord?*" She doesn't drop her eyes, even though she's supposed to. She lets them drill into his blue ones, because she wants him to *see* her concern and resentment.

"Once upon a time," the Prince starts, and Kaylor has to grit her teeth to stop her eyes from rolling, "A rebellion rose against my father. The castle was attacked by a group of nobles and their misinformed... *lackeys*, all sorcerers, who tried to take his crown from him. And now—"

"Now every sorcerer in Sarenia has to register and give a token, under pain of death or imprisonment, so he'll know if they're planning to betray him. I *know*. Kindly get to the point, my lord."

Prince Casteor frowns at her, but keeps going: "My father has... certain intelligence that another rebellion is rising."

"So you're going to attack all of your people just so you and your father can stay in power." She remembers all those people: the boarded up shops and orphaned children, their parents dragged away by the town guards because they could do something King Shirot didn't like. *All of those people* —and the Prince might ask her to kill them one day. Kaylor feels sick to her stomach.

Casteor's frown deepens. "No. Don't be stupid, *Lady Kaylor*. These plans were made because the King thinks that one—or more—of the cities will fall to this... *rebellion*. And what happens then? It's good to have these plans, just in case." It sounds innocent enough, but Kaylor can't be sure she's not imagining the sort of hungry half-smile that's lurking on Casteor's face. Almost as if he *wants* it to come to that. She's suddenly so full of disgust with the Prince—and with herself for everything she's done for him—she can hardly bear it. She wants to leave, she wants to *get out*, and she wants *nothing* more to do with him and his harebrained ideas.

But she can't do that now. All she can do is argue. So she does. "Pardon me my lord, but honestly…the life's gone out of the cities. I don't see a way any one of them could be a threat: even if the people there are planning on rebelling, all of the cities—*all of them*, every single one—are half deserted! You've chased off or imprisoned so many of your subjects—many loyal subjects, I might add. You *need* those people, they're farmers and craftsmen and merchants—what are you going to do when they're gone?"

The Prince's blue eyes glitter with disdain, his mouth set in a thin line. "Less than half of my people are sorcerers. Surely you noticed that on your travels? And sorcerers are allowed to live freely, as long as they do it *legally*. All they have to do is register with one of the lords in the cities, where they will be given a token."

"So you can track all their movements and force them into your army if it tickles your fancy."

"Why, yes. Many sorcerers have powers that can be used to keep Sarenia and its people safe. Why would they not want to fight for their country?"

Kaylor stares down at the maps, caught. It's not right, she *knows* it's not right, but she's run out of steam and can't think of a rebuke. "What are you planning, Casteor?" she asks quietly.

Prince Casteor smirks back at her, for once not upset

that she's called him by his first name. The expression reminds Kaylor uncannily of…oh, never mind. She's left that part of her life behind. "Do you understand now?" he asks.

Kaylor swallows. "I don't."

"Good. You're not meant to."

She glares across the table, torn between picking up one of the candles and throwing it at the Prince's face or ripping a chunk of her own hair out. "Well, whatever it is you're planning, I don't agree with it," she snaps. The Prince raises an eyebrow at her, and Kaylor finally gives in to the urge to roll her eyes, "My lord."

"It's a pity," he says, leaning across the table to stare right at her, "about that earring you had to give me, isn't it?" He clucks his tongue, "Such a pity, that you can't do whatever you want. Don't forget, Kaylor, that if your actions start to stray," he brings his fingers up and snaps them in front of her face, and Kaylor flinches despite herself, "it will burst into a thousand glittering pieces, and I will know that I have been betrayed. Now," he stands back up, his eyes dropping to the maps, "you are dismissed."

Kaylor straightens her uniform as she steps down the hallway towards her quarters, boots clicking against the hard stone. Emblazoned on the front of her shirt is a red roc on a purple sky, the insignia of the King's—of *Prince Casteor's*—

family. It suddenly seems revolting, that she's parading around in this. Like it doesn't belong on her anymore. All those stupid things he'd told her, reeling her in with tales of battle and glory when it all still seemed so abstract. They'd go after Husifi, to kill the dragons that had murdered his aunt and young cousins, he'd said. And then Telegarath, a land of ice and snow across the sea, from where his ancestors fled, a place they'd liberate from an emperor who still believes in slavery. And on from there. Kaylor thought she could make a difference in the lives of these people, that she was needed here to help the Prince, and that maybe she'd been pulled out of her world and on to the next for that very reason.

That was before she found out what the King had done to the sorcerers. Before she'd taken her tour of Sarenia to draw the maps, before she'd met the people, seen the beggars and the empty streets. Before she knew what she was, and what the Prince was. Now, Kaylor just wants to go home.

She reaches her door and opens it. Her room isn't much: a small bed is tucked into the far corner, next to a nightstand with a water skin and a small stack of coins sitting on top of it. A table and two chairs, covered in papers, sit next to a tiny window set deep into the stone. A small dresser takes up most of the opposite wall. The floor is bare rock but for the scruffy orange rug next to the bed. Kaylor slumps down into one of the chairs, running her hands through her tangle of frizzy blond hair.

This room has been her official quarters since the day

she arrived in Valliseg and participated in the tournament, which was last summer. She's been here for more than a year. A *year*.

When she'd first started living here at Shaltac Castle, she'd been thrilled that the Prince himself wanted to work with her. It was the first time she'd ever been in a real castle, and it was full of knights and nobles and royalty, and the Prince had so many wonderful ideas.

Kaylor picks a pen up and watches the ink drip down the end and back into the ink pot. Most of the papers on her desk are maps, but some of them are reports. She's supposed to write up everything she does when she goes out on missions for the Prince. And she does—mostly. She should work on them now, but…she doesn't *want* to. She doesn't want to do *anything* that might help the Prince.

She glances over at the earring sitting on her end table. Its mate is wherever Prince Casteor keeps the tokens faithful sorcerers give him. She had to give it up just after her first fight, when her powers had shown themselves for the very first time. She'd watched as one of Prince Casteor's men, a Cursemaker, had woven a spell into the tiny orange teardrop earring that would keep it whole unless it's owner acted against the will of the crown.

Prince Casteor will know if she betrays him, and Kaylor will have to flee, or suffer King Shirot's punishment for sorcerers who break their oaths or refuse to take them: prison, or death.

Kaylor leans her elbows on the table and buries her face in her hands. Why is *she* the one being saddled with all this?

Not for the first time, she wonders why Prince Casteor even asked her to help him. She's not a noble, not really a commoner even, though she hasn't told anyone that. She's an outsider, she's not from Sarenia, and she's sure people have noticed at least that much. How can the Prince possibly think he can trust her?

She rubs at the corners of her eyes, and that's when she sees the envelope. It's sitting on top of the papers piled on her desk, her name written in looping cursive on its front. Kaylor picks it up, flipping it over to look at the back. There's nothing on the outside except for her name. She sticks a fingernail through the upper edge and rips it open, then pulls the letter out to read it.

Hello Kaylor,

I know why you're here. Not why you're at the castle, and not in the city—I know where you're really from, and why you're not there anymore. I know where your friends are—yes, Anna and Sarah are here too.

Kaylor's breath catches in her throat. She hasn't told *anyone* about Sarah and Anna—granted, one or two of the guards in Morento might guess about Anna, but Sarah…who sent her this letter?

One of them is going to ask something of you, and I know you're going to want to go to her. But there's something I need to inform you of first.

There's someone waiting for you. He should be at the Chatty Sphinx, or somewhere in the forest surrounding it. You know what's in that forest and why it's so dangerous, but he doesn't. It is imperative that you find him, and that you tell no one else that he's here.

Sincerely,
A friend

Someone knocks at her door.

Kaylor folds the note up, shoves it under some papers, and gets to her feet to go answer it. Her heart pounds in her throat. If she's right, the letter is implying that there's someone else from…America, Colorado, *home*—along with her and Anna and Sarah, here *now*, lost in the forest. The knock comes again, and Kaylor realizes that she's frozen, her hand hovering just over the door handle. She gives herself a mental shake and pulls it open.

She immediately schools her expression into one of snooty haughtiness. "Sir Redbrak," she says, "To what do I owe this pleasure?"

"My dearest, most gentle Lady Kaylor," the knight bows so low Kaylor has to step back a couple of times to stay out of his way, "Sir Martic wishes to see you."

Kaylor snorts and raises an eyebrow, dropping her act, "Does he now?"

"Shocking, I know," says the knight, straightening up to his full height, which is well above Kaylor's, and grinning, "It must be a very grave matter indeed."

"He didn't tell you?"

"Does he ever?"

"Good point." Kaylor brushes past him out into the hallway. She isn't surprised when he follows her.

"Any idea what he might want?" Redbrak asks, shaking his arm and straightening out the blue band of fabric tied just below his shoulder. Kaylor has one of these too—it means they're new knights with limited training, that they haven't seen real combat or done anything of note yet.

"None. He knows I'm working for the Prince at the moment, right? He doesn't want to assign me anything new, does he?"

Redbrak makes a face. "I should hope not. The festival's in two days, the turning of the seasons. He *can't* want to start us on some new assignment *now*."

It's a long walk down to Sir Martic's office. The crown has accepted so many new knights in the past year that *all* the tiny rooms in this wing of the castle are full.

When Kaylor asked one of the older knights about it, he told her that most of these rooms are meant to be used for storage, or servants, which is why they're much smaller than the senior knights' quarters. There are more knights living in Shaltac Castle now than ever before, and that doesn't even count the officers and senior knights who live outside, throughout the city.

Redbrak stops at the end of the hallway. "Don't let him eat you alive."

Kaylor smirks back at him, "He won't. He's still scared of me, remember?"

That gets a laugh out of Redbrak. "Then at least try not to threaten him again. Your friends—and the goddess Larosri herself of course—require your presence at the festival."

Kaylor rolls her eyes. Redbrak grins and backs away, sending her a mock-salute. Kaylor, sad to see him go, waves as he rounds the corner down another hallway. But she has to get this over with.

She stops in front of a large oak door, sighs, raises her fist, and knocks.

Nothing.

She waits for a few minutes before she knocks again. Still nothing. She purses her lips and grips the handle, swinging the door open, stepping inside and closing it behind her.

A severe looking man with longish gray hair and a scruffy, thinning beard sits behind a desk cluttered with papers. A bright red strip of fabric tied around his upper left arm signifies his rank as a superior officer. He looks up as Kaylor walks in, and she dips her head to him. He doesn't return the gesture, instead going back to writing on one of the papers on his desk. He does this every time he calls one of the newer knights in, and it drives Kaylor crazy. She clears her throat. When that doesn't work, she shuffles her feet across the floor, making as much noise as she can fidgeting. He still won't look up.

"Sir Martic?" she snaps, "You requested my presence? As soon as possible?"

Sir Martic glances at her again before waving at one of

the servants flanking his desk. The servant bows and moves to a door at the back of the office. Kaylor has always assumed that it leads to a closet, or the cellar, or a private room with some nasty hidden thing of Sir Martic's in it, but what's really there is a small sitting room. A boy around Kaylor's age perches on the edge of one of the plush, dark green chairs. Sir Martic's servant whispers something to him and he nods, getting up to follow the servant. His copper-colored skin and dark hair are a little rougher than she'd expect from someone in the castle, but his clothes are new and clean. He has a sharp Denadian nose, large eyes, and a full mouth. A golden hoop earring dangles from one of his ears, and something around his neck catches the light as he bows to Kaylor.

A small cross—pure silver—attached to a sterling silver chain, with tiny letters etched across the charm: *Anna Thomas*. Kaylor would know that necklace anywhere.

Chapter Eleven

ANNA

66th day of Summer
Year 1452

A few miles from Tallipeg
Altibrl Sea

nna Thomas stands on the prow of a navy blue ship that sways and rocks in the sea water, not far from shore. The ship is small and slender, with three off-white sails and an enormous carved swordfish protruding from her nose, so large that the forecastle cuts into its back. Anna stands just behind it, peering over the railing and out to the water beyond. She's a little too short for the battered, dirty-brown trench coat blowing around her ankles, but then again she's a little too short for almost anything. Including the large black tricorn perched on her head. At least her old skirt fits her, even if it is crusted with dirt and salt by now. She's worn it, and a few identical copies she's had her helmsman Choffson make for her, almost every day she's been here. Her step-siblings—especially Bella, the brat—would tell her the entire ensemble made her look like a child, or a gremlin, or something else stupid and offensive. But frankly, Anna doesn't give a shit what Bella thinks: she never has. Or maybe that's not quite true—part of her wants to wear the hat and the trench coat *because* her step-sister would hate it.

Lines of dock spider out in front of her, leading from the shipyard all the way to the shoreline, where they meet the towering stone walls of the city. Anna lifts a telescope to her eye.

The *Dragon's Breath*, a crown trader, drifts in the water between Anna and the city, ripe for the picking. The ship's bright gold lettering is stenciled over a thick, pearly-pink shade of jewel paint. She inspects it through her telescope for the seventh time this hour, baffled that they haven't left a lookout on board. It's a big ship, and there are sorcerers about in the harbor—it's captain shouldn't have left it without one.

"Captain," a young boy interrupts her thoughts, tugging on her sleeve. His name is Zer, and he's a nine-year old orphan Colf asked her to look after. Anna turns to him and he motions for her to bend closer so he can whisper in her ear, "Where's Patrick?" he asks, "He's been gone for so long."

She straightens up to look down at Zer, frowning, "Patrick can take care of himself, I'm sure he's fine. I sent him…away, to retrieve something for me. He'll be back soon."

Zer tilts his head and raises his eyebrows, planting his feet firmly on the deck.

Anna closes her eyes and represses a sigh. What exactly does he want to hear? She told him the truth, all that she knows. What more does he want from her?

Much to Anna's relief, another member of her crew—Hisef—steps forward. "See that ship over there? The pinkish one?" Hisef crouches down to Zer's height, pointing at the *Dragon's Breath*, "It's packed with fruit and meat they're shipping to Morento. We haven't had fresh fruit for weeks, how would you like some tonight?"

Zer's face lights up, breaking into a grin. He nods eagerly.

"Captain," the boy says, turning back to Anna, "Will I get to go too? You wouldn't let me last time. I could be a real help if there's any fighting you need done."

Anna has to suck in her cheeks to keep herself from laughing, but Hisef only looks down at the boy, his face grave.

"Someone has to stay behind and protect the ship, just in case," he says.

Zer gives him a skeptical look, but nods anyway. *One of these days, he's going to realize that's a ploy.* But Hisef's so good with the boy, Anna's certain he'll just come up with another excuse, and Zer will eat it up like pudding.

"Come on," says Hisef, "The Captain's a little busy at the moment, we should go tend to the ship."

Hisef winks at Anna as he leads Zer away. He knows she isn't very good with kids and that Zer tends to get on her nerves. She nods at him in thanks, then walks down the length of the ship to the helm. Yorren and Choffson, her first mate and helmsman, are waiting for her.

Anna has six people to man her ship: Wrom, Hisef, and Zer, three young sorcerers chased out of their country by their own King; Choffson and Yorren, remnants of the old crew before Anna took power; and Patrick, a Denadian stowaway who decided to help her with the mutiny. She wishes she hadn't had to send Patrick away, but she wouldn't have trusted anyone else with the task she gave him. Patrick's smart, quick, and slippery, and Anna's confident he'll be able to get out of any situation he gets himself into. He'd be helpful *here*, now.

It's late in the evening, maybe an hour or two before the sun sets. At this point the harbor is nearly deserted: no other ships block the way for a fast escape. Anna made the decision to try and board the *Dragon's Breath* two days ago, when they first arrived at the harbor. They need supplies, and they haven't yet stolen from any ships in Tallipeg. There's a place they can flee to and hide once they've stolen the goods. It's all set up, planned out, and should be an easy raid. But something about this leaves a sour taste in Anna's mouth. Maybe because two guards are patrolling the decks of the *Dragon's Breath*—even if there's no lookout, no one is stupid enough to leave a ship unguarded—clearing wielding swords and bows. Maybe because this is a dock, right next to a city full to the brim with knights, guards, sailors, and other citizens. If one of the guards on the ship sounds an alarm, she has no idea how many people will come to their aide.

She's only been captain for a couple of months, and most of what she's been doing is illegal trade, salvage, and ferrying fugitives. She's only been in one real skirmish before, and even that hadn't amounted to much. She'd barely fought one opponent before her crew had subdued the others. At least, thanks to Patrick's training, Anna's proficient in a sword fight. She knows she can defend herself if it comes to that. That doesn't mean she wants it to come to that.

Choffson grunts at her in greeting as she takes her place next to him.

"What do you think?" she asks, looking first to Choffson and then to Yorren on her other side, "Is the raid still a good idea?"

"We do need the supplies," says Yorren, "And we can make do with fog, I think."

"They haven't finished unloading," says Choffson, "and it's almost night. No doubt the Captain will let his crew take a break and head to the taverns this evening."

"Right," says Anna, thinking through the plan again, "It'll be fine. It will work."

Two hours later, once the sun's down and it's dark enough to conceal the faces of her crew, they dock the *Annihilator* not fifty yards from the *Dragon's Breath* and Anna orders her ship's ramp deployed. It folds down until the end lands on the docks, ready for loading.

Anna leaves her hat in her quarters and ties her trench coat securely over her distinctive shirt and skirt, hiding them from view. She leads Yorren, Hisef, and Wrom down onto the dock and motions for them to come closer.

"Does everyone know what they're doing?" she whispers. She examines each of their faces as they nod, studying their expressions. Yorren's confident but still a little skeptical, as always. Hisef is grave, but otherwise sure enough to settle Anna's nerves. Wrom is nervous, but not so much that she'll mess up: it's her turn to do the hard part. Anna herself does her best to hide her reluctance behind steely determination.

They set off for the *Dragon's Breath*.

As they walk, Anna beckons over her shoulder with her fingers, calling upon the power she's just recently discovered. Icy tendrils of damp air snake down her back, over her shoulders, and around her sides. Soon Anna and her crew are enveloped in a dense cloud of fog.

She stalks down the dock while the other three trail behind, eyes glued to the ground as it drifts out of the fog three feet in front of her. *The second left is the Dragon's Breath.* Footsteps clatter across the wood ahead, and Anna lifts her head in time to see another group of sailors walking straight at them. She ducks her head down, averting her eyes as they pass. What are these people doing out here at this time of night? Anna and her crew will have to be more careful— they don't want to be seen, especially not on the way back to the *Annihilator*.

After twenty more steps she turns left. She's been trying to count their steps in her head: she's taken 142. Not far at all. The bow of the *Dragon's Breath* looms before her, the sheen of its pale paint shining through the night and the fog. Anna stops next to it, craning her neck and listening hard. Light footsteps echo across the deck above, but only one set. She allows herself a small smile. Just one guard: the crew must either be off ship tonight or sleeping.

Anna beckons the rest of her own crew forward. They duck behind the *Dragon's Breath*, and Wrom steps forward so that Hisef can boost her up and onto the deck. Anna holds her breath as she waits, pressed against the ship's side, with Hisef and Yorren. The sound of voices drift down from above: Wrom's high voice and the gruffer one of the guard. A loud crack stops the conversation. Anna holds her breath. Moments later, Wrom unhooks the ramp and folds it down.

"There were two of them," Wrom explains as Anna and the others start up the ramp, "I managed to subdue one, and knock the other out. I Cursed them both—they won't be able to move 'til morning. They're blindfolded, so they can't recognize any of you later."

Anna gives her a curt nod, "Good job, Wrom. Now we need to get to the cargo hold." She stops on the prow to watch the harbor, letting the fog dissipate so she can see the path back to the *Annihilator*. There's nothing in their way, but her hands won't stop shaking. What if a troop of city guards walks by? What if they've changed the patrols and assigned some to walk the docks at night? In Anna's mind, they appear out of the blackness like ghosts and run straight across the harbor at the *Dragon's Breath*.

"Captain!" Yorren whispers from behind her, jarring her out of her thoughts, "Wrom has bread and flour, there are fruits and vegetables in here as well. How much do you want us to take?"

Anna frowns, turning back to scan the docks for guards. "Take as much as you can carry in one trip. We'll come back again if we can."

She steps over the legs of the guard Wrom has bound and gagged. His head shakes back and forth, trying to dislodge the blindfold. Anna feels a twinge of pity—he might get punished for his negligence, or even lose his job tomorrow morning—but she pushes it away, burying the feeling in a satisfied smirk.

She shrouds them in fog again as they carry the crates of food down the ramp, onto the docks, and back to the *Annihilator*.

Chapter Twelve

SARAH

66th day of Summer
Year 1452

The Four-Eyed Griffin

Sarah swallows down the last of her food and tries not to be too obvious as she glances over her shoulder at the strange man in the corner. He's still there. Jash is happy to stand around and talk with her when he's not serving any costumers, and he's offered to walk her home after his shift ends in a couple of hours, but Sarah wants to get back as soon as she can to check on Nellie. She's just going to have to avoid the less crowded streets and hope the stranger won't follow her. She gets to her feet, determined not to look at the strange man again, and walks through the front door out onto the street.

Despite the inn's closeness to the docks, most of its patrons are people who live in Husifi or spend enough time here to explore; it's tucked away from the general public behind another row of taverns and shops. The main streets by the docks are packed with sailors and traders, pirates and foreign travelers. Husifi is the only place to buy Jewel Paint —a sticky substance made of sap and minerals that hardens into a strong, water-proof crust—and people flock from all over Sarenia, Telegarath, Thethria, Denadia, and even Gorthrofen to dip their hands in its lucrative trade. It's the reason almost all of the ships in the Altibrl Sea and the buildings in Husifi are painted bright colors: hulls and roofs are coated with jewel paint to eliminate leaks. The area by Husifi's lone harbor is always full of people, looking to drop off shipments or fill up their empty ships with more goods to trade. Crowded inns, taverns, paint shops, and supply stores line the main streets.

Sarah heads down the streets again at a brisk pace, towards home, but stops when something snags the end of her pants. A fluffy black cat rubs his face against Sarah's leg and then reaches up to paw at her.

"*Sarah,*" the cat blinks, "*I thought you didn't like it down here by the docks? When did you and the dragon get back?*" Sarah reaches down to scratch the cat behind the ears.

"*Just a few hours ago. Have you been down here in the taverns all day, Tiff? You weren't at home when we got back.*"

"*They give out the best scraps here. There's a lot of fish. You know I love fish.*" Sarah laughs and stands up to keep walking, but Tiffany winds around her legs, purring loudly. There's a colony of feral cats that runs through the streets of Husifi, and Tiffany has always been Sarah's favorite. He was the first one she'd talked to.

A week or so after Sarah had arrived in Husifi, she'd been hanging out with the cats down at the market. Four of them seemed to like her: Fiona the tabby cat, Mark the scruffy orange one, Charlie the white, and Tiffany, the rambunctious young black cat.

Tiffany had been snuffling around the bottom of the fish stall. He'd paused in his search, craning his neck to sniff the air, and announced, *"I wonder if the stuff they sell the humans tastes better than the scraps they throw us down by the docks."* Sarah had hummed and started to answer.

"I think—" and then she'd remembered that this was a cat. She stared at Tiffany, unblinking, for several seconds, and then whipped around to look over her shoulder at the rest of the market. It hadn't been crowded that time of day; no other person was anywhere near her. The kitten had *talked*.

"Tiffany," she whispered, "Did you just *say* something?"

The kitten trotted up to her and deposited a tiny scrap of fish scales in her lap. *"How come you're not eating? Here, have this. I'm full already."*

Sarah dusted the fish scales off her lap with a sharp smack of her hand, scooting backwards and away from the cat. *"You can talk?"*

Tiffany blinked. *"Obviously. If you can understand me, you must be one of those 'speaker' types. There's a few of them around. How come you haven't answered me before?"*

"I'm a what-type?"

"A speaker."

When she questioned him further, the kitten didn't seem

to know much more on the subject.

Sarah ran home to go and ask Nellie, who seemed surprised that Sarah didn't know she was a Speaker.

"*It's how you can talk to me,*" Nellie explained, "*And why you can speak any language you like with little or no training.*"

"*I guess I just thought I was really good at learning languages,*" Sarah said with a shrug. She'd been top of her class in Spanish at school, and had taught herself both French and German at home. "*But wait—how come I've never heard a cat speak before? I used to hang out with the strays back home sometimes. And what about dogs? My sister had a dog. Do they talk too?*"

Nellie shook her head. "*I don't know exactly how it works, but I do know that some languages are easier than others: you have to listen to some for longer before you can speak them. And not all Speakers can speak all languages. Some of them only get as far as the human ones. But others can speak Dragon and Griffin and Sphinx, and some can even talk to cats, like you.*"

For a while, she was a little disappointed that it wasn't because of her unusual intelligence that she could pick up languages so quickly. But then she started to spend time sitting by the docks and listening to people speak in languages she couldn't understand, picking apart the words and sorting them in her mind, and marveling when she woke up the very next day fluent in those languages. It was incredible, and Sarah couldn't get enough of it. She followed foreigners around almost non-stop for a week, picking up Sarenian, Thethrian, Denadian, Telegarathian, five or so dialects of Gorthrofenese, and even some Onoran, which was supposed to be a dead language. She talked to stray cats and dogs, birds, lizards, snakes, and even a moth once.

During this time, Tiffany unofficially adopted her and Nellie, deciding to sleep in their cave at night and following Sarah everywhere. It took a few more weeks for Sarah to realize that Tiffany was, in fact, a male cat. But when she later offered to change his name, the cat refused, stating that he already had it memorized and why did Sarah think it was a feminine name? Sarah tried to explain it to him, but he couldn't grasp the concept. Cats don't have gendered names, or at least the cats of Husifi don't. So Tiffany's been Tiffany ever since.

As she stands there petting the cat, puzzling about the stranger at the inn and trying not to look back, Sarah's nerves get the better of her. She straightens and turns to watch the door of the *Four-Eyed Griffin*.

"*Sarah? Something bothering you, little sister?*" Tiff paws at her feet.

"*I'm not your little sister, I'm much older than you.*" Sarah answers, brushing a bit of hair out of her eyes so she can see better. She scoops Tiff up into her arms and keeps walking.

"*I grew up faster. I have better instincts. You looked after me when I was younger, now it's my turn to look after you.*" the cat chatters on, but Sarah isn't listening. A cold shiver runs down her spine. Someone's watching her. She turns around and searches through the crowd in the street until she sees him. It's the pale man with the furs from the *Four-Eyed Griffin*. His gaze meets hers, and he starts forward, pushing his way through the crowd.

"*Sarah?*" Tiffany asks, sounding as worried as a cat can sound.

Sarah starts down the alley, letting Tiff leap out of her arms on the way. Footsteps pad through the dirt behind her. She looks over her shoulder and sees something moving through the shadows. She speeds her pace into a brisk walk. The warm night air blows against her cheek, tugging a strand of hair out from behind her ear. Why is he following her? He's obviously not from around here: with all those furs, he looks as if he's never been to Husifi before in his life. The alley dumps out into another street, the dirt turning to cobblestones. Someone else is walking up ahead of her. Maybe Sarah knows them, maybe they can help. She tries to catch up. The woman in front of her slows down and glances over her own shoulder. Her face is pale under the light of a street lamp, but full of freckles and sunburned on her nose and the tops of her cheeks. Long red hair is braided into a circle around the top of her head. She stops under the street lamp and takes something out of her pocket. *What should I do?* Should she tell this woman about the strange man behind them? She only has a few more steps...

But the woman looks up, gazing past Sarah as if she's invisible, and stares hard down the street at the stranger.

"Colf!" Sarah catches the angry whisper under the woman's breath, even from several yards away. Tiff still trots along at Sarah's feet, not troubled in the slightest.

"*Who are those people?*" he asks. Sarah puts a finger to her lips to try and shush him, and leads him a few steps further to another alley. They duck inside, and Sarah stands facing the street, heart pounding in her throat, feet spread apart in what she thinks is a fighting stance. She wipes her hair out of her eyes. No one's coming. Soft voices float through the air. Sarah creeps forward and peeks around the corner of the building, toward the strangers. The woman is still standing under the lamppost, and the man wearing the furs is with her. Their heads are bent together, and they're talking in urgent whispers. Sarah can't make out anything they're saying. She moves a little bit closer, flattening herself against the building, into the shadows. Tiff wanders out into the middle of the street, tail straight up and ears pricked. Sarah tries to wave him back, but he won't look at her, instead staring at the two in the street with alert intensity. *That cat's going to get himself killed.* But she's close enough now that she can hear bits and pieces of the conversation.

"...not...I *left for a reason*..." says the woman's voice, in Sarenian.

"*You...can't abandon...started*..." answers the man.

"...your *rebellion, not mine*..."

Soft footsteps pad against the dirt to Sarah's left. She freezes. Five or so silhouettes pass in front of her in the darkness, heading for the two people under the lamppost.

The new figures melt into the night. Sarah can just make out a few of them moving in the shadows. They're surrounding the people under the streetlamp.

"*Colf!*" one of the figures says, "*We've been looking for you for a week! You're going to have to come back with us.*"

The woman pulls her hood up over her head, stepping behind the man wearing the furs—Colf, Sarah assumes—who stands and faces the one talking, his face a mask of anger.

"*I don't know what you mean. I'm here under the King's orders.*"

The soldier laughs, the light of one of the lampposts illuminating his face. It's the pirate—the one who warned Sarah earlier that she was being watched.

"*Liar,*" he says. Two other figures leap forward from the shadows, each grabbing one of Colf's arms. He wriggles free with relative ease, shaking the men off to the side. The woman's gone. "*We've got to get you back to Valliseg now, where you belong.*" Colf glares at the other man until he steps forward and whispers something in his ear. Colf's stare hardens, but he holds out his hands and lets the soldier tie them together. Something tugs on Sarah's arm. She almost jumps out of her skin when she sees the strange woman standing next to her.

"*We have to get out of here,*" the woman says in Gaentuki, "*You can trust me.*"

Chapter Thirteen

KAYLOR

66th day of Summer
Year 1452

Shaltac Castle
Valliseg

I have procured you a servant," Sir Martic's voice drones from across his desk, jolting Kaylor from her thoughts about the necklace, "One who hopes to learn from you, and to compete in the tournament next year." Sir Martic stops, still not looking up from his papers, to dip his pen in a pot of ink, "He asked specifically for *you*, the gods know why. Oh, and Lady Kaylor," Kaylor blinks as he looks up—*finally*—from whatever it is he's doing, "He's a mute."

If she'd been less preoccupied with what the boy had dangling around his neck she'd have snapped at Sir Martic for his lack of attention. But the boy's eyes twinkle with mischief as he smirks back at Kaylor, and suddenly she has a strong urge to punch something. *If this kid has done something to Anna*...well, she'll find that out in a minute. With a jerk of her chin to indicate that he should follow her, Kaylor strides out the door.

This is more or less a routine thing for the knights of the King's Guard: more wealthy assistants are called squires, and less wealthy are brought in as servants. There has to be some way to train both since everyone is allowed to compete in the tournament, and either class would be offended if they weren't included. It's apparently a good deal more complicated, but that's the extent of what Kaylor understands. But she has a feeling that this boy isn't here to train with her.

The boy has Anna's necklace. Kaylor's friend has never parted with it in her life, or at least not since Kaylor's known her. It belonged to Anna's mother.

As soon as they're far enough down the hallway, where Sir Martic won't be able to hear them, Kaylor springs into action, turning and slamming the boy up against the wall, her drawn sword pressed to his throat. His hands fly up into the air on either side of his face and he swallows, Adam's apple bobbing up and down centimeters from the sharp edge of the sword.

"Where," Kaylor whispers, "did you get that necklace?"

He stares back at her with frightened eyes, then opens and closes his mouth, but no sound comes out. It takes Kaylor a minute to remember that he's a mute. She steps back, letting her sword fall to her side, and studies him. He dusts himself off while his eyes track her movements.

Kaylor lets out the breath she's been holding in. There's nothing else for it.

"Come on," she says, "My room's that way. There's a pen and paper in there." She walks him down the hallway with her hand clamped around his elbow, struggling to keep her thoughts from swimming through speculation about her friend.

A year ago, there had been three of them. Anna, Sarah, and Kaylor. It was a hot summer day in the park, and they decided to go out to their quiet space down by the lake. Sarah saw something move in the reeds and got to her feet, grinning back at them. And then Anna after her, and Kaylor at the back. They walked in a line, gripping each others' hands. Until the ground dropped out from beneath Kaylor's feet, her scream swallowed up into the crushing noise around her, and they were gone. Kaylor wasn't in the reeds anymore and Anna and Sarah were gone.

She thought she'd lost them forever. Until one day when she'd been traveling through Morento, a southern port city of Sarenia. She caught a glimpse of fabric, the gaudy floral pattern Anna's skirt had been the day they had been separated. Kaylor had plowed through the crowd, desperate to see her friend, and eventually caught a glimpse of Anna. Her friend's face was thinner, harder, and heavily freckled, shadowed under a large black tricorn with an enormous purple feather. She was talking to several other people across the crowded square and Kaylor couldn't get to her. In moments, she had vanished.

She went back to the guard house to talk to the knights stationed in Morento, hoping they might point her in the right direction to find her friend. She was surprised when they recognized Kaylor's description and immediately began to question her about Anna's whereabouts. It was then that Kaylor learned what Anna had become.

They weren't on the same side anymore.

She'd had to make one of the most difficult choices she's ever made, and she'd gone with the Prince and her oath instead of her friend.

Kaylor steps in front of the boy to open up her door, and then forces him inside with a hand between his shoulder blades.

"Where did you get that necklace?" She waves her hand at a sheaf of blank paper and a pen on the table. He edges over to the other side of the room, putting the table between Kaylor and himself, then grabs a pen and starts to write. He slides the paper to Kaylor when he's finished. She picks it up.

Anna Thomas gave it to me.

The note is written in English, not Sarenian or Denadian. Anna must have taught him to write it. Kaylor frowns and passes it back. "You expect me to believe that she gave that to you, of her own free will?" she motions at the necklace, "Where is Anna? And who are you?"

My name is Patrick. Yours?

She glares at him. Does he think this is a game? "Where's Anna?"

Your name.

"If I tell you my name, will you tell me where she is?"

Maybe.

Kaylor shakes her head. He should know her name already, if he really did ask for her to train him, shouldn't he? Across the table, his face is stretched into a smirk. Kaylor scowls, remembering the mind games Anna used to play with everyone around her, even her closest friends. She knows by now that it's best to just go with it, no matter how absurd it seems. "Fine, then. I'm Kaylor. Lady Kaylor Williams. Now will you please just tell me where my friend is?"

Patrick's face splits into a wide grin, and he nods, reaching out across the table to grab the paper back from her. "Did Anna send you here? To come and get me?"

Patrick nods as he scribbles away across the paper. As he slides it back to her, some of the clutter on the table shifts and exposes the envelope Kaylor received that morning. She swallows down the lump in her throat. Whoever wrote that letter was right: Anna must have sent the boy to ask for Kaylor's help.

She was in Tallipeg at the docks on her ship the Annihilator when I left. She is on her way to Husifi. She wants me to bring you. She will be there in five days' time.

"Does she need my help?"

Patrick shrugs, and sticks the pen into the middle of the ink pot, letting it plink against the bottom. A billion questions swim through Kaylor's head. *Anna's* ship? At the docks in Tallipeg? What's Anna doing with a ship? And why did she send this boy here to get Kaylor, instead of coming herself? Is she hurt? Is she in trouble? Did Prince Casteor or one of his men finally manage to catch her? Should she ask this boy any of that, or will he even answer if she does? Would Anna even trust him enough to tell him the truth?

The guards in Morento said that Anna was a pirate, stealing goods and provisions from the crown by attacking their ships, often slipping onto them at night to steal the merchandise and leaving no other trace. Though they had little concrete evidence against her for stealing, there was no doubt that Anna worked against the crown. There was solid proof that she consorted with unregistered sorcerers, going so far as to ferry them across the sea to Denadia.

But Kaylor made the wrong choice before, she can see that now. If Anna's in trouble, Kaylor will have to go and help her: no matter if her earring breaks and she loses her position as a knight. This is *Anna*, who's brilliant and crafty and loyal to a fault, Anna who's as good as her sister, and Kaylor would never be able to forgive herself if something horrible happened to her.

And then there's the matter of the letter. If the writer is right about Anna, they might be right about the boy stranded in the forest. Kaylor will have to take a detour. "I'll meet you in Tallipeg. There's something I need to take care of first."

Patrick shakes his head furiously and picks the pen back out of the pot.

We will not catch her. She will be leaving tomorrow. We need to go across the plains.

"Across the *plains*? How? You know about the dragon patrols and the sphinx, right? The centaurs, too, and the firefalls," The Terrible Plains are just as dangerous as Caimig Forest, if not more so, during the day.

Not through Thutia and the firefalls, down the river. We can hide in a boat. I have a way to make us invisible.

"You…can make us invisible?" Has Anna sent her an Illusionist? Kaylor suddenly has a lot more respect for the boy standing in front of her. He's almost certainly not registered, and yet here he is, right under the nose of King Shirot himself. If he's caught, he could be killed. She grimaces, regretting how she pinned him to the wall and dragged him down the hallway earlier. "Look…I…I'm sorry. I didn't know you were working for Anna, I thought you might have stolen the necklace."

Patrick shrugs, his smirk softening a little.

She has to admit, traveling with someone who can make them disappear at a moment's notice would make things easier. But she has loose ends to clean up, and a boy to save. Kaylor shakes her head. "I can't go with you. I need to go through Tallipeg, to—pick something up." She swallows, looking down at the papers spread across the table, the work she's been doing for the crown. If she leaves for Husifi, it's more likely than not that she'll never come back. And if she does, she'll be a wanted woman, a fugitive. Does she really have to do this? What were all of those arguments Casteor had seduced her with, so long ago? Why had she turned her back on Anna the first time? *Because I thought it was the right thing to do.* But now she knows better, and there's no time: Anna might need her. And the boy in the letter. Kaylor knows first hand what it's like to be stranded in that forest. When she first came to Sarenia, she escaped the clutches of a vampire by the skin of her teeth. She can't stay here while she knows someone out there needs her help.

Patrick's frowning at her now.

It can not wait?

"It can't."

He nods, but he still doesn't look happy.

I will go to Husifi alone. I can ask Anna to wait for a few days but she will not like it. I believe you should go with me but I will not stop you from going another way. I will see you there.

Kaylor nods, and opens the door for Patrick to leave. Hopefully she'll meet Anna before her friend can get to Husifi, but if there's trouble and she doesn't make it, Patrick can tell Anna she's coming. She gives him quick directions to the servant's quarters and tells him he can use her name to get supplies or a bath or whatever else he might need, and then she hurries him out.

She leans against the back of the door, sliding down until she's sitting on the floor, and lets her head drop into her hands.

I'm going to see Anna again. God help me.

Chapter Fourteen

SARAH

66th day of Summer
Year 1452

Streets of Husifi

e have to get out of here," the woman says in Sarenian, *"You can trust me."* Sarah blinks at her in the darkness, not sure what to do. When people have to tell you to trust them, it usually means you can't, doesn't it? Besides, this strange woman was just talking to the man Sarah was running away from.

"Ennia," the woman tugs on her sleeve, backing into the alley and pulling Sarah after her, *"My name is Juanna Ariet. I'm here to help you find your friends."*

"My friends?" Sarah asks. All her friends are here, now, in the city. What is this woman—Juanna—talking about?

"Your friends," hisses Juanna, glancing around Sarah at the street as if to make sure no one's there, *"The two who came here with you. Tersa, and Conrina,"* she shakes her head, letting out a noise of frustration, *"You might know them as something else."*

"My friends…who came here with me? I didn't come here with anyone, I—" but then she remembers the day in the reeds

116

last summer, down by the lake, and the thought hits her like a ton of bricks. "Anna and Kaylor? *Are they here too?*" Oh, *no...*

"*Yes—yes!*" says Juanna, tugging at Sarah's hand now, "*We need to get out of here, and quickly.*"

Sarah bites the inside of her cheek and considers. Juanna isn't acting like she wants to hurt her—Sarah doesn't even know for certain that the strange man following her wanted to hurt her. And she seems to know a lot about Sarah already. She might even know where she lives.

She can always scream. If one of the guards that patrol the rooftops at night hears her, they'll come down right away to see what the commotion is, and they can save her.

Juanna watches her anxiously, eyes darting up and down the street. Sarah nods, and Juanna's shoulders sag with relief. She grabs Sarah's hand and leads her down the street, to the front of a small, vacant paint shop. Juanna starts to hurry inside, but Sarah plants her feet.

"*Why do we have to go in there?*"

Juanna bites her lip, looking up and down the street again. "*I can't....we shouldn't talk out here. I won't hurt you, I promise. I'm Sarenian—if they catch me doing anything criminal, they'll kick me out of the city.*"

"*If they* catch *you*," Sarah mutters, but she follows the strange woman inside. She *has* to know what Juanna's talking about.

Stacks of barrels, line the walls, smudges of bright paint on their fronts marking their colors. She follows Juanna behind the counter at the back and through a door.

This woman can't be telling the truth, can she? If Sarah had known that Kaylor and Anna had followed her…she would have tried to find them. She would have stopped at *nothing* until she knew they were safe.

They're in a small room, stacked with more barrels and paint. Juanna shoves a blue barrel aside and crouches down to unhook a latch embedded in the floor. She pulls a trap door open and slides down into it, motioning for Sarah to follow. Sarah jumps down after her.

They're in a cellar, probably where the owners of the shop live. Juanna leads her down a narrow hallway and into a small room containing a desk, a basin, and a cot. A young forest dragon is curled onto the cot in a tangle of coils and limbs, tiny horns barely beginning to sprout on his over-sized head. His scaled side rises and falls with his breath. Sarah's surprised they haven't woken him. Juanna sits on the bed next to the dragon and gestures for Sarah to take the chair by the desk.

"How long have you been here?" Juanna whispers, glancing briefly at the sleeping dragon.

"How long have I been where?"

"This world."

"How do you know I'm from another world?"

Juanna laughs, reaching back to scratch the little dragon behind the ears. He grumbles in his sleep, coiling up tighter around himself.

"My father is a Powersenser. He recognized you, from before. He knew you when you were very young. Your name is Ennia, isn't it?"

Sarah blinks at her, *"No. My name is Sarah."* Maybe she

118

has the wrong person. How often do people from 'other worlds' show up here? But then…what about Kaylor and Anna? Is there some other girl with two best friends from another world, one who grew up with this Colf person? There must be. Relief swamps her. Sarah's friends aren't here.

Juanna stops petting the dragon, settling her hands back into her lap. Her eyes narrow as she scrutinizes Sarah.

"I've heard of young children sometimes having memory problems when they're Vanished. Your two friends don't go by their real names either. I wonder if that's what happened to you," she purses her lips and adds, *"My father is never wrong."*

"I'm not from here," Sarah blurts, *"I have parents, and a family, back home. This…Colf, he never could have known me as a child. I grew up somewhere else."*

Juanna's eyes dart away, settling on the dragon nestled into the bed beside her. *"When you were very young…something happened to you. You weren't meant to be part of…anything, not then, but Colf put his trust in the wrong people. They took you away from here, away from your family and your world, so you would grow up somewhere else,"* she shakes her head, *"They had their reasons, but I can't say that I agree with them."*

Sarah stares at the floor, thinking hard. She doesn't remember much of her early childhood. Her parents have never said that she's adopted, but she's had suspicions for a while now. Her brother and sister look like their parents, with the same noses, eyebrows, and the same shaped eyes. And her hair, which is long and straight while the rest of her family's is tightly coiled ringlets. But Sarah has always been different. Her mother always told her she got her looks from her grandparents, who she hadn't seen more than twice before they died when she was eight. It could be true, she supposes, but she'd need more proof to believe it.

But she has some other questions she wants answered. *"What did those men want with your father? Colf? And why didn't the guards stop them?"* That sort of ambush isn't permitted on the streets of Husifi, and Sarah wonders why the guards let it happen. Especially since the soldiers after Colf were from the south.

"I told you he's a Powersenser? Powersensers are…not nearly as common as other sorcerers. King Shirot uses my father to track down sorcerers still living in hiding in Sarenia. The king doesn't care about most of the refugees, since he believes that as long as they're not in his country, they can't hurt him. But there are still people hiding out in the Nedlim Mountains, and no one can find the Shydo in the Winter Swamps. Shirot won't rest until he's found them all. He forces my father to help him. Sometimes he escapes," she sighs, *"As for the soldiers, they were members of the King's Guard, in, I'll admit, a very poor disguise. I don't know why they were allowed to do that openly in the street, only that it's not the first time it's happened."*

Sarah's heard before about the Mad King of the South, trapping and killing the sorcerers in his own country because of his paranoia. Husifi's now home to a growing community of refugees. If this Colf is a sorcerer, and he's escaped from under the King's command, then *"Why doesn't he just leave? Go to Denadia, or somewhere beyond? How can they force him to do that? Can't he just lead them on false trails? Lie about where the other sorcerers are?"*

Juanna looks down at her hands. *"He would, but…they have…something very important to him, and if he doesn't do as they ask, they'll…destroy it."*

There's a loud knock on the bedroom door. Sarah jumps. Juanna squeezes Sarah's shoulder, then gets up to unlatch it. A plump Gaentuki woman in a bright blue dress grabs Juanna in a tight hug, then steps back to look at her, her hands gripping Juanna's elbows.

"Juanna! A group of Sarenian soldiers just walked by outside. Did they see you? Are you okay? Oh!" The woman speaks rapidly in Gaentuki, but stops short when she sees Sarah. *"Who is this?"*

"I'm Sarah."

"Is she part of this rebellion your father's trying to start again?" she asks.

"No, Ellata. Well, not yet."

"What do you mean not yet? You aren't recruiting for him, are you? I thought you wanted nothing to do with it?"

"I don't. But…" she looks at Sarah, meeting her eyes, *"…Sarah deserves to know what's going on. She's been involved in this against her will as well."*

Ellata turns back to Sarah, scrutinizing her. The young dragon snorts in his sleep, pulling a paw up to cover his face.

"Is she one of those children, the ones that Colf—?"

"She might be." Juanna murmurs, so quietly that Sarah almost doesn't hear it.

"One of what children?" Sarah asks, just as quietly.

"Do you have somewhere safe to go for the night?" Ellata

pushes past Juanna into the room, her eyebrows furrowed as she looks Sarah over.

"I do," Sarah says, fidgeting under the force of Ellata's stare, *"But do you know where I can find my friends?"*

To Sarah's surprise, Juanna beams at her, *"I don't think you'll have to find them. My father is bringing them here."*

What? *"He's bringing them* here? *How? When?* Why?"

"It will be best for my father to explain all of this to you—he knows much more about it than I do. Once my father is—liberated, or once I know a little more about the situation, we can sit down for a talk." Sarah opens her mouth, but Juanna *holds up a hand to silence her,* "Tomorrow is festival day. Meet us back here the day after."

"How do you know he'll be back by then? You know some things. You said you know who my friends are."

Juanna sighs. *"I do. But I've told you almost everything I know. The three of you were taken from your parents when you were very young, and my father made a mistake while he was trying to get you back,"* she shakes her head, *"I'm sorry Sarah, but that's all I know. Come back later, and hopefully we'll have more for you. My father is nothing if not persistent, and he plans to be here after festival day,"* Juanna reaches over and grabs Ellata's hand.

"Sarah?" says Ellata, giving Juanna's hand a squeeze and then letting it go, *"Did you need someone to walk you home?"*

"I...um, that's okay. It's not that far from here."

"Okay," Ellata sticks both of her hands in the pockets of her skirt, *"I'll show you out. Just...if you need any help, with anything, Juanna and I are usually at the shop."*

Sarah swallows. *"You're sure you can't tell me anything else?"*

Juanna nods and squeezes Sarah's shoulder. *"Come back later, when I've heard from my father. I'll tell you everything he tells me."*

Sarah nods. Ellata steps forward and takes her hand, leading her out of the shop.

Sarah doesn't know how she manages to get home. She honest-to-god doesn't remember. She's so lost in her thoughts the entire way back she doesn't notice when Tiffany scratches her leg to try and get her attention. She's too *worried* to pay attention to *anything*.

Now, she sits on her bed, rubbing at the scratch and staring at the wall. Tiff yowls as he wanders about the cave, wanting to play. Sarah tunes him out.

"Sarah," Nellie peeks her head into the room, *"What's gotten into you? Can you at least get your cat to quiet down?"*

"I—" Sarah starts, and then stops, and then starts again, *"You remember what I told you about where I'm from? About those friends I had? Kaylor and Anna?"*

Nellie nods, stretching her neck further into the room so she can rest her head on the end of Sarah's bed. Sarah reaches out to scratch behind the dragon's horns.

"Well…I think they're here, in Sarenia. I noticed someone watching me in the Four-Eyed Griffin, or, someone else noticed, and…" Sarah relates the whole story, trying not to leave out any details. Once she's finished, Nellie turns to look at her out of one golden eye.

"So you need to find these friends of yours."

"Yes. As soon as possible."

Nellie hums deep in her throat. *"It's late. Go to sleep, and meet this Colf person after festival day. I'll go with you if you want, to keep you safe. If he really is bringing them here, can we do more than wait?"*

Sarah bites her lip, twisting the blankets between her fingers. *"I suppose not. Just—I'm worried, and I don't like sitting around."*

Nellie lets out a small chuckle, *"None of us do, young one. None of us do."* Sarah looks up and gives Nellie a brief smile. The dragon regards her for a few seconds, and then retreats from Sarah's room.

Chapter Fifteen

ANNA

66th day of Summer
Year 1452

A few miles from Tallipeg
Altibrl Sea

Once Anna's crew is back on the *Annihilator* for the night, after five more runs for goods on the *Dragon's Breath*, Anna can let out a breath of relief. They've managed the raid without any significant problems, despite Anna's misgivings. They haven't been caught at this yet, but that just means it'll happen sooner rather than later. There are already rumors going around, and the *Annihilator*'s presence in Morento has already been connected with the nighttime raids. It's only a matter of time now. At least it didn't happen tonight. Anna's a little shaky and lightheaded from the constant stress she's been under for the past day and a half. She hasn't been sleeping well lately, either.

There is one thing, though. They'd dispensed with the guards Wrom had tied up by locking them securely into the *Dragon's Breath*'s cargo hold, but another sailor had shown up and tried to tackle Hisef on their way back to the *Annihilator*. Yorren and Hisef managed to subdue and gag him, but he'd seen the ship, and the crew aboard it, so they had to take him with them. Anna's nerves were so frayed after that she wouldn't allow another trip back to the *Dragon's Breath* for the rest of the supplies. In fact, she's making them leave the harbor now, in another blur of dense fog.

"Captain Thomas?" someone calls, and Wrom emerges onto the deck out of the mist, holding the hands of the prisoner behind his back. He tries to twist free, but she forces his wrist sideways, making him bend over in pain.

"Yes, Wrom?" says Anna, tucking her hands behind her back and plastering an exaggerated scowl on her face, "Who is this?" She's already been told, of course, but she wants the prisoner to feel unimportant.

"This is the one we caught," Wrom says, holding the sailor in place, "Says his name's Jesan. You wanted to speak to him?"

"Ah, yes," Anna stares up at them both, crossing her arms and studying the sailor. People tend to get uncomfortable when Anna stares at them for too long. Sometimes she can get them to spill their secrets just by looking at them. It's a trick she uses to her full advantage. The sailor is sun-burnt, greasy, and otherwise dirty, his clothes ripped and worn. Nothing more than a typical crewman. Anna turns back to Wrom, "Does he know where he is?" She needs to know if he knows the name of her ship. If he doesn't know, Anna might be able to let him go.

"No, Captain. But he claims to be the first mate on the *Dragon's Breath*."

Footsteps clatter across the deck behind her, until

Yorren stops by her side, "Probably enhancing his rank so that we'll try to ransom him, 'stead of just throwing him overboard," he mutters into her ear.

Anna turns back to the sailor, and stares him full in the face, grabbing his chin and forcing him to look at her when he won't do it on his own. His eyes are fearful. Sweat drips in cold tendrils down his forehead. "Hmm…No, I don't think this one's worth anything. You can toss him if you'd like, Wrom."

The sailor's eyes widen in panic, and he struggles, trying to break out of Wrom's grip. Wrom looks back at Anna in confusion, opening her mouth to speak, but Anna holds up a hand to stop her.

"Okay—okay! I'm not the first mate. Just don't…I know what's in the water, please have mercy!"

Anna sighs deeply, lifting her fingers to tap against her mouth, then looks back at the sailor, staring him down. "I don't tolerate lies on my ship, Jesan. I suppose…if you're willing to tell us the truth—" the sailor nods, swallowing, "—then I can let Wrom leave you in the brig, for now. Thank you Wrom, that will be all." Wrom hurries off, the sailor in tow. His legs tremble, and he doesn't struggle when Wrom leads him down the stairs to the brig.

"That's a load of crap," says Yorren. Anna turns around to smirk at him.

"I know. He doesn't look stupid enough to be a first mate, does he?"

Yorren scowls. "I meant about the lies, Captain."

"Oh," Anna says with a shrug, "Should I rephrase that?

I don't tolerate lies that don't benefit me. Is that better?"

"Fine," says Yorren, still scowling.

"We're outlaws, Yorren, what do you expect?" Yorren opens his mouth to retort, eyes livid, but Anna interrupts him before he can speak, "Will you go and supervise over there, please? I don't trust Zer not to drop any of that." Anna waves her hand over the ship, in the direction of the boy, who's struggling with a box at least as large as he is. Yorren swears and hurries across the deck.

Sure that Yorren's got it well in hand—he is her first mate for a reason—Anna heads up the stairs to where Choffson is leaning against the wheel. She turns to survey the crew as they move about on the deck.

"It was a good raid, Captain," says Choffson from behind her.

"It was. No one was caught, no one had to so much as lift a sword, and I swear we've never been quieter," she frowns, "Still, we had to capture that sailor. I can't ignore that. Someone else might have seen us and kept quiet, or this sailor—Jesan—might get word back to the guards about us if we let him go." She taps her fingernails against the railing, and then a thought hits her. "Yorren!" she yells from above, stealing her first mate's attention away from Zer, "Tell Wrom to check that sailor for trinkets. Anything that looks like it could be Cursed."

Yorren salutes her mockingly from below, and she returns the gesture.

"Oh, and Choffson?"

"Yes, Captain?"

"Set our course for Husifi. We're to meet with Colf there, as soon as possible."

"Uh…Captain?" Choffson shuffles, tearing Anna's attention away from the rest of her crew.

"What?"

"I thought…don't we still have a, uh, special shipment to pick up?"

Anna turns so she can study Choffson's face. More refugees? But Colf was the one who organized that. Does he want her in two places at once?

"Is that now? I can't possibly get them all the way to Denadia, then return and go to Husifi, without taking another couple of weeks."

Choffson's expression is quizzical. "Are you sure Colf wants to meet with you now?"

"Yes. I—I must have forgot. About the refugees, not the meeting." Anna shoots Choffson a look as he opens his mouth, she assumes to correct her. A cold feeling crawls down Anna's throat. How could she forget about more refugees? They might have been out there for days— shivering in the cold wind kicked up by the sea at night, expecting a boat with beds and rooms and shelter over their heads: one that never showed up. "How long have we been meaning to pick up those refugees?"

Choffson scratches his head. "Not long. The date in the message was set for tomorrow."

"Huh," says Anna, staring out over her crew again. Colf isn't usually that disorganized. "Something must have gone wrong."

"What are we going to do?"

Anna taps her fingers against the railing again, making a racket as she thinks it over. "Husifi is just as safe as Denadia, isn't it? We'll pick them up and take them with us there, and any who want to stay can. Any who want to go on to Denadia will have to wait for us to finish with Colf."

Colf. Always on Colf's leash, always doing what he says. Anna's fingers curl into fists around the railing. He's why she's still here in the first place, he's the reason they have enough provisions. If they weren't ferrying the refugees across the ocean for him, they could get enough from raiding, true, but Anna's tethered to Colf for one other reason: information.

Anna has scattered memories of her life dating back to when she was seven years old, but most of the ones before that are clouded and subtle, like they're hidden behind a curtain. But it's shear: there are small holes in a few places, worn down thread in others. She remembers a smile and a laughing face, a cascade of tidy brown curls just like her own. She remembers a car, bright red, pulled up against the curb, a deep frown marring the normally happy features and creases around sad brown eyes. Her mother used to tell her she had her father's eyes, but Anna knows they're not the same green. She's checked. And her nose is different, too, than either of her parents. She thinks she took after one of her grandparents: on her mother's side, of course. But they live in Europe, and any memory she had of them is gone with Anna's mother. Or, that's what she's been told. "Europe" is starting to look an awful lot like Sarenia.

Colf knows something, and he's keeping it from her. He told her—when she met him not long after she was dumped into the ocean on this new world—that her mother was alive, that he knew her. He found Anna again, months later, after she took charge of the Annihilator. That was when he gave her this task: ferry the sorcerers across the ocean, and he'll give her information. And perhaps along the way she'll find who she's looking for amongst the refugees.

Anna wonders if it would be better just to go it alone. But Kaylor and Sarah are here too, she's sure of it, and Colf has some of that information too. She knows because Colf let it slip in front of her, and she's been bothering him about it ever since. She's gotten him to tell her where Kaylor is—but only because he believes Anna can't get to her friend at the palace. Which is where he's dead wrong. But he hasn't told her about Sarah. No matter: she's sure he knows more than he's saying, and she'll get him to tell her soon.

And that means something big. If Anna's mother is from this world, if Anna's from it too, then that's why she's here. If her friends are here, that means they must be like her. They must have come from this place just like Anna.

She's already sent Patrick out to get Kaylor. And once she finds them, they can all be together again just like they have been since sixth grade, and Anna's world will be one step closer to equilibrium. And then she can be rid of Colf, and her work with the refugees, and her friends can help her find her mother.

Chapter Sixteen

KAYLOR

66th day of Summer
Year 1452

Shaltac Castle
Valliseg

*T*here's no time to lose. But Kaylor can't just leave—the Prince can't know that she's going. She'll have to sneak out. So she waits for night to fall, passing the time by flipping through papers on her table and staring out of her tiny window. Clouds gather in the sky outside, but they're wispy and insubstantial. Tonight should be clear enough for flying. She just has to hope no one will look up and see her.

She has one of the castle servants bring her dinner to her room, but she can't bear to eat more than a few bites. She's too sick with worry—over Anna, mostly, but also because of the letter, the helpless boy it mentions, and how fast all of this is happening. Just yesterday, she was training in the yard with the other knights, knocking Redbrak off his feet and cutting down dummies with practice swords. This morning, she was at a briefing with the Prince. What if she's doing the wrong thing, leaving the castle like this? Could she do more good here trying to convince Casteor that his plans are stupid than she could running after a friend she already abandoned? She has the same argument with herself several times while she waits for nightfall, but always decides to do the same thing: she needs to help Anna, no matter what the consequences.

So that evening, after the castle's inhabitants have retired to their bedrooms, she creeps out of her quarters with a travel sack slung across her back. She's packed the money, her water skin, a bedroll, a knife for skinning, a knife for throwing, and an extra change of clothes. Her sword stays strapped to her hip, the sheath buckled securely to the belt around her waist. She considers leaving her chainmail and uniform, but the guards or servants are less likely to stop her if she's dressed like a knight. As for the chainmail, she doesn't particularly want to face the creatures in Caimig Forest without it.

She debates for several minutes whether to take the orange teardrop earring sitting on the bedside table. Eventually, she sticks it in her left ear, back where it was the day she landed in Sarenia. It will be her reminder of the oath she made—the oath she's about to break. The other one's still with Prince Casteor. She wonders how long it'll take for it to burst.

She makes her way as silently as she can down the hallway, edging past the doors to the rooms of her fellow knights. The only way she can get past the guards unseen is by going through the atrium: an enormous, roofed garden. In there, vines and crawling plants cover the walls three stories up to a row of large, open windows. The walls outside are craggy with statues, window sills, and fancy lines of architecture, making them easily climbable.

Kaylor slips through the door into the airy indoor garden, tiptoeing over the rough sandstone under her feet. The quiet trickle of the fountain at ground level echoes up through the curved walls. Her quarters are on the second story, and so is the walkway she's on. Here, immovable glass covers the many windows lining the wall. To get to the open windows, she'll have to climb the ivy to the walkway above her.

Kaylor swings out over the railing, gripping one of the smooth pillars between the levels tightly. She grabs a section of the ivy and tugs, hard—it doesn't budge. Trusting that it will hold her weight, Kaylor scales the plants twining around the pillars, making her way to the upper level.

She makes it outside without any problems. Still, Kaylor scans the open gardens around the castle once her feet hit the ground, making sure that no one's out and about to see her. A bright, full moon illuminates the castle's outdoor gardens before her, making it easier to find the path she wants to take. The stables are behind the armory, just through a small courtyard with some statues and hedges. It's a church: Sarenian places of worship are outside, under the sky and the trees. Eleven statues stand in a circle around a central pedestal, where six larger, more elaborate statues face them. The Imperial Six at the center, the other gods surrounding them and waiting for instruction.

She hesitates for a second under the statue of Sheolida, Kaylor's patron goddess. It's said that all sorcerers receive their powers from a corresponding god, and if that's true,

134

Kaylor's powers come from this one. Her cold marble brow is furrowed, her right hand clasped around a stout sword and her left up and extended, ready to cast a shield. Kaylor lets out a breath, and glances at the other five gods in the center. Larosri, goddess of storms, watches her out the corner of her eye, her long hair and full dress billowing in a non-existent wind. Gweligen, goddess of languages, a snake twined around her right arm and a hawk perched on her left shoulder, smiles down more kindly. Together, these three goddesses are the Triplets.

On their right are Lefyrin and Theoloden, gods of life and death respectively. Lefyrin's right hand is held up in the air, in the act of releasing a small, delicately carved sparrow. His left hand is clasped in Theoloden's right. A nearly identical sparrow, slumped and clearly dead, is cradled gently in the god of death's other hand. They are the Old Ones, the First Gods.

Reygreon, the Lone God, patron god of Flamestarters and god of fire, takes the last place in the circle. His eyes are somehow colder and harder than any of the others, and both of his hands hover just in front of his chest, cradling a small lick of flame.

Kaylor's never been very religious, but she can't help but feel as though the statues are alive and watching her. She tries to push aside her guilt as they stare down at her with judgment written upon their cold, marble faces. She has a good reason for doing this.

Still, she lets out a breath of relief once she's out of the hedges. She can see the silhouette of the stables now, out across a wide green yard. Large wooden posts stick out of the ground at intervals, but there are no fences to keep the horses in.

Kaylor makes her way to the back of one of the stall doors and leans over it.

"Ratha!" she whispers. A large white nose hits her on the forehead, pushing her a step back. She laughs, patting Ratha's nose, "Did you miss me? I've missed you. It's been, what, a whole day?" Ratha nickers as Kaylor reaches up to scratch between his ears.

She steps back and reaches over the stall door. With a soft clink, the lock opens and the door swings forward.

Ratha steps out, unfurling a pair of magnificent, pure white, feathery wings. The faint moonlight ripples through the iridescent feathers as Ratha stretches them. Kaylor hugs the pegasus's face as he steps forward, pushing her another step back.

It isn't long before she's got a saddle strapped to Ratha's back: one of the big ones with extra straps, meant for two people. She settles in and straps down her legs, leaning forward against Ratha's neck.

"Ratha," she whispers into the pegasus's ear, "Up."

The pegasus tosses his head and starts forward, gaining speed as he races across the grass, and soon they're in the air.

The sprawling expanse of Sarenian countryside rushes along miles beneath them. The river glints in the bright moonlight, cutting through the city and on to the forest. No matter how many times she's taken Ratha out flying over

Valliseg, she's never gotten used to the sight. Or the feel of the air as it rushes and whistles past her face, whipping her hair up into a tangled mess. She lets out a breathless laugh as Ratha veers to the side to avoid a wisp of cloud.

In a couple of wing-beats they're floating over the dense Caimig Forest, with hardly a gap in the trees to show the ground beneath them. She looks toward the coastline in the distance: the great, walled city of Tallipeg a jagged outcrop against the unusual sapphire blue of the Altibrl Sea. That's where Anna is.

A few hours later, Kaylor commands Ratha to descend. Her legs have been asleep for a while, and now she can barely feel them. They're heading for a small, familiar clearing in the forest below. Kaylor's landed here several times before, when she's had to travel between the capital and Tallipeg, or vice versa. She leans forward onto Ratha's back as the altitude decreases, bracing herself against the padded saddle with her forearms in case the landing isn't as smooth as it should be. Ratha glides forward just above the ground, hooves churning beneath him until they connect with the grass. They circle the clearing a few times while he slows down, his breath coming out in labored puffs. He stutters to a stop, shaking his wings out before he folds them back into place against his sides.

"Right," Kaylor lets out a deep breath, reaching down to scratch Ratha's shoulder, "We're almost there."

She unbuckles the straps and dismounts, then leads him forward through the trees, keeping her muscles tensed as they head down the overgrown path. Her left hand hovers over the hilt of her sword while she grips Ratha's lead with her right. There are Gauekos and vampires about in the forest at night, and she'd rather not be caught unawares. As they go, bits and pieces of wood and stone litter the ground in increasing amounts of rubble. Eventually they make it to a small wooden building, still miraculously standing, nestled into the dense forest. Kaylor leads Ratha around the side to a sheltered space she cut out of the bushes for him last time she was here. She ties a rope to Ratha's halter and attaches the other end to a nearby tree. She sighs, stroking Ratha's head. She won't be able to groom him tonight: it'll have to wait until morning. She can't be out and about right now, and Ratha shouldn't be either. Still, she unbuckles his saddle and slides it off as quickly as she can.

According to the people in Valliseg, this place was built as another stop for travelers: like the *Chatty Sphinx*, except on a larger scale. Unfortunately, they couldn't protect such a large settlement from the creatures in the forest. Wickfen Village was deserted within a year.

Beside her, the pegasus snorts and paws at the ground. "I'm sorry, Ratha," Kaylor says, reaching up to play with a strand of his mane, "But we had to go through the forest. It'd be too hard to hide from Casteor in Thutia. No one's going to find us here." She gives him a pat on the neck, "You have to get to sleep now. You know the drill." She reaches into her pocket and digs out a small handful of black seeds, holding them out to Ratha on her flat palm. The pegasus lips them eagerly off her hand.

After collecting her supplies from the saddlebags and

giving Ratha one more goodnight pat, Kaylor ducks in through the front door of the building, scraping away a stray cobweb as she goes. It's been a while since she's been here. This is where she landed, after something—or someone—pulled her to Sarenia from her home.

"Wickfen village," she murmurs to herself. She forces her voice a little lower and affects a Sarenian accent, *"You're lucky the Gauekos didn't get you out there, Kaylor. Or the vampires."* That's what Keripen told her, when she'd shown up on his doorstep in a torn-up t-shirt, neon-colored tennis shoes, and a bright orange miniskirt. She lets out a breathy laugh. So much has changed since then.

This boy—the one in the letter she found earlier that day—is he here? It's too dangerous to search in the middle of the night. She hopes he's been able to dodge the dangers of the forest while he's been here. She'll look around the village in the morning, and then she'll go to the *Chatty Sphinx* and ask Keripen if he's seen anything. But part of her wants to go out and search now, Gaeukos and vampires be damned. As little as a month ago, she wouldn't have even thought about it; she'd be out there scouring every inch until she found her quarry. Someone could be out there, someone who doesn't know how dangerous this forest is at night, and what happens if he gets hurt? What happens if he *dies*?

But what if you die while you're out looking for him, Sarah's voice says in her ear, *What if he's already dead, and you die too because you went out looking? What if you die, and he makes it through the first night, but he's lost in the forest and can't find a way out? Do you really think he'll make it through two nights in a row? Better to bide your time, go in the morning.*

Kaylor closes her eyes and works on slowing her breathing. She'll wait. She has to wait.

She rolls out her bedroll then digs the black seeds out of her pocket, then lays them out on her palm. There are only five left. She frowns down at them. "Remember," she mutters to herself, "the Gaeukos only go after you if you're awake." She always does that—talks to herself—when she has to travel alone. It makes her feel less lonely. One time, months ago, she started talking to herself in Sarenian. It scared her as soon as she noticed: she immediately forced herself to say something in English, just to make sure she could still remember it. Now, she doesn't let herself speak Sarenian unless she's talking to another person; she can't lose that part of herself, she just *can't*. It's a little bit of home.

She pops one seed into her mouth and tips the rest back into her pocket. She settles under the blankets again and is asleep within seconds.

She jerks awake not long after the sun breaches the horizon. Fingers of pink and purple streak through the sky above the ruined house, barely visible through the dense branches of the trees. She packs up her belongings and sets them outside the entrance, creeping through the doorway and across the leaves so as not to wake Ratha.

Moss, lichen, and leaves coat the ground and the deserted buildings. Kaylor scours the village, from the tiniest shack to the old town hall, and ventures into the trees as far as she dares in every direction. There's no sign of a boy. If he's made it to the road or has found any people to travel with, he's likely at the *Chatty Sphinx* or on his way to it. She's got to move on.

She makes her way back to the ruined house, and soon after, Ratha launches himself into the air again with Kaylor fastened into the saddle. She keeps her eyes glued to the forest below her as they glide over the trees, peering through the cracks in the leaves. She doesn't see hide nor hair of the boy.

They land in another clearing several hours later, just as the sun is setting. It's late. Too late. She decides then and there that if Keripen hasn't seen this boy, she'll venture back into the forest tonight and she won't come back until she finds him. She dismounts and leads Ratha down a rough and obscure deer trail until they reach the road, eyes darting back and forth the whole way, looking for any sign of movement. There's nothing. Kaylor swallows. She can't go looking yet—she needs to drop Ratha off and go inside first. Besides, if he's this close, the Naracos can keep him safe.

A gate looms ahead of them in the darkness. Two large cats pace back and forth in front of it, ready to fend off any terrors that might emerge from the forest. Kaylor dismounts and leads Ratha forward. The first cat bounds over to meet her, and Kaylor has to fight the urge to flinch. They aren't going to hurt her, she knows that, but she hasn't yet been able to shake the urge to turn and run whenever she sees them. The cat stops a few feet from her, tail swishing back and forth in large arcs, raising its nose to sniff at the air. Kaylor holds out a hand, and the Naraco tilts its head to nuzzle against it, purring loudly. This one's name… starts with an S, she can't remember. She grins down at it while it walks around her side, rubbing its face on her elbow. The other one bounds forward, not wanting to miss out on the attention. Behind her, Ratha snorts and stamps his feet in discomfort. He's met the cats before, but he doesn't like them much. It's a credit to his training that he doesn't startle or bolt.

Kaylor reaches the gate with her Naraco escort, Ratha trailing a little behind, and pounds her fist twice on the rough wood. A few minutes later a tiny door swings opens to reveal a tired young face. Immediately the door closes again and the gate unlatches, swinging inward to let Kaylor and Ratha through.

Keripen's nephew launches himself forward to give Kaylor a hug.

"Lady Kaylor," he says, "Uncle will be delighted to see you!"

Kaylor laughs, extricating herself from the boy's

embrace, "I'm sure he will be. Is he awake?"

The boy—his name is Ashard, she thinks; or was it Arden?—nods vigorously, bending around her to take Ratha's reins, "I'll wake him. He'll want to know you're here. I'll go and put Ratha in the stable, you can go and wait for him inside."

A tiny sliver of guilt pinches Kaylor's gut. Of course, Keripen's nephew remembers her *and* her pegasus' names, and she isn't even sure what *his* is.

She leaves him to take care of Ratha and makes her way to the inn, pushing the unlocked door open with ease. The Naracos will keep any harmful creatures out, and the creatures in the forest keep the harmful strangers out, so it's never been worth Keripen's effort to lock the front door.

The main dining room looks exactly the same as it did the last time she was here—tables spread throughout the open room, the light of the fire on the far end dancing across the wooden walls. Candles still burn on the chandelier and in the lights along the wall. It's empty at this time of night.

Kaylor winds her way between the tables to the hearth, where a large, plush rug covers the wood just in front of the fire. She crouches down on the rug a few feet from the warm glow of the flames, and that's when she realizes that she isn't alone.

A boy, probably around her age, sits staring at her from the shadows under one of the tables with cold, crystal-blue eyes.

She smiles at him, trying to cover her shock with

friendliness, "I'm Kaylor," she says, "I'm a traveler, from Valliseg. Who are you?"

"Tyler," he says in an American accent, "My name's Tyler."

Chapter Seventeen

SARAH

67th day of Summer
Year 1452

Sarah's House
Husifi

oday is the last day of summer. There are six seasons, and at the end of each, there's a festival day for one of the gods. Specifically, one of the Imperial Six. There are seventeen gods, and the Imperial Six are the ones that make the laws of man, time, and nature. This is the festival of Larosri, Goddess of Storms, and today Husifi is a buzzing hub of non-stop activity.

The real festival doesn't start until the evening and doesn't end until the early hours of the morning. Sarah floats through the whole thing in a haze.

Nellie wants her scales painted in blue, gray, and black—the colors of Larosri—so Sarah obliges, letting her hands glide over the dragon's side while her mind wanders. She remembers following Kaylor and Anna down the street by the park, on the walk home from school through their quiet neighborhood, past the old oak tree Anna used to climb. She remembers riding down that same street in the car Kaylor "borrowed" from her brother, munching on french fries and milk shakes on their way to one of the crowded parties Kaylor used to drag them to. Anna, who keeps at least six bobby pins buried in her hair in case she has to pick a lock; Kaylor, who once jumped off the roof onto a trampoline because her older brother dared her to.

They're getting into trouble *right this minute*, Sarah knows it, and she's stuck here painting the scales of a fussy dragon on festival day.

After four o'clock, once it's cool enough to venture outside, Sarah's nerves are eating at her so much she can't concentrate on anything. She decides to head down to the paint shop and demand more answers, whether Juanna wants to give them to her or not.

When she gets there, it's closed and locked, the windows barred with thick planks of wood. Many of the businesses do this in Husifi, as a precaution against the kind of rowdy fun that isn't tolerated on most days of the year. Criminals get past the dragons most easily on festival days. Sarah wants *answers*, dammit, and she wants them *now*. But she can't break into the shop. Maybe she'll see Juanna at the festival.

That night at the festival, even though Sarah scans every crowd, peers into every corner, she doesn't catch sight of Juanna's head of red hair. Nellie runs off to romp with a few of her dragon friends, and Sarah slips away.

She finds Tiffany in her room, curled in the corner, avoiding the crowded streets. Sarah scoops him up and heads to bed, exhausted despite her anxiety. But when she goes to climb in, her hand crinkles against the fabric.

There's something on top of the covers. It's an envelope, and it's got her name written on it. Sarah picks it up and slides her finger under the flap to open it.

Hello Sarah,

My name is Mr. Lee. I don't know if this letter will reach you in time, though I can only hope it will. There is a very dangerous man on your trail. His name is Colf Ariet.

Your friends are here, in Sarenia, and are on their way to Husifi, no doubt as a part of Colf's plan. When they arrive, Anna and Kaylor should have three boys with them. The six of you are the reason Colf thinks he can overthrow King Shirot, or the Mad King in the South as the Gaentuki call him.

Now, I know this sounds like a noble goal, but before you follow Colf's plan blindly, there are a few things you need to know about him, his cause, and yourselves. I have set a meeting place with Anna; she will tell you where to find me when she arrives. I can answer any questions you might have.

Sincerely,
Mr. Lee

So Colf really *is* behind a rebellion in the South. And that's why Juanna claimed that Sarah is involved against her will: *The six of you are the reason Colf thinks he can overthrow King Shirot.* So…does that mean Colf is the reason Sarah and her friends are here? Did he pluck them out of their lives in Colorado and bring them to this other world? Is that what they need to know about him? Or is it something else? Who are the three boys with Anna and Kaylor? And what things about themselves can this Mr. Lee tell them? Kaylor and Anna will both want to meet him, Kaylor so she can decide on the most righteous course of action and Anna so she can obtain more information. Still, they'll need to be on their guard. There's no way to know for sure that this isn't an ambush. If Sarah, Anna, and Kaylor are already marked as a part of this rebellion, it's possible someone is after them.

Sarah folds the note, smoothing the creases until they're sharp, and tucks it under her pillow. She'll have to be on her guard tomorrow when she talks to Juanna.

She wakes the next morning with a large lump of furry cat sprawled across her chest. She pushes Tiffany off, blinking her bleary eyes up at the ceiling. An impending sense of doom is hanging over her head, and it takes her a few minutes to remember why. *Kaylor and Anna.* Sarah groans, rolling over onto her side. But Juanna told her to come back today, and she'll be damned if she doesn't show up on time.

Sarah gets up and dressed without bothering to wake Nellie. Tiffany trails along sleepily behind her as she winds her way through the streets toward the paint shop.

"*Sarah,*" Tiffany whines, "*Why are you up this early? Sunrise was several hours ago, and you didn't wake up then. It's time to go back to sleep now."* He yawns, shaking his fluffy fur out until it stands on end, *"Humans are so strange."*

Sarah huffs a quiet laugh, but doesn't answer. The empty windows of the paint shop glint in the sunlight as she ducks in through the narrow doorway.

Ellata is waiting for her behind the counter. As Sarah walks into the shop, she motions for Sarah to follow her, and leads her to the back room where the entrance to the cellar is.

Sarah thanks her and clambers down the ladder into the hallway. Juanna appears at the end and beckons Sarah forward, into a different room. Instead of a bed and a desk, this one has a worn wooden table and two chairs. There's a tall Sarenian man with an enormous pair of spectacles sitting in one. It's not Colf. Some of the tension drains out of Sarah's body. The man smiles at her and stands up.

"It's Sarah, Juanna tells me?" he says in Sarenian, glancing at Juanna, who sits down in one of the other chairs. He plays with the hem of his shirt, then taps his fingers on the table. *"It's a pleasure to meet you, finally. My name is Cremon. I'm a…*friend *of Colf's. Juanna here sent news of his capture, so my brother sent me along to try and explain some things. Colf will be back soon, he just needs to convince the King he has a valid reason to be in Husifi."* He holds his right hand out for her to shake.

Sarah nods, taking his offered hand. Instead of shaking it, he grips it with both of his and smiles from ear to ear. *"I'm so glad we've finally managed to find you: my brother's been out of his mind with worry."*

"*Um…sorry?*"

Cremon chuckles. "*Oh, it's no fault of yours. Colf is the only one to blame here, but we'll get to that in time. Now,*" he says, "*I understand you want to find your friends?*"

Sarah nods, and sits down in the chair across from him. "*As soon as possible.*" She shakes her head, trying yet again to shut down all the horrible scenarios she thought up last night and the day before, "*Who knows how much trouble they've gotten into without me.*"

Cremon laughs, uncrossing and re-crossing his legs as he does. "*I have it on good authority that they've managed quite a bit. Kaylor's been working as a knight, with the Prince in Shaltac Castle—*"

"*With the Mad King of the South?*"

His mouth twitches in amusement. "*Well, yes, I suppose you could say that. Except, if everything's going to plan, she'll be leaving his service very soon. As for Anna, Colf has been in contact with her for quite some time now. She's been ferrying refugees to Denadia; on Colf's orders, of course.*"

That's bad. If Sarah and her friends are associated with the rebellion, even indirectly, Kaylor shouldn't be right at the center of Shirot's kingdom. If they're already suspicious of Kaylor before she deserts, they might catch her before she leaves. Or if they think she's valuable, they might try twice as hard to find her. As for Anna—being a pirate isn't exactly the safest profession. Sarah leans her elbows on her knees and buries her face in her hands. "*Are they okay?*"

She can hear the sympathy in Cremon's voice when he answers, "*Of course. Colf's been keeping tabs on both of them, to the best of his ability. They're both fine, and in any case, will be here soon so you can see for yourself.*"

"*Wait a minute, you said Anna was ferrying refugees? Anna herself, she's not helping someone else do it?*"

"*Well, Anna is the captain, so yes.*"

Oh, *shit*. So they're hunting Anna, too. And if Anna's been given leave to order people around, people who are willing to do anything she asks them—it's kind of a scary thought. Sarah loves her friend, but Anna can be relentless, cold, and a little too sure of herself at times. A combination that's gotten her into trouble more than once. "*And how, exactly, did Anna become the captain?*"

Cremon shifts his legs around again, "*It was rather clever of her, actually. The old captain wasn't a very nice man, see, so Anna decided to take things into her own hands. She got a flock of sirens to help her overthrow the captain and his men, and then managed to talk them out of the price she owed them.*" He shrugs, "*It seems a little underhanded, but I don't know all of the details.*"

Sarah stares at him, dumbfounded, for what feels like several hours before she can come up with anything to say.

"*So—let me get this straight. You're saying that Kaylor is a knight—a rogue knight now, and the Prince and his men are after her—and Anna's the captain of a pirate ship, but only because she made a deal with sirens?*"

"*I suppose you could put it like that.*"

"*Oh, shit. I need to find them. Now.*" Sarah starts to get to her feet.

"*Sarah—they're not your responsibility.*" Cremon says, leaning forward and reaching out as if to put a hand on her shoulder.

Sarah recoils, standing up. They don't understand how this works. "*I—you just don't know what it's like, having them both as friends. Kaylor will do anything—anything!—if she thinks it'll be fun, or if someone makes her think it's the right thing to do. And believe me, it's easy to convince her if you say it the right way. And if Anna thinks doing something dangerous will help her get what she wants, she throws caution to the wind! I've spent years talking them out of doing* stupid *things, years covering for them and getting them out of trouble when they get themselves into it!*" Sarah shouts, dropping her pigtails when she realizes she's tugging on them, "*I'm the level head, the mediator, the realist. They've never known what to do without me,*" she says in a small voice, "*They've told me that, again and again.*"

Cremon and Juanna stare at her, frozen, their eyes wide. "*Sarah—*" Juanna starts, but Cremon motions for her to be quiet. He can tell she isn't finished yet. Sarah stops, taking a deep breath, trying to clear her head. "*I have to go and get them. I have to go and get them* now."

"*Sarah, wait—*" Juanna makes a grab for her arm as she storms out, but Sarah dodges it. She's relieved that Anna and Kaylor are alive, but—she can't trust them to take care of themselves. She never could. She scrambles up the ladder, pushes past Ellata, and breaks into a run down the street. She hears Juanna and Cremon calling after her, but she doesn't stop. She can't.

"*Nellie,*" she pants, skidding to a halt just inside the entrance to their cave, "*We have to go. Now!*"

Chapter Eighteen

ANNA

1st day of Tivar
Year 1452

Coast North of Tallipeg
Altibrl Sea

𝕬 pale, shivering hand reaches out to grasp Anna's as she stands at the top of a ladder. She helps Hisef pull the man onto the deck, where the commotion of the other refugees nearly drowns out his murmur of thanks. Anna gives him a curt nod before she turns back to the ladder, holding her hand out for the next lost sorcerer.

A mother urges a young, skinny child up in front of her. The child declines Anna's help, scrambling over the rail on his own, but the mother smiles warmly as Anna takes her hand and helps hoist her over and onto the deck. Anna can't help but smile back for a moment, letting her concentration slip. She mentally shakes herself and peers into the woman's face, looking for any similarities between it and her own. There aren't any. Anna turns to the next refugee.

It's been so long that Anna can barely remember what her mother looks like. But she does remember some things: the bronze skin, dark brown hair—darker than Anna's own —and brown eyes. She had freckles too, Anna's sure she had freckles. But none of the women she's seen fit the bill.

Anna continues to help Hisef and the rest of her crew pull people onto the boat until everyone's safely aboard. The refugees had to make a camp to wait for the ship: the remains of a fire and a few meager possessions are scattered over the beach in the cove. This cove is well hidden behind a rolling arc of grassy hills and several large rocks that block the wind. It's as sheltered as it's going to get along the western coast, and that's why Colf has the refugees meet Anna here. And last night was an important festival night: any guards, travelers, or civilians would be drawn to the parties taking place in the cities and towns, their attention on the goddess Larosri and not on tracking down a stray group of refugees. In fact, Anna would have been celebrating her birthday last night if she'd grown up in Sarenia. It's not her actual birthday, but Anna is a Stormbringer and Larosri is the goddess of Stormbringers. Sorcerers in Sarenia are honored on the festival days of their patron gods. *Not that there are many of them left*, Anna thinks wryly. Still, the gods are tied to the seasons as much as they are to the sorcerers, so even non-sorcerers, or *Noarlea*, would have been out to celebrate the end of summer and the beginning of Tivar.

She stops to watch Yorren, Hisef, and Wrom pull the smaller loading-boats back up onto the ship. They lash them into the center of the *Annihilator*, between the masts, so that they're as out of the way as they can be. Satisfied with their work, she leaves to check on the refugees.

The people have crowded into five of the six rooms

reserved for them under the deck, huddled together in the corners and by the windows. Anna grasps a hand here and murmurs a quiet word there, letting them know where the food and blankets are and that they can come to her with any problems. Yorren, Hisef, and Zer will be down later; they're more easy-going and approachable than Anna is, and most of the refugees prefer to deal with them. All the same, Anna is the Captain, and it's her duty to make sure they're settled.

Half an hour later, she retires to her cabin, locking the door behind her. She settles into the chair behind her desk, sliding open the top drawer and removing a thick stack of paper bound in a neat leather case. She sets it down on the desk with a loud thump and shoves her arm back into the drawer, scraping around at the back and sides before she finds a small, dirty, clear plastic pen. She holds it up to her face, frowning at the short band of ink along the bottom. This is her last ballpoint pen. She grimaces. She might have to switch to a quill soon.

She taps the pen on the table, forcing her attention back to the papers in front of her.

Captain's Log

et

Collecte des Faits et des Schémas

She smiles to herself, stroking over the words with a finger.

Property of Captain Anna Thomas
Privé: quiconque est trouvé lisant ce sera tué.

The death threat is more symbolic than anything: she wouldn't kill anyone for looking through her book. That doesn't mean it wouldn't make her angry, even though it's not likely they'd be able to understand it. Sarenian is close enough to English that someone might be able to read it, but Anna hasn't heard anything like French in this place. She's glad she remembers it well enough from classes in school. Of course, if she finds Sarah, she has no doubt that the other girl would be able to read it. Anna's friend is fluent in French, Spanish, and—though she'd spent less than a day trying to learn it—German.

Anna lifts the first half of the paper stack, setting it down on the desk beside her. She flips through the pages of the remaining half, past neatly written paragraphs in English (all dated) and on to scattered pages of diagrams, sketches, and notes in French. She runs her finger across the bullet points in the left margin of the open page, and stops near the bottom. She jots something in the margin next to one of the bullet points:

26 réfugiés, soir de 1e de Tivar: 9 hommes, 12 femmes, 5 enfants.

26 refugees, evening of the 1st of Tivar: 9 men, 12 women, 5 children.

There's a knock on her door. Anna jumps, then stacks

the papers, fastens the case shut, and slides the package into her desk drawer in one practiced motion. She shuts the drawer, locks it, and gets up to answer the door.

"Captain?" Zer stands before her with his hands tucked behind his back, "Hisef says to tell you that dinner's almost done. Are you going to eat with us?"

"Tell them I'll be right there, I just have to finish with something."

"Okay, Captain," Zer salutes her, no doubt copying the gesture from Yorren, then retreats back to the kitchen.

Anna walks back over to her desk, collapses into the chair behind it, and sighs. How many of those refugees are going to want to get off in Husifi? She's done so much for Colf already. If he doesn't have more information for her this time, Anna might have to ditch him and his refugees and just look for Sarah without his help. If everything goes to plan, Kaylor's going to meet them in Husifi, and with *her* help, they can get things done faster.

Anna reaches up to finger the silver cross necklace she always keeps around her neck before she remembers that it's not there anymore. She gave it to Patrick.

She sent Patrick to get Kaylor because there's no one else she can trust. He's the one who got her out of the brig and helped her take over the ship. If he weren't a mute, she would have made him her first mate.

Or maybe not. Though he would have deserved the title, he's also inexperienced. He was a servant for a wealthy estate back in Denadia before he arrived on the ship, or something like it. The *Annihilator* was the first ship he had ever been on.

She'd found him hiding in one of the barrels in the cargo hold. He'd been running from someone. From what Anna can get out of him, it's his former master's fault he's a mute. Anger boils up in her chest at the thought of anyone after Patrick, especially someone who has power over him like that. It's no small wonder he ran away.

Someone pounds on her door again. What does Zer want now?

"Zer, I said I'd be there in a minute!"

"Captain…" Hisef's voice floats through the wood, his tone uncertain, "I think you're going to want to see this."

Anna's on her feet and out the door in a flash. If something's worried the eternally calm Hisef, it's got to be something big. Half the crew is standing at the edge of the boat, looking out over the side, toward a line of rocks not far from the ship.

"Captain," Yorren asks, "Should we pick them up? Did we miss a few? Colf's note said twenty-six, I counted twenty-six…" he trails off as Anna pushes past him to stand on the prow, wanting to see what's out there for herself.

Standing at the top of the rocks, now pointing and waving at her, are two figures—two boys, maybe around Anna's age. One jumps up into the air, waving his hands above his head.

"Anna!" his voice floats to her faintly through the wind, "Are you Anna Thomas?!"

PART 3

REUNION

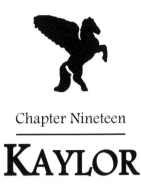

Chapter Nineteen

KAYLOR

1st day of Tivar
Year 1452

The Chatty Sphinx

"Tyler," he says, "My name's Tyler."

Somewhere in the back of her mind, Kaylor's aware that she's gaping. The boy—*Tyler*—stares back at her for a fraction of a second before his eyes drop to the floor.

"I—You're—What are you doing here?" Kaylor blurts, in *English*. Because he sounds *American*. The boy's hair is so pale it's almost white. Paired with his blue eyes and pale skin, he looks almost like he's from Telegarath. He fiddles with his fingers, almost wringing his hands. Is this the boy from the letter?

"I...I'm going to the city." He stares hard into the fireplace, eyes fixed on the dancing flames.

"Which city?"

He looks back down at the rug, and something about him strikes her as very familiar. *This* is who she's supposed to find, she's certain. "Well, um—the one that's not in the forest."

Kaylor laughs. "There aren't *any* cities in the forest." He

161

smiles a little back at her, but he doesn't hold her gaze for very long, and doesn't attempt to explain himself. "Hey listen, do—"

The wood of the stairway creaks behind them, and Tyler shrinks down into himself, his eyes wide. Kaylor twists around, grabbing the hilt of her sword, ready to fight whatever might have made the noise, but it's only Keripen.

"Kaylor?" he asks, stopping in his tracks halfway down the stairs.

"Keripen!" She leaps to her feet and runs to him, enveloping him in a tight hug. His shirt is scratchy against her cheek and smells like freshly baked bread. Keripen was one of the first people in Sarenia to offer Kaylor any sort of kindness, and he's the only person she's told about her real home.

"Tyler," Keripen releases her and takes a step back, stern gray eyes still studying her face, "Will you give us a moment?"

Kaylor looks back at Tyler. She doesn't want to let him out of her sight, at least not yet. She's supposed to look after him, isn't she? That's what the letter said. But she also needs to tell Keripen about what's going on: he might be able to help her.

Tyler clears his throat, then frowns. "Sure. But um…you took my backpack? For safekeeping? Can I, uh, have it back now?" He mimes taking a backpack off and setting it down. Kaylor stifles a giggle—she forgot how weird a Sarenian accent sounds, how different Sarenian people talk. She must have looked just as funny gesturing her way through conversations last summer as Tyler does now.

"Oh," Keripen chuckles, then says slowly, "There is a chest against the back wall. I gave you a key, but I think you were lost in your thoughts when I told you," he pauses to scratch his beard, and Tyler goes a little red. "I think Agred left you bedding as well." Tyler frowns, puzzling through Keripen's words. Just as Kaylor opens her mouth to translate, Tyler nods, face still flushed, then hurries off into the back room.

She shakes her head, smiling. "Where did you find him?" she asks in Sarenian, "Do you know where he's from?"

"He showed up at the gate," Keripen says, sitting at a table and pulling another chair out for Kaylor, "Agred found him gawking at the Naracos."

Kaylor sits, trying to picture the moment in her head. Shit, Keripen's nephew—his name is Agred. *Agred Agred Agred.* She'll have to try harder to remember that.

"But Kaylor," he says, sounding a little concerned, "What brings you here? I thought you were done drawing the maps?"

She stares down at the wood grain in the table, tracing it with a finger. She's going to have to tell him at some point; might as well be now. She takes a deep breath, "Keripen, I quit. Well, as good as quit, anyway. Casteor's planning something...I can't condone what he's doing. There was a letter...I'm supposed to find someone who's lost in the forest. And then this servant boy showed up, with Anna's necklace—have I told you about Anna?—and I can't help but think that she might be in trouble, that she sent him to get me because something's gone wrong and she needs my help."

There's no judgment or consternation in Keripen's expression, to Kaylor's relief. Maybe she made the right decision after all. "It sounds like you've had a stressful couple of days. What's this about a letter? Am I right to guess you've found this lost person?" Keripen nods in the direction of the back room, where Tyler's disappeared into the shadows.

"I think so." Kaylor pulls the letter out of her pocket and hands it to Keripen.

The innkeeper studies it, eyebrows furrowing in concentration. "It's not signed," he says after a few minutes.

"I know," says Kaylor, "But they were right about Anna asking me for help, and they know where I…about my travels. *You* haven't told anyone about…about where I'm from, have you?"

Keripen frowns. "I swear to you, I haven't told a soul," his frown deepens as he studies the writing, "But…I think you can trust the person who wrote this."

"Why?"

"The only thing they've told you to do is to try to find someone lost in the forest—" Keripen's eye smile at her over the letter, "—and if Tyler is that person, I very much doubt he's a spy or anything like it. As for Anna, you've made your decision, and I take it you understand the consequences?"

Kaylor nods, swallowing. "I have to get out of the

164

country."

Keripen meets her eyes. "If you can ever make it back, you will always be welcome here."

"Thank you," Kaylor tries to convey exactly how much that means to her in those two words. The *Chatty Sphinx* has always felt more like home than the castle in Valliseg, though she's spent less than half as much time here.

"The boy," Keripen says, shifting in his seat, "You can't fit two people on one pegasus for a long trip, Kaylor, you know that."

"You can if you have the right saddle," Kaylor grumbles.

Keripen shakes his head, "Kaylor," he reaches across the table to grasp her hands in his, "You're heading to Husifi, aren't you?"

Kaylor nods. "I'm supposed to meet Anna there."

"And what are you going to do with Ratha once you get there?"

"Well, actually, I was planning on making it to Tallipeg first, and taking a ship from there. The wind can be rough over the Altibrl Sea, I don't want Ratha getting hurt. Then —he'll go wherever I go, I suppose."

Keripen steeples his fingers on the tabletop. "Will he behave around the dragons?"

Kaylor chews on her lip, flinching when she bites it too hard. "I'm almost certain he will. He gets on okay with the Naracos, and he won't even shy away from *manticores* when he smells them..." she winces. Ratha's stubborn courage has put them at risk more than once. But he's trained like a warhorse—better even—and he's got her out of bad situations in the past. Which is why she's reluctant to leave him behind.

Keripen nods, looking thoughtful. "Maybe he *will* be able to stomach it. He sounds a little too brave for his own good." Kaylor hears the thought at the end of the sentence, even though Keripen doesn't say it aloud: *Just like you.* "You can always leave him here for a while, if you'd like."

"I—" That might be a good idea. She doesn't want to do it, she'd never want to leave Ratha alone anywhere, but...

"You would have to hide him. The King's Guard are the only people in Sarenia permitted to work with pegasi, you know that. You will have to leave him outside the city while you look for a ride, and you will have to find a ship with a crew that won't want to steal him from you."

"Because I'll need a pirate ship to take me to Husifi."

"Or a foreign ship. From Denadia or Thethria, most likely, but you may want to try your luck with a Telegarathian ship if there's one in the harbor."

"They transport horses all the time, right? I'm already smuggling myself out, I might as well take Ratha too."

Keripen sighs, "Normally, I wouldn't advise it, but... flying on a pegasus to Tallipeg is safer than letting you travel on the ground as a fugitive. And, I may know of someone trustworthy you can meet at the port in Tallipeg. She owns a ship—she can take you to Husifi, if she's going that way. She would be willing to transport a pegasus, if you decide to take him with you. I will send her a sparrow, so she knows to expect you."

Kaylor gasps. "A *Sight Sparrow?*"

The little creatures, animated and controlled by a Lifebringer, are used to send messages quickly over great distances. Scrolls or papers are folded up tightly and tucked into a compartment built into the tiny sparrows' backs'. The birds can be kept in a cage until they're needed: they won't expire until they achieve their goal, or the Lifebringer who animated them dies. There's a Lifebringer at Shaltac Castle whose sole duty is to animate Sight Sparrows so the King can use them as messengers.

Kaylor lowers her voice, "You have a *Lifebringer* here?" No one's supposed to be doing that sort of thing—creating magical objects like Sight Sparrows—unless it's done in service to the crown. Has Keripen been hiding fugitives at the *Chatty Sphinx?*

Keripen's eyes twinkle in the firelight. "Ah, no. I had the sparrow made years ago—before the Mad King banned the open practice of sorcery. But you should go and talk to Tyler. To confirm that he's the boy mentioned in this letter." Kaylor opens her mouth, wanting to ask more questions about the Sight Sparrow and whatever friend Keripen's sending her to meet, but Keripen silences her with a look. "It's late. We'll talk tomorrow morning over breakfast?"

Kaylor nods, swallowing her words. "Good night. I should…I'll go check on Tyler. I can just sleep in the back room too, for now, I'll pay you for lodging and for Ratha's stabling tomorrow morning."

He shakes his head, "I won't accept your money, you know that. You're like the daughter I never had," Kaylor opens her mouth to protest, but Keripen shakes his head with a fond smile, "Good night. You need to rest up for your journey."

After Keripen climbs the stairs to his room, Kaylor heads down the hallway into the back room, hoping Tyler hasn't gone to sleep yet. She finds him sitting in one of the chairs in front of the fire, peering over the tops of his knees, which are tucked up against his chest. The look he gives her is almost a glare.

Kaylor swallows. "Um…hi. I hope it's alright if I sleep in the room here? I have my own bedroll and everything…"

Tyler nods, biting his lip and looking back at the fire. "It's fine. Agred just left, he said you might be able to…" he trails off, grimacing.

"Show you how to get to the city?"

"Yes."

"I—" Kaylor's voice falters, "—I can, yes."

He nods again, solemnly, and turns back to the fire. Kaylor sits on the other chair. It's quiet for a few minutes, and the silence bothers Kaylor more than she'd like to admit. Tyler glaces at her, and then turns back to the flames again, leaning forward with his elbows on his knees.

"Where are you from?" Kaylor asks him.

He glances a couple times between her and the fire, as though trying to figure out what to say. She takes pity on him.

"I'm from a place very far away," she says, "Further than the mountains or even across the sea. I don't know if you'll know it—it's quite different there than it is here."

"Oh?" Tyler says, finally tearing his eyes away from the fire.

She gives him a minute, but when he still doesn't give her an answer, she presses onward: "There are many, many more people there than there are here, there are giant buildings that reach into the sky, and there isn't…there's not nearly as much open land. Nearly everyone goes to school, and almost no one rides horses to get from place to place."

Tyler's eyes brighten as she talks, a small smile growing on his face. "And there are many more books, and little devices with light-up screens that can give you all the information you would ever want to know. And almost everyone knows how to read and write," he adds.

They're both grinning now. "How long have you been here?" Kaylor asks.

"Just a couple days." He twists his fingers together anxiously for a moment before he asks, "Where *is* here, exactly?"

"Sarenia, that's the country. Or, what would translate to a country in m—our world. And um, right now we're in the Caimig Forest, between Tallipeg on the coast and Valliseg—the capital—the other way. We're in the province of Angota. Does that help? At all?"

Tyler smiles and nods, "A little. We're…not in the middle ages, then?"

"Um…not really, I don't think so. There are some things that are different. Like the Naracos, and the manticores, and the sorcerers."

"The innkeeper and his son—the language they speak, I

recognize most of the words. It's like an obscure dialect, but it's still mostly English. If this is a different *world*, then why…why would they speak something so similar to what *we* speak?"

She's never even thought about that before. If they're somewhere as far from home as she thinks they are, it doesn't make a lot of sense. "I don't know."

"How come—why do you have a sword?"

"Because I'm a knight."

"A *knight?*"

"Well, it's not quite the same as it was in medieval Europe. At least, I don't think so. Weren't they only nobles, or something?" Tyler nods at her eagerly, so she continues, "Then it's different. Here, there's a contest that happens once every four years that anyone can enter. First there are contests in each city, and then the, uh, preliminaries take place in the capital of each region: Larroc in Normath, Guinsia in Diag, and Valliseg in Angota. Then the winners of those—the top twenty, or thirty? Something around there, I think—anyway, the winners all travel to Valliseg, where the final contest is held. The crown has scouts that watch you fight, and so do the Lords of the cities. After the contests, the contenders are ranked, and the King gets his pick of the best fighters to train to be members of the King's Guard. The Prince can pick people for that, too. The Lords get to fight—or, argue—over who's left. The last tournament happened last year, it was going on when I got here."

"Do you work for the King? Or one of the Lords?"

"The King, or more specifically the Prince. Or— I *did* work for the Prince." Kaylor reaches up to finger the orange teardrop still dangling from her left ear.

"Why don't you work for him anymore?"

Kaylor stares down at her hands in her lap. How can she explain that in a way someone else can understand, when she's still wrestling with it herself? She should show him the letter. But she doesn't—it might scare him, and she doesn't want to do that. "I—one of my friends is in trouble. With the King," she clarifies, "And I care more about her than I do about being a knight."

"Is that why you're here? Are you going to find her? Is she from...where we're from?"

"Yeah, all of those."

His face seems to light up in the firelight as she answers his questions, his legs slowly unfolding so his feet can settle on the floor. He balances his elbows on his knees and rests his chin in his hands.

"...can I come with you?" he murmurs, so quiet she almost doesn't hear him.

He's still staring into the fire, but he's turned a little more towards her now. He sneaks a glance over at her, sees that she's watching him, and flushes. "It's just...I have nothing else to do. Nowhere else to go. And maybe I can find out more about this place, if I travel. And you're a knight. You're a trained fighter, and there are some... *nasty* creatures out there."

Kaylor barks out a laugh. "Of course!" She can't help but make fun of him a little, though. "I mean...I'll bring you to the city, and then we'll see."

His eyes narrow and he tries to glare, but he ruins the effect with a slight smile.

Chapter Twenty

ANNA

1st day of Tivar
Year 1452

Coast North of Tallipeg
Altibrl Sea

nna freezes, staring out over the water at the strange boys on the rocks. *Who are these people?* How do they know her name? She peers closer, holding a hand out behind her until someone presses a telescope into it.

They're standing next to each other, one in all black tights and a loose shirt, the other in rough, bluish pants and a coat and...sneakers. He's wearing sneakers.

"Hisef! Wrom!" Anna barks, "Get one of the boats, we're bringing them aboard!"

She waits at the railing, watching with rapt attention as Wrom and Hisef paddle the loading boat closer to the rocks. Could these boys be from Anna's home? Or did this boy steal the tennis shoes from someone? No—the rest of their outfits are too modern and alien to belong here in Sarenia. Anna practically bounces on her toes in excitement. She hasn't seen someone from home in over a *year*. Are these two here for the same reason as Anna and her friends? She'll have to ask Colf. She'll need to convince them to go with her to meet him in Husifi.

"Captain?" Someone whispers in her left ear. She turns to find Choffson standing behind her, shifting from foot to foot. "I, er...found this, attached to your door, a couple nights ago," The helmsman presses an envelope into her hand, "I figured you might not want all the others to see it. I meant to give it to you yesterday, but with the refugees and all..." he shrugs, scratching at the side of his head.

Anna frowns, tucking the envelope inside her sleeve. "Thank you, Choffson. Try and remember sooner next time."

She doesn't have time to look at it before Wrom and Hisef are back with the boat and the two boys. The four of them climb up to the deck with Yorren's help. One of the boys, his bright ginger hair crusted with salt, spins around in slow backwards circles, taking in the ship and the crew. The other boy, an Asian kid who almost looks Shydo with his gray-tinted skin and squarish face, is more subdued; merely staring at the ship and the crew instead of spinning around theatrically. It strikes Anna that she and her pirates might be the first people these boys have seen in Sarenia. Which begs the question—how did they manage to find *each other*? Anna, Kaylor, and Sarah all came through at the same time, in the same place, and wound up in completely different locations. Maybe one of the boys grabbed the other when they were pulled through? Or maybe someone brought them through together, on purpose, if that's even possible. But more importantly, how do they know Anna?

The red-haired boy's eyes find her, and he stops

spinning. "Are you Anna?" he asks, stepping forward until he's only a few feet from her, "Anna Thomas?" He has an American accent. It's been so long since Anna's heard one, she'd almost forgotten what it sounds like.

The crew watch him like a nervous pack of wolves, hands moving to rest on sword pommels as scowls decorate their faces.

"I am," says Anna, "Do I know you?"

"I—" Darn frowns down at the deck, "I don't think so. I don't know. But—" he looks back up at her, "I saw your picture, in the newspaper. You were with two other girls, Sarah Miller and Kaylor Williams. They're looking for you," he takes another step forward, "I mean, your family's looking for you."

Anna takes a step back. "Maybe," she says. She wouldn't put it past her father to go looking, no matter how distant and negligent he's always been, but she doubts her step mother or siblings have anything to do with it. They've never cared much about her. Her step-sister Bella, always jealous of anything that belonged to Anna, once tried to steal the silver cross necklace that Anna's mother gave her. So Anna had to carve her name into it. And despite the obvious evidence, her father never realized—or ignored all the signs because they didn't match up with the sparkling perfect world he'd constructed in his head—that Anna didn't get along in the *slightest* with her step-family.

But Anna doesn't want to give these boys any information about herself yet, not what she can't help. She barely knows them—she has no idea whether she can trust them. She needs to know more about them first. "What are your names?" she asks.

"I'm Darn, and that's Alex." The ginger boy gestures to himself and then to his friend. The Asian boy gives her a small wave and a dimpled smile.

"Darn?" That's an odd name. It's too odd to be a lie.

"Huh? Oh, well uh, my real name's Max. I just—it just never really fit me, I just go by Darn."

Those are American names. At least, Alex and Max are. And this—Max, or Darn, or whatever—mentioned a newspaper. The other one—Alex—stays a little behind him in the shadows. She notices he hasn't said anything yet. His gaze switches between parts of the ship and members of her crew, never settling anywhere for longer than a few seconds.

"Are they spies?" Zer whispers, wide-eyed, to Hisef.

"They're not spies," Anna says, raising her voice, the white lie forming in her mind even as it slips out over her tongue, "I think I *do* know them. Colf was supposed to send someone to meet us, I remember that now," she turns to Choffson, "I think this is why we had orders to pick the refugees up on the way to Husifi—Colf knew I'd forget about this." She turns back to the rest of the crew, "They're refugees too, but they had to be more discrete. They have some...*important* information for us. So, if you all wouldn't mind, I'd like to have a private audience with them in my cabin."

She raises her eyebrows and glowers at the rest of her crew, who are *still* standing around gawking, until they break up to attend to their ship-board duties. Yorren shoots Anna a disparaging look as she leads the boys back into her cabin, but she pays him no mind. He knows she's lying, but he won't say anything in front of the crew. She'll have to deal with him later.

She shuts the door and locks it as soon as they're inside. She hops up and perches on the desk, picking the pen up and tapping it against the wood. "So," she says, crossing her legs under the desk, "You're from Earth, aren't you?"

"We're from *what?*" Darn almost yells at her, his eyes bugging out of his head.

The other boy—Alex—shoots Darn a look, "We're ob-obviously not...anywhere that's...known. Where are we, then?" He takes a step sideways and a little in front of Darn, almost as if he's trying to shield him from her. *Well, that's interesting.*

"And how do we get back?" Darn adds. Alex nods.

Anna studies both of their faces, trying to glean some insight into their heads. Alex is warier than Darn in this moment. He suspects her of something, and he's trying to protect Darn from it. Either they know each other well and Alex wants to protect his friend, or Alex has a Kaylor-like hero complex. She'll have to figure out which. "You're in Sarenia," she decides to tell them, "To be specific, you're floating on *my* ship in the Altibrl Sea," she turns to Alex, "If I wanted to hurt you, you'd be dead already."

"I must be going nuts," Darn mutters.

"You're *n-not,*" Alex snaps.

"As for the second question," Anna continues,

pretending to ignore that interesting little exchange, "I'm not sure there *is* a way to get home."

Darn stares at her in disbelief, and Alex stiffens next to him.

"W-what do you mean?"

"I'm not sure there is a way," Anna says, keeping her face blank and impassive, "But if you want, I can take you to Colf. He might know how you got here, and he might be able to help you get back." He might have another tidbit of information for her if she brings him these two boys.

"Who's Colf?" Darn asks, straightening his shoulders.

"He's why I'm here. And he may have something to do with you as well. Crossing worlds doesn't just happen—someone has to bring you over. A special kind of sorcerer, called a Vanisher. Colf knows one of them." She doesn't mention the stories of ships appearing out of nowhere in the Bay of Monsters or Ganerly Ocean, nor the tales of strange people stumbling out of the Forgotten Wood every decade or so. They don't need to know any of that.

Alex glances over at Darn, then turns back to Anna. "We'd b-better find this C-colf then."

Check. A thrill of satisfaction shoots up her spine at how easily they fall into place. It's always like this with her various plans and schemes–which is part of why she's always plotting away. Everyone–well, everyone but Kaylor and Sarah, and perhaps not Patrick–is a piece on Anna's game board.

"I should be able to take you to him. In fact, we're heading there right now. You're welcome to come with us."

Alex nods. Darn stares hard at her, and says, "Yeah, sure. And this is the only way to get back?"

Anna shrugs, making sure it looks casual. "He's the only lead I've got."

Darn frowns at her, but nods anyway. Anna stifles a smirk. *Checkmate.*

The envelope up her sleeve slides back down and hits the desk, brushing against Anna's wrist. She'd forgotten about that. But she can't open it in front of these two.

"Okay," she says, "That's settled, then. You'll come with us to Husifi and meet Colf. One of the crewmen will show you to your quarters: just tell them I want you housed with the other refugees." She slides off the desk and walks to the door, pulling it open and holding it still, letting them know they're expected to leave. Darn gives her an odd look as he brushes past her. Alex stops and opens his mouth, as if he's going to say something, then snaps it shut and shakes his head, following his friend through the door. Anna shuts it and locks it behind them.

She sits at the desk and pulls the letter out, ripping the envelope open and straightening the creases in the paper.

Hello Anna,

My name is Mr. Lee. I'm sure Colf's told you much about me, but he hasn't told you everything. I know for a fact he hasn't told you anything about your mother, and that he's keeping that information from you because he wants you under his control. You no doubt already know this.

There's something I need you to do for me. There are two boys who will be stranded in the Altibrl Sea just north of Tallipeg on the first of Tivar. I'll enclose more specific coordinates. I want you to find them before Colf does. You're supposed to meet with him in Husifi a few days from then, correct? Your friend Sarah is there. If everything goes to plan, Kaylor will be there as well. She should have one other boy with her.

Colf wants you, Sarah, Kaylor, and these boys to help him with something neither I nor your mother condone. Of course it will ultimately be up to you what you do, but I can give you some answers before you make that decision. Once Sarah and the boys are with you, find an inn called the Four-Eyed Griffin and meet me in the alley outside the back entrance just after noon. I will be there from the 4th to the 7th of Tivar. I will answer every question you have to the best of my ability.

Sincerely,
Mr. Lee

So…this *Mr. Lee* person is responsible for these boys. Though he must not be as important to Colf as he seems to think, since he's never been mentioned to Anna before. She snorts out a laugh. At least now she knows why the boys are here. Colf wants them.

And Sarah—if the writer is to be believed, Sarah is in Husifi. Anna might get to see *both* of her friends again very, very soon. She tries to temper her excitement with a healthy amount of suspicion and caution, but she can't suppress it. She might get to see her *friends* again.

She can't help but admire the writer, whether he's telling the truth or not. The letter is well-played. He's offering Anna the two things she wants most: her friends and information. All she has to do is show up and meet him. Many a fool has been lured into a trap with bait like this. Anna will have to be careful.

Chapter Twenty One

DARN

1st day of Tivar
Year 1452

Altibrl Sea

Darn leans against the outside of the cabin, surveying his surroundings. This ship…is not what it's supposed to be. And neither are the people on board. It's old-fashioned, but not in a familiar way. Like they're on one of those restored historic ships Darn visited with his family when they were in Florida—except it's blue, and it's narrower, and it just doesn't *look* right.

And then there's Anna Thomas. Darn still has a clear memory of the picture from the newspaper burned into his mind's eye. The unsettling sense of familiarity he felt the first time he saw those three girls won't leave him alone, especially now that he's actually met Anna. She's the girl in the photo—he's *positive*. She's even wearing the same skirt and blouse. The hat and the coat are new, though.

It's kind of funny, actually, because the hat and coat dwarf the girl wearing them, but somehow she's still intimidating. Every time she looks at him, her green eyes bore into his, like she's dissecting his soul and is only mildly fascinated with what she finds there. Like he's a bug on the wall that's an interesting color.

And now he's thinking in metaphors. Darn shakes his head, trying to knock the pieces of his reality back into place. "I must be going nuts."

"You're *not*," says Alex.

That's the other thing. Why the hell would *Alex*, of all people, be here with him? "You could be a figment of my imagination, for all I know."

Alex frowns at him, leaning back against the railing of the ship. "Sometimes it's h-hard to tell the d-difference."

Darn watches Alex for a moment. The other boy watches the pirates go about their business, his expression calm and almost serene. Alex hasn't seemed bothered by any of it. Not even the weird horse-dolphin they'd seen in the ocean. "How are you so sure, then?"

Alex smiles weakly at him. "You g-get better at it with p-practice."

What's *that* supposed to mean? It strikes Darn that he doesn't know much about Alex at all. Maybe he isn't all that right in the head, which honestly would explain a few things. Still, for whatever reason he feels like he can trust him. Or at least like he can trust him more than he can trust Anna.

After a few minutes of staring at the ocean, just when Darn is so bored he's starting to think the grooves on the wood of the railing are the most *fascinating* thing he's ever seen, Anna trots down the steps from the helm and heads straight for them. She's frowning, her eyes searching the waves.

"We're being tracked," she says, "I'm going to…there's going to be a storm, for a little while. You're going to want to get below the deck. The left room at the end of the hallway's still empty, you can use that one." Her frown deepens as she fiddles with the hilt of the sword strapped to her hip.

Darn looks up. No clouds. Barely any wind. "What storm?"

She turns to face him, staring him down with a terrifying glare. "There's going to be one," she says, "Trust me."

Next to him, Alex pushes himself off the railing and nods. Why is he listening to her? There aren't any clouds in the sky, there's *no sign* of a storm. None of this makes sense, and no one has a good explanation. *How* can they possibly trust Anna, and *why* should they? Darn gives Alex a look.

Alex shrugs. "She knows th-this place better than we d-do."

Great. "So what if she tells us to jump off the ship into the mouth of an erupting volcano? Will you just do it, because 'she knows the area better'?"

Alex's face goes blank, his jaw muscles so tight they jut out against his skin. Anna doesn't react at all, which is unsettling. In the back of his mind, Darn *knows* he's being unreasonable because he's stressed and he's hungry, but he can't quite bring himself to care. "Oh, fine. Better safe than sorry, I guess. Just call us back out when the storm doesn't hit," he waves his hand at the empty sky. Anna doesn't even flinch at the jab, which unsettles Darn even more. Instead, her impassive eyes follow them closely as they slip down the stairs.

It's dark and dank below the deck. There's a narrow central hallway, flanked by several doors into smaller rooms. The two at the front are marked with large X's drawn on torn out sheets of lined notebook paper, and have "Crew Only" written underneath. One of the rooms doesn't have a door—it's packed with sealed barrels, crates, and several canvas bags. Most of the other doors down the hallway are open a crack. Darn peeks into one as they go by, and four sets of wide eyes stare at him out of haggard faces. He jerks away and doesn't look in any of the other rooms.

"Who are those people?" he whispers

"I think Anna s-said something about r-refugees," Alex mutters. He leads them to the end of the hall, to the only other door that's open all the way. Four hammocks hang side-by-side in the small room, and a chest is chained to the ground under the window. A few iron hooks and railings are nailed to the ceiling.

Alex settles down cross-legged on the floor against the wall. Not sure what else to do, Darn flops down into one of the hammocks, letting his arms and legs dangle over the sides. It's quiet but for the swish of the waves against the side of the boat and the creak of the boards around them. Is this boat even safe?

Darn's parents used to talk all the time about getting a boat, going back down to Florida and staying there for a few weeks, sailing around in it. That never happened. They're always too busy for a trip like that. Though they'd probably pay for Darn to go, probably with Trish and her family. He imagines that sort of boat is very different from this one.

"Have you ever been on a boat?" he asks Alex.

The other boy leans back against the wall and pulls his knees up to his chest. "N-no."

"Oh. I have, but not any big ones. I went whale watching once—that was kind of cool."

"See an-any hippocampuses?"

"Ha," Darn says, picking a thread out of the hammock and throwing it at Alex, "No. Mostly just dolphins. And a humpback whale."

Alex swallows and looks down at his knees. "You're lucky," he whispers.

Darn hums in assent. "My parents are pretty well off. Mom's an accountant, and she inherited a lot of money from my grandparents. Dad owns a record company. He's got some pretty good artists, but no one too huge. So we're not millionaires, but…we're not poor either."

"Oh."

"What about your parents?" Alex bites his lip and stares at the floor. Maybe he shouldn't have asked. "Look, if you don't want—"

"N-no, I—my dad's a m-mechanic. M-mom—used to work in a d-department store, but…I d-don't really know anymore. She doesn't—we don't r-really…" He trails off. Darn gives him a minute before he asks anything else.

"Are they divorced?"

"N-no…but th-that might happen, some t-time soon."

"Oh. I'm sorry."

"D-don't be." Alex sighs heavily, "It's n-not your f-fault."

They lapse into silence. Darn fiddles with the threading of the hammock, trying desperately to come up with something else to say, and failing. Now that they've been talking about parents, Darn misses his. Never mind that they're likely still at work at this time of day, that they probably won't be home until after Darn's asleep. If his mom were here, she'd know what to do: or she'd at least have a plan to figure it out. Darn would be able to leave it to her, just go along for the ride, safe and certain that it'd all turn out alright just like it always does. He can't imagine what it's like for Alex, what it would be like to have to live without her in his life.

A few minutes later, a member of Anna's crew, the young boy, shows up with a plate of food in his arms. Darn clambers out of the hammock, his mouth already starting to water.

Despite the minor language difference (Darn can only understand about half of what the boy says without having to stop and think about it) he manages to get the boy's name—Zer—and convince him to stay and eat with them. The three of them spread the plates out on the floor and scoop food into them. Darn piles his plate full of fish, mashed potatoes, and bread until it spills over onto the floor. Alex's mouth twitches when Darn scoops a drop of mashed potatoes off the floor with the tips of his finger and makes a face at it. He wipes it on Zer's filthy shirt. The boy doesn't seem to mind, but it makes Alex shake his head and try to hide a smile. So Darn makes it his goal to make Alex laugh.

He plays word games with Zer and makes fun of Anna, imitating her voice and even getting up to strut around like she does. Zer's laughter echoes down the hallway, but Alex never does more than smile. Zer clears away the dinner and announces with an air of great importance that he has to go and help keep the ship afloat.

All the while, raindrops clatter and fade in and out over the deck. Darn lays back in the hammock as they pound a soothing rhythm overhead.

He jolts awake and then drifts back to sleep several times before the rocking of the ship shakes him into alertness. He stares at the wall for a long time, slamming his hand against it each time the ship creaks, stopping his hammock from swinging too far to the side. He turns Anna's words over and over in his mind: "*I'm not sure there is a way to get home.*" Home. Somewhere that's clearly not here, or anywhere near here. Darn still misses his parents. And what about his friends at school, his relatives, Trish—what's he going to do without them? Will he ever see them again?

His hand hits the wood with a loud thump. A crack of thunder booms outside the boat. Rain and footsteps splatter noisily over the deck above them. A flash of lightning floods the hallway with light through the door they've left open. Anna's voice rings out over the racket of the storm, "Take a' *navegats* in! Don't touch a' wheel, Zer, that's not yar job! Where is Choffson?! We need a *dol* as straight as possible—we don't want a be any place near a' cliffs yet!" Her accent sounds just as thick as the rest of her crews'.

Darn wrinkles his nose. It smells salty and fishy and a bit like sweaty people, too. And he's getting restless. He can't talk to Alex over the storm without shouting, and there isn't much else to do in here but sit in the hammock as the ship jostles around. Speaking of Alex, Darn's new friend is starting to look queasy.

"You alright?" Darn shouts. Alex nods, but then leans forward, resting his elbows on his knees and his head in his hands. Maybe Darn should find Anna, or one of her crew. There's got to be people who get sea sick sometimes, maybe they know how to cure it. Or make it a little better, at least. Darn gets up and walks out into the hallway.

The ship rocks again, sending Darn skidding toward the opposite wall. He slams his palms into it to keep from falling, then leans against it as he stumbles down the hallway and up onto the deck. Thousands of raindrops fly at him and drench him from head to foot. The downpour soaks through his hair and clothes and stings at his eyes, blinding him. He has to grab onto a large wooden pole to avoid being blown away. He can hear Anna yelling out commands to the crew, but he can't make out the words she's saying over the roar of the storm. A flash of lightning illuminates the ship for an instant, and Darn recognizes the wood he's gripping as one of the masts. Several crew members dash about wildly, tugging on ropes. He probably shouldn't distract them right now. He'll have to take care of Alex on his own.

He half-falls, half-staggers back down the stairs. The *Annihilator* rocks forward, knocking him off his feet. He flings his hands out in front of him before his head can hit the ground. He sits heavily on the floor and leans back against the wall, trying to get his bearings. Going upstairs probably wasn't a very good idea. At least now he knows Anna wasn't lying about the storm.

There's a bucket a few feet away, just in front of the stairs. If Alex has to throw up, he should at least have something to throw up *in*. Darn crawls over to it on his hands and knees, not wanting to get knocked off his feet again. He brings it back to the room.

"Thanks," Alex takes the bucket and bends over it, breathing heavily through his nose. Out of nowhere, the rain pounding down on the deck lets up, the ship steadying to a slower, rocking rhythm.

"*Tha's* another Stormbringer!" Anna yells from above. A *what*? Darn needs to talk to Anna—he needs some more answers. He wants to know how she knew about the storm.

"Okay?" he asks Alex.

Alex nods, still a little green, but no longer bent over the bucket. He'll be fine.

"I'm going…I want to talk to Anna about something. I'll be right back?"

Alex nods again, swallowing a few times.

Darn nods back, then stalks out of the room. When he emerges from the stairway, Anna sees him and motions him over. "Were you both okay down there?"

"Alex is a little seasick, but otherwise, yeah. What's a Stormbringer? Does that have something to do with the—" Darn waves his hand at the sky, "—with that storm? And how it's gone now?"

"Good. I'm afraid Alex will just have to wait out the sickness, we don't have anything for that right now," she says, watching her crew intently and not meeting Darn's eyes, "We're a bit farther out to sea than we want to be, but we should be able to make it to Husifi in a day or less."

"Where's Husifi? And what's a Stormbringer?"

She shoots him an unreadable look. "It's in the mountains. We're going there to find Colf."

"Oh—right. The guy who can help us."

"I'm not making any promises, but there's a chance he'll be able to send you back, yes." Send *you* back. Not send *us* back.

"Aren't you coming with us? If he can send us back, I mean."

"No. At least, not yet. I…have to find someone first."

"Find who?"

"It's complicated." Anna's voice goes cold. He isn't going to get anything else out of her right now.

Darn turns away, sighing heavily and running a hand through his hair. Maybe he'll have better luck with one of the crew.

Chapter Twenty Two

TYLER

2nd day of Tivar
Year 1452

The Chatty Sphinx

yler has to resist the urge to pinch himself when he wakes up the next morning. This isn't a dream—that much is clear by now. The thatched wooden ceiling of the inn and the hard ground under his back remind him that he isn't even *close* to home.

It doesn't seem as incredible anymore as it should. Really, it's only natural that he should end up here, in a place like this, a day after he set his hands on fire. And the letter from Mr. Lee. This has to be real. He's really here.

Kaylor shifts on the ground a few feet away from him, muttering something in her sleep. *Kaylor Williams.* She's one of the people mentioned in the letter, along with Sarah Miller, Anna Thomas, Alex Scott, and Darn Harrison. Tyler stayed up late last night, reading the letter over and over again by the fire while Kaylor slept. He has it memorized. One person down, four to go. And from what he's heard, Kaylor's on her way to meet one of her friends, Anna. He's assuming this Anna is Anna Thomas.

He sits up, pushing a mound of scratchy blankets off onto the floor, and debates whether he should wake Kaylor. The only part of her visible over her blanket is her tangled blonde hair. Should he grab the approximate location of her shoulder and try to shake it? Should he nudge her with his foot? Should he call her name until she moves? He can't pick; he doesn't know what he's supposed to do.

He's saved a few minutes later when Agred clatters down the stairs and startles her awake with the noise.

They want to try and leave before the other guests get up, so the whole morning is a blur of activity. Keripen makes them porridge because there's no time for anything else. Kaylor scarfs down three bowls like a starving dog— she doesn't even put honey in it first. Tyler adds two spoonfuls of honey and some milk to his, and it still tastes bland. He has to force himself to swallow each mouthful without gagging. Kaylor stays behind to exchange a few words with Keripen while Agred and Tyler fold the blankets and pack the bags. When they're finished, she walks across the room and out the back door, throwing Tyler a quick smile on her way. He gets the broom and gives the floor a quick sweep before heading out after her.

She's waiting for him, holding a set of reins in her hand. Next to her is a magnificent stallion, his coat such a clear white it reflects the sunlight in a pale rainbow of colors.

She grins and nudges the horse with her elbow, "This is Ratha."

Ratha bobs his head, wickers, and stretches a pair of wings up a little above his head before settling them back

193

down onto his back. Tyler gapes. "He's…a…"

"Pegasus, yeah. We'll get there much faster if we're flying."

"I…I've never even ridden a horse before," Tyler mumbles. This…okay, so most of the other things Tyler's seen here in Sarenia aren't all that pleasant, but…if there are other things here like the pegasus before him, he could stand to stick around for a while.

Kaylor grabs him by the arm and pulls him forward, beaming. "That's just fine, since staying on a pegasus is much easier than staying on a horse—or, it is when you have the right saddle—and that's all you're going to have to do. You're taller than I am, so you should ride behind me. Stand over there, next to Ratha's foreleg—right there. Now grab that strap with one hand and the back with the other, put your foot here—there you go—okay, now swing your right leg up and over his back."

But before he can swing his foot over, Ratha walks forward a few steps, and Tyler hops along after him, foot stuck in the stirrup. Kaylor snorts and tries to cover it up with a cough. Blood rushes to Tyler's face. He grabs the front of the saddle again and manages to swing his leg up and over.

Kaylor's grin softens, "Really, you're taking this a lot better than I did. I freaked out and wouldn't listen to what anyone said. For days."

She's not just talking about riding horses. Tyler isn't sure what to say to that, so he busies himself fiddling with the straps under his legs. Kaylor shows him how to fasten his calves into the straps, then hooks a belt around his waist and clips a line from that to the back of the saddle. Then she mounts up in front of him and straps herself in, about ten times faster than it took Tyler to do it.

The pegasus trots down the path, gate rolling and unsteady. Feathers brush against Tyler's shin, tickling the skin under the scratchy pants. Dense green vegetation boxes the dusty dirt road in on either side. Kaylor clicks her tongue, jerks the reins, and then shouts, "Ratha, up!"

The pegasus launches himself into the air. Tyler grabs Kaylor around the waist, squeezing his eyes shut against the air rushing past his face. Kaylor lets out a loud whoop.

Once they're in the air, Ratha's flight is much smoother than Tyler expected. Riding on a pegasus is one of the strangest feelings he's ever had in his life. He's never ridden on a horse before. He's never *flown* before. The wind whips past his face so fast it's hard to breathe. The ground races along below him, trees blurring into a sweeping mass of green. It's kind of fun, actually.

"So did Keripen find you in the forest?" Kaylor yells.

"No, I found the road and I walked!" Tyler tries to yell over the wind, but his voice comes out strangled and raw.

"What?"

"I found the road and I walked!"

Kaylor laughs, "I can't hear you over the wind! Hang on —we're gonna try something." She leans forward and whistles shrilly, three times in succession. Ratha's muscles flex and he angles upward, toward a dense wall of clouds. Half a second later, a blast of moisture hits Tyler in the face. Ratha speeds up, and Tyler reaches out a hand to run his fingers through the damp air. He blinks as the pegasus clears the cloud bank seconds later, emerging out the top into a vast, white world enveloped in brilliant, golden sunlight. The wind isn't blowing into Tyler's eyes anymore; instead, it's buffeting gently against his back. Ratha's wings glide up and down through the air in lazy loops, letting the wind carry him forward.

"Awesome, huh?" Kaylor glances at him over her shoulder, grinning, "I don't think I'll ever forget the first time I got to fly on a pegasus. What was I asking you again?"

Tyler clears his throat, "I walked. Um…Keripen didn't find me."

"You didn't land in the village?"

"What village?"

"The village—well, at least, it *was* a village. That's where I landed. A caravan found me an hour or so later." She adjusts the reins in her hands, tugging to the left, "They were heading for Tallipeg, to watch one of their friends fight in the tournament."

"Was that the one you fought in?"

"Well, sort of," Kaylor says, "That was the preliminary round. I stayed with Keripen while that was going on. A bunch of people stopped at the *Chatty Sphinx* again on their way to the finals: one of the preliminaries happens in Tallipeg, but the winners of that have to go to the finals at the capital. Keripen sent me on to the city with one of the contestants because there was someone he wanted me to meet—" Kaylor pauses for a second, "I never actually *found* that person. I should have asked Keripen about that before we left today. Anyway, that was the one I fought in—the finals, in Valliseg."

They ride in silence for a while. Tyler stares at bits of cloud as they float by, marveling at their airy fluffiness. Despite the amazing scenery, the silence starts to bug him. It's a weird feeling: he's been used to silence for most of his life, why is it bothering him now? He scrounges around through his thoughts for something—anything—to say.

"How did you win?" he blurts, spitting the words out before he can lose his nerve.

"What?" she asks.

Tyler clears his throat, "How did you win? The tournament, I mean?"

She laughs, but seems to brighten at the chance to talk about it. "I didn't win, that would have been impossible. I came in thirty-sixth. And I did it by accident, actually. I got there with the contestant Keripen sent me with—Lady Faria. She insisted I share her tent that night since I didn't have my own, and I didn't have money to rent a room in the city. That morning, I got out of the tent and one of the King's administrators was there and he must have thought I was Lady Faria, because the next thing I knew he and his men were ushering me off through the camp, and then he pushed me through a door into the ring."

She tells him the rest of the story, taking both hands off of the reins to flail them about as she talks. She hesitates when she comes to the details of her first fight, but then plows onward smoothly, attributing her win to how athletic she's always been (she's been a dancer, a wrestler, a gymnast, and even dabbled in karate for a month or two) and how lucky she was that she'd been paired with a clumsy, untrained farm boy for her first fight. Tyler's certain there's a little more to it, but he won't press her for details. It's obvious she wants to keep some things from him, and he doesn't blame her for that.

She goes on to talk about how the Prince saw her fighting and set her apart from the others, deciding to sponsor and train her himself, and how she's still not sure why. "It's not that impressive, really. I just had a lot of luck on my side."

"*I* never would have been able to do that."

She glances over her shoulder at him, her smile wide and friendly. "Thanks. I don't think I could have survived a night all by myself out in that forest, not when I first got here."

Tyler flushes, unsure what to say to that. He struggles to find something to break the silence with, and forces himself to blurt out the first thing that comes to mind, "I'm—just curious. Aren't knights generally—not female?"

Kaylor laughs at him. "You're in a different world now Tyler, hadn't you noticed?"

He can't help but smile back a little bit, and he's sure his face is getting red but he doesn't know why.

The rest of the ride is quiet, with the exception of Kaylor's interjections about pegasi, interesting looking clouds, or questions about the general goings-on back in

Aurora. Tyler tries his best to answer all of them, though he can't tell her anything when she asks him about her family. He doesn't recognize any of the names she gives him.

When they dive down through the cloud bank, the trees are gone, faded into the distance behind them, and in their place are fields of tall grass dotted with small, thatched farmhouses. Pressure builds in Tyler's ears as they descend, and they pop painfully when Ratha hits the ground. Kaylor lets out a breathless laugh and starts to unbuckle the straps around her legs. Tyler follows her lead. She commands Ratha to stay, and starts to walk up a nearby hill. Tyler follows her.

"Over there," Kaylor says once she gets to the top, pointing ahead at something in the distance, "We're almost there."

Tyler stops next to her, slightly out of breath, and looks. The city looms before them, one or two miles away. It's like nothing Tyler's ever seen before. Grey stone walls tower up over the tall grass, a wide dirt road leading to a single wooden gate. Beyond the wall, a squarish, light blue castle with cone-shaped roofs and slit windows rests, surrounded by a smattering of stone and wooden houses.

"Welcome to Tallipeg," says Kaylor.

Chapter Twenty Three

ALEX

2nd day of Tivar
Year 1452

Altibrl Sea

lex crouches against the wall, staring at the bucket still settled in his lap. The ship isn't rocking as much anymore, but his stomach is still roiling and his head's spinning. Thankfully, he's managing *not* to cough up what food is left in his stomach. His throat is painfully dry and his lips are chapped. He could do with some water. He looks up, opening his mouth to ask Darn if he's thirsty too, and finds the room empty. Panic rises in his throat, and he tries to wrestle it down. Darn's fine—the storm's gone, and he couldn't have gone far: they're floating on a ship in the middle of the ocean, after all. Still, if only for his own peace of mind, he'd better go and check.

He gets to his feet, forcing his shaking legs to behave and carry him out the door. The people in the other rooms down the hallway—refugees, Anna called them—huddle in the corners, wrapped in tattered cloaks and stained blankets. One or two peek out at him as he walks by. Alex smiles and waves at a little girl before she ducks behind the arms of her parents, who watch him with wary eyes. How horrible would that be—to be ripped from your home, made to run from somewhere that's supposed to be safe. Alex doesn't miss the irony in that thought: he's here, ripped away from his own home and his parents and his sister, and…he might not be as upset about it as he should be.

He starts up the stairs to the deck.

Relief floods him when he sees Darn leaning against the mast, talking to some of the other people on the ship, including the kid who brought them food last night. Darn's making a face and waving his arms over his head in an exaggerated imitation of…something, making the boy giggle. Alex watches them for a moment, then looks over the rest of the ship. It's smaller than Alex thought it would be—he's never seen an *actual* ship before. They aren't exactly everywhere in Denver. Anna stands on the upper deck just in front of the wheel, watching over the ship and the ocean beyond. Something about her sets Alex's teeth on edge, but he can't put a finger on what.

He catches her eye and waves at her. She grimaces at him, and goes back to watching the ocean. He walks over to stand next to her.

She spares him a sideways glance before she returns to her ocean gazing. "I can tell you have questions—just as many as your friend does—but you're too polite to ask. I'll answer them for you, I don't mind."

"I—I have a lot."

She cracks a smile—not a smirk or a grimace, a genuine smile, even though it's small. "I have plenty of time."

"H-how did you know th-that storm was coming?"

"Because I made it."

"You—you *made* it? You mean y-you moved it, or you…c-created it?"

Now the smirk's back. "Both."

"*How?*"

"I'm a Stormbringer."

"A what?"

"A Stormbringer. A kind of sorcerer."

Sorcerer? Alex goes quiet for a minute, trying to digest that. Could it really be true? Not where Alex is from, no. But why not? Alex himself can…he swallows, stopping those thoughts in their tracks. Thinking about *that* will lead him down a dark trail to the locked box in the back of his mind, and he doesn't want to go there right now.

"Here," Anna says, stretching her right hand out in front of her, "Watch."

Steam starts to rise out of her palm, floating off the skin and up into the air. Slowly it forms into a tiny storm cloud, twisting and raging inches above the palm of her hand. Thunder crackles and minuscule drops of rain drip down onto her skin. Alex crouches so the tiny storm's at eye level, his mouth falling open.

Then Anna folds her fingers inward, against her palm, and it vanishes. "Believe me now?" she asks.

"I n-never didn't," Alex says truthfully, still staring at her hand. He's seen stranger things.

Anna frowns at him. "Right," she says, "that's not all we can do, though. I can conjure fog, control where lightning strikes, and even change the strength and direction of the wind," she stops, studying his face with piercing eyes, "but that's not the only thing a sorcerer can do. There are different kinds—*seventeen* different kinds. What you are determines what you can do. There are Illusionists, Mindinvaders, Flamestarters, Ghostspeakers—"

Alex swallows and looks away—he can't help but do it —and Anna stops talking. "Are you—?"

"I d-don't...I don't know."

It would explain a lot.

But Anna puts a hand on his arm. "I was only going to ask if you were alright," she says.

Relief floods Alex's veins. She doesn't know: she couldn't possibly have guessed from just that tiny, stupid little slip-up. But...if Anna's a sorcerer, and she's not from this other, magical land, does that mean they exist at home too? Could Alex be one of them? *Maybe I'm not crazy. Maybe I'm not alone.* He lets out a shaky breath, and then asks, "W-why did you make it? The s-storm?"

Anna turns, stalking across the helm to look over the back of the ship. "Look there," she says, pointing out over the water. Alex moves next to her and squints, eyes roving over the endless cerulean waves.

"There's a—something, o-out there," he says, following her finger, "I don't—I c-can't tell what it is."

"It's a ship," Anna murmurs, "And they're after us."

"The refugees."

Anna nods. "Yes. And me, Zer, Wrom, and Hisef. They're catching sorcerers, but just the ones who refuse to register and bow to *Shirot's* every whim." She spits out the name like it's poison on her tongue.

"Shirot?"

"The Mad King of the South, that's what everyone calls him. At least, everyone with any sense. It's a fitting name."

Alex hesitates, and then asks the obvious question. "Why th-the Mad King?"

"For a few reasons. It's got something to do with imprisoning the sorcerers, something to do with recklessly trying to start wars, and a lot to do with how paranoid he is. He thinks everyone's out to get him: that there are assassins and rebellions everywhere," Anna pauses for a second to wipe a sweaty curl off her brow, "And he thinks the only way to save himself from all of these supposed enemies is to conquer them, or kill them."

"You sure s-seem to know a l-lot about it."

Anna smirks and winks at him, "Let's just say not *all* of his fears are unfounded."

Oh. If Anna's sneaking refugees out from under this Mad King's nose, it makes sense that she's working for a rebellion. But...something about her still doesn't add up.

"Y-you haven't been t-trying to get home?"

Her mouth twists into a sour sort of scowl. "No. I don't think I ever really belonged in that other place—it might have been your home, but it wasn't mine. I have reason to believe that my mother is from here, not there, and I think she came back here when I was seven. I have to find her."

Something like hope—or maybe more like dread, he can't quite tell—starts to rise in his chest. What if Alex *isn't* actually from Korea? What if he and Lilly *weren't* actually turned over to an orphanage because their birth mother couldn't take care of them? What if Alex's birth parents are *here* somewhere, and if so, why did they give him up?

When he finally looks back at Anna, he finds her watching him, waiting for him to finish thinking. "Any more questions? Or is that all you have for me?"

"D-do you have any w-water?"

She laughs. "Yes; we do. You and Darn can help yourselves to what's in the storeroom by the sleeping quarters. There's food there, too." She looks back across the deck at Darn, scowling, though her eyes still seem to smile, "You should go and get him, he's keeping my crew from their duties." Alex turns to do as she says, but she stops him with a hand on his arm. "If you have any more questions, I'd be happy to answer them for you."

Alex smiles at her and nods. Maybe he shouldn't feel as uneasy as he does about Anna. Maybe she really does want to help them.

Something in his gut tells him he can trust her, and it's never been wrong before.

Chapter Twenty Four

KAYLOR

2nd day of Tivar
Year 1452

Tallipeg

aylor leads Ratha and Tyler through the gentle slopes of the hills, far enough from the road that the people on it won't be able to tell that Ratha's a pegasus. She hopes. Keripen gave her a folded sheet before they left this morning, which is now wrapped in a billowing mass over Ratha's back and tied together under his belly, hiding his wings from view.

Before Kaylor and Tyler left the inn, another Sight Sparrow had fluttered in through the window and landed on Keripen's desk. This captain he knows is waiting for them at the docks. But to get to the docks, they'll have to make it through the city.

Kaylor has three choices that she can think of. One, she can keep her uniform on and walk openly through the city, pretending nothing is wrong. Though that plan is shot if her earring has already burst and the Prince knows she's betrayed him. Two, they can try to disguise themselves and sprint through the city, hoping that no one will notice them.

Three, they won't enter the city at all, but will instead fly Ratha around the wall and land on the docks out back.

"Didn't you say Husifi's in the mountains?" Tyler asks, pointing off to the right at the distant peaks of the Fodomos, "Couldn't we just fly there? Do we need to take a ship?"

"That *would* be the easiest way, if it weren't for the dragons," Kaylor says, grinning when Tyler's mouth twists into a grimace, "The Gaentuki can be pretty territorial. Also, anywhere there are mountains there are griffins, and griffins are one of the only things that can hunt and kill pegasi without breaking a sweat. Plus the border's always crawling with guards, and I don't want to be seen, even flying overhead. We'd only go that way if there weren't any other options."

Kaylor continues to walk a few paces before she notices Tyler isn't beside her anymore. She stops, tugging on Ratha's reins.

"Do you have a hat?" Tyler asks.

"A hat? Why?"

"If we go through the city—Your hair—" Tyler waves his hand at her head, "There are guards here too, right? They'll recognize that. Can you…do you have a scarf you can cover your face with?"

"I have a hood. I think I can disguise myself, I'm more worried about Ratha."

Tyler runs a hand through his hair, his arms in nervous, awkward angles. "What if we didn't disguise him? Do all of the knights know each other? Are all the pegasuses—

pegasus—pegasi kept at the castle?"

Kaylor thinks she knows where he's going with this. "No, the guards here only know me because I've been here before. They don't know everyone at the castle. We can pretend you're a knight from Valliseg!"

Tyler jerks a sharp nod. "Right. Am I going to have to…"

"Here," Kaylor says, already shrugging her cloak off and working her surcoat over her head, "I think I might have broader shoulders than you, but it should fit okay," she frowns, looking him over, "The mail goes down to my knees, and the surcoat covers that, so those should be long enough. Though the sleeves might be a little short."

"If—do you have gloves? Or a strip of fabric? I, um, have an extra set of clothes in my backpack, if you need them. But they're the ones I came here in, they're kind of ripped, and…not from this world."

"Here, yeah, we can tear the sheet Ratha's wearing apart. You can tuck the ends of the sleeves into that. I don't think I need to borrow anything—I'm wearing a shirt under the chainmail, you know. I'll make something to cover my face, too."

A few minutes later, Tyler leads Ratha down the road, fiddling with the fastenings on Kaylor's scabbard where it's strapped to his hip, his eyes darting between the people passing them and the gate ahead. He's not comfortable in Kaylor's uniform, and it shows. Kaylor tugs her hood down further over her face, tucking a loose strand of hair back into the tight bun at the base of her neck.

"Put your shoulders back," she whispers through the fabric covering her mouth and nose, "don't hunch over so much. And try taking bigger steps."

Tyler swallows and forces his body to cooperate, throwing his shoulders back so far he's looking at the sky. Kaylor stifles a laugh and nudges him with her elbow. "Not *that* far."

A minute later, a young maiden passes them on the road, giving Tyler a shy smile as she walks by. Tyler's face jerks into a surprised grimace. The girl's face goes blank as she scutters off. Kaylor bursts out laughing. "Maybe don't try to smile at people," she says, once she's got her breath back, "Just...I don't know, nod, or something."

The guards at the entrance aren't people Kaylor recognizes. They stand on either side of the gate, scanning the crowd as it flows steadily into the city. No one's getting pulled aside today. Kaylor lets out a breath of relief. They're going to make it through.

One of the guards looks up, sees Tyler, and waves. Tyler gives him a very practiced, formal nod, and Kaylor has to snort into the back of her fist. At least he didn't try to smile this time.

Once they're through the gate, Kaylor pulls the scarf down off of her face. It's easy to get lost in the crowd now, away from the gate guards, but she keeps her hood up just in case. They wind their way through the streets, avoiding guards or anyone dressed too expensively to be a peasant. Kaylor points out the general direction of the docks, and then lets Tyler go ahead of her. The crowd at the market parts when Tyler walks through with Ratha, his face tilted almost comically upward as he strides through the plaza.

Despite the crowd at the market, the rest of the city is next to deserted. Windows and doors are boarded up, some with signs fastened to the fronts and others without. A small crowd in the middle of a square catches Kaylor's eye, and she stops Tyler and drags him over to look at it.

There's a newly erected bulletin board at the center of the crowd, gleaming white parchment nailed to it's face.

SORCERERS ARE DANGEROUS

Anyone found or seen practicing magic of any sort should be reported to a guard or knight immediately.

Every sorcerer in Sarenia must be registered with the Lord of their city or the King. Failure to provide proof of registry will result in immediate arrest.

UNCONTROLLED SORCERERS CAN AND WILL KILL YOU WITHOUT HESITATION

If you find an unregistered sorcerer and fail to report it, you will be considered just as guilty as the sorcerer.

Anyone handing over an unregistered sorcerer to the crown will be rewarded handsomely with gold in an amount consistent with the sorcerer's power.

"Is that why you're here?" an older woman in the crowd asks, her steely gray eyes fixed on Tyler.

He opens his mouth and then closes it, at a loss. Kaylor elbows him in the ribs. *Just say something, damn it.* She doesn't want to talk in case one of the guards is around, so Tyler's going to have to improvise. She should have known this might happen.

"I, uh, yeah. I mean, sort of. The King's been—sending reinforcements, out to the cities. Just in case." Tyler says. Kaylor winces under her cloak. His Sarenian accent is frankly awful, barely passable, and he doesn't use all the right words. But she really shouldn't blame him. He's only been here a few days. Hopefully the townspeople won't be too suspicious.

The woman's eyes narrow. She backs away, and then spits on the ground at Tyler's feet. The rest of the crowd gasps, tripping over themselves to get away from her. "You took my husband," she snarls, "He did *nothing* wrong. *Nothing*. He was a *Healer!*"

Tyler gapes at her while a couple of her friends rush forward to hold her back.

"She didn't mean it, sir, she really didn't," says a young boy tearfully, "She's just ill, is all."

"Come on," Kaylor says, grabbing Tyler's arm and pulling him aside, "We need to get out of here."

Kaylor's hands stay clenched into fists the rest of the way to the docks. It hits her that the sign isn't just about other, token-less sorcerers King Shirot has more or less always been hunting down, but about *Kaylor* now, too. She's on her way to becoming the very thing that scares the King the most. A rebel. A rebel *sorcerer*. She's not sure how she feels about that.

They're supposed to meet Keripen's contact at one of the inns down by the docks. There are two: the *White Mare* and the *Skipping Centaur*. Kaylor's stayed at the *White Mare* before, when she hasn't wanted to bother with the over-crowded guardhouses. They're to meet Keripen's friend in the considerably louder and seedier *Skipping Centaur*.

They tie Ratha to a lamppost just outside, close enough that they'll be able to see him through one of the windows, and Kaylor leads the way in.

It's crowded: all the stools in front of the counter are occupied, and several people are sitting on window sills to eat. Good. That means they can hide in the crowd. Except —well, guards almost *never* go inside the *Skipping Centaur*, much less knights of the King's Guard. A hush falls over the crowd as Tyler steps in through the door.

"Lady Kaylor?" A woman in a dark cloak with a wide hood says in a light Thethrian accent. She detaches from the crowd before them and approaches Kaylor, "Is that you?"

Kaylor watches the people around them gradually return to their drinks, still quiet. "Why don't we talk outside?" Is this Keripen's contact? She must be—how else would she know Kaylor's name?

The stranger nods. Kaylor grabs Tyler's elbow and leads them out. Once they've fetched Ratha and found a less-crowded nook, the stranger holds out a hand for Kaylor to shake. "My name is Captain Darkin. I'm a friend of Keripen's. He didn't mention he was sending me two sorcerers, or I might have suggested we meet somewhere more discrete."

Kaylor gapes at her. *Is it really that obvious?* But…Kaylor hasn't done anything suspicious, she hasn't made any shields

212

for...for several days now, actually. "How did you *know*? I mean, I haven't...why would you think I'm a *sorcerer*?"

Chapter Twenty Five

TYLER

2nd day of Tivar
Year 1452

Tallipeg

𝕴 am a Powersenser," she says, "*Dith* Keripen no *minse* ya?"

"How—*Y'aught* not a be saying that in public!" Kaylor sputters. Tyler sets his jaw, glancing back and forth down the street. No one seems to be paying them any attention, but that doesn't mean they aren't. If there's a reward for bringing in unregistered sorcerers, they need to…*Hang on.* She'd said *two* sorcerers. Implying that *Kaylor* has some of these powers, too.

Captain Darkin studies them with narrowed eyes. "I am a foreign captain. *Si* a' King *dith* arrest *khuile* foreign sorcerer who *dith* come here *a* trade, he would be in a large sum more trouble than he at present is. 'Long as we art not from here, 'r transporting other sorcerers from here, he does not seem a *ware*," she grimaces, "he *dith* not start arresting us, *hath* he?"

"Oh," Kaylor says, her eyes fixed on something just over Captain Darkin's shoulder. "I guess I did not think *schetk* that. *Ach* we aught to get going—it is most *temp* f'r a' dock guards a switch *gluases*, *y si* they try a stop us they may recognize me."

The Captain nods, then turns and leads them through an alley between the *Skipping Centaur* and a boarded up building, past a thin wooden wall and down a set of stairs. The docks expand out in an arc before them, glittering blue water lapping at their edges. Tyler's never seen the ocean before, but he doubts the one on Earth is this blue.

The boats floating in the water aren't anything like what Tyler's seen before. Some have large, billowing sails, others have stiff, triangular ones, and still others don't seem to have any. But even more peculiar are the colors. There are bright red ships, cobalt blue ships, sunshine yellow, burgundy, deep purple, indigo, and bronze. Not a single ship is a regular wood color. And the figureheads—oh, the figureheads are fantastic! Every ship has something different, ranging from lions to mermaids to antelope to things Tyler doesn't recognize in the slightest. And they're all very large. Some of them take up the entire front of the ship, their backs hollowed out to make room for the decks.

Ratha doesn't like it much. He snorts in Tyler's ear and scuffs a hoof on the ground. Kaylor reaches back and tugs the reins out of Tyler's hand.

The Captain takes them to a reddish-orange ship with a magnificent carved creature leaping out of the front. "It's a manticore," Kaylor whispers when she catches Tyler staring, "Quite rare, but very dangerous."

The ship—the *Zephyr*, Darkin calls it—is more roomy

than it looks from down on the docks. People bustle across the deck moving various boxes and crates, all sporting swords or other weapons strapped to their hips. Tyler steps aside as one pushes past him. Kaylor, her hood down and the scarf gone from her face, is talking with the captain, smacking her fist against her open palm and grinning as she does. Tyler picks at a link of chain mail on his sleeve. It's heavy. He's wearing it over the scratchy shirt Keripen gave him, and it isn't very comfortable. When's Kaylor going to want it back?

He wanders over to stand at the edge of the deck, drumming his fingers on the wooden railing. The blue ocean beneath them swells and ripples, splashing up against the sides of the boat. It's captivating. Someone coughs to his left, and Tyler catches sight of a small girl in dirty clothes leaning against the same railing not far from him. She sees him watching her and looks down at her sleeves, playing with the loose threads of her dress. She starts to hum. Tyler doesn't see her parents, or any other people for that matter, anywhere near her. It worries him. She looks so small in her dirty rags. If she's on this ship, shouldn't her parents be too? Did they let her come up here by herself? Probably—they might be downstairs, or wherever the cabins for passengers are located. He turns back to the water.

"Art ya a noble?" a small, clear voice asks. Tyler turns to see that the girl has scooted closer.

"What would make ya think that?" he asks. She giggles, kicking her feet up and leaning over the edge of the railing.

Tyler tenses, ready to grab her if she slips and falls.

"Well, y'art quite clean," she sets her feet back down on the deck and grins at him, "Ya look quite like a' lords that live in a' castle. Y'art *wear-ag* knight's cloth."

The corners of Tyler's mouth twitch, but he can't quite bring himself to smile. "I…did…borrowed? I did borrow these from um—from mine friend—we had to sneak into… a' city. I'm not from here," he shrugs, then decides to play along, "*Ach*, I did not know my parents, so I suppose I could be a noble."

The girl pats him on the arm. "I am sorry."

"It's alright."

"Mine parents did leave too, ya knowe," she says, staring out at the water, "Mine father can move *aguc* with his *fagers*, so a' guards dith take him hence *y* will not let him come home."

She tells him about her mother too, how she couldn't find work in the city and had to travel to Valliseg to join the Prince's army so she could send money and food back to Liana. When they didn't pay her enough, she sent a letter to Liana's uncle in Denadia. That's where the girl's going now: to meet her uncle. She hesitates for a moment, and then says softly, "I am sure yar parents shall come back *en final*. They probably dith do a' same *thig*. They art *come-ag* back, I knowe," She glares up at Tyler from under her bangs, as if daring him to say she's wrong. He gives her a small smile. He remembers when he was her age, when he used to dream about his parents coming back to liberate him from foster care and take him home to live a perfect life. Those fantasies got him through countless sleepless nights when he'd been younger. But…what if his parents are *here*? What if they're still alive? What if something like one of those fantasies is coming true, right before his eyes? A warm feeling grows in Tyler's chest.

"'O course they will."

She smiles back at him, her teeth crooked and a little yellow.

"I like ya. Y'art not like *huile* a' other adults. They *minse* me not a *lis schetk* it." Tyler isn't quite sure what that means, but he nods anyway. "Mine name's Liana, *uiell*."

"I'm Tyler."

"Liana? Liana, where art ya?" The cook emerges at the bottom of the stairs, scowling and beckoning to the girl when he sees her.

"I am sorry," Liana says, pushing her way off the railing and starting across the deck, "I am sorry, *ach* a' Captain says I has't a help out in a' kitchens. Y'art *com-ag* with us a Denadia?"

"I don't think so. I has't a…friend who wants to take me with her…on an adventure."

"Oh, that girl with a' cloak?" she says, looking a little crestfallen, "*Ach* shall ya come *y* visit later?"

"I—Maybe."

Liana beams, then lurches to her feet as the cook calls her again. She waves at him as she darts down the stairs to finish her chores.

Tyler turns back to the water. He wonders what happened to Liana's father. She said he could move water with his fingers—at least, that's what he thinks she said. Was he a sorcerer? He remembers what Captain Darkin said earlier. About *two* sorcerers.

Mr. Lee mentioned Kaylor in the letter. Are the four other people sorcerers too? *Are my parents sorcerers?* Is that why Tyler never knew them? Did they send him away, to keep him safe? He still hasn't told Kaylor about the letter. Maybe he should.

Chapter Twenty Six

DARN

2nd day of Tivar
Year 1452

Altibrl Sea

𝕴 can not *creid* ya *wert afeard* o' a hippocampus," says Zer, disgusted, "*That* is silly. They art harmless."

Darn snorts, tempted to cuff the kid over the head. "How was I supposed to know that? I've never seen one before."

"Ya nev…never…*seen?*" asks Zer, peering at him curiously, "I do not knowe what y'art *say-ag.*"

"I," Darn points to his chest.

Zer tilts his head and rolls his eyes. "I knowe *that.*"

Darn grins, "Have never," he shakes his head and puts his hands up, "seen," he points to his eyes and then around at the ship, "one before," he jerks his thumb over his shoulder.

Zer frowns. "*Y'ast na begu* one *afore.*"

Darn shrugs, "Sure."

"Zer!" calls one of the men—Hisef, if Darn remembers right, "Y'art meant a help me mop a' deck!"

"Sorry!" Zer squeaks, throwing Darn a rueful look as he

scampers off. Darn looks around to see if Alex is upstairs yet, and finds him standing a few feet away, grinning as he watches Zer go.

"Hey," says Darn, "You're not gonna throw up on me, are you?"

Alex's grin turns crooked, dimpling one of his cheeks. "No," he says, "A-anna says you were b-bothering her crew."

Darn spares a glance at the helm where Anna stands watching over her ship. "So what if I am?" Anna still gives him the creeps. He feels like a rat trapped in a maze, like she's keeping them here because she thinks they can help her get something she wants.

Alex's voice breaks through his thoughts. "I think she j-just wants to help us. To g-get us h-home."

Darn thinks Alex might be too trusting. "I don't know, Alex," he says, "I don't think we can trust her. Just—keep an eye on her, don't let her manipulate you."

Alex grins back at him. "I th-think she just makes you n-nervous because we're not—not—" he frowns, "we're so far from home."

Darn kicks at the deck with the black shoes, the shoes from the Peter Pan's shadow costume he wore to that party weeks—no, only days, only two days ago. He has the black t-shirt from the costume, but all he has for pants is the morph suit: he uses the arms to tie the upper half around his waist. They feel like tights and he looks ridiculous, but no one has any clothes to lend, and at least they don't have holes in them.

"Yeah, sure. But I'd rather get out of here as soon as

possible."

The rest of the day is uneventful—Darn spends most of it walking aimlessly around the deck or laying in the hammock, staring at the ceiling. The rest of the crew are polite enough, but it's clear that they don't want anything to do with him. He'd talk to Alex, but the other boy's slipped into a melancholy mood, spending much of the day staring out over the ocean and only acknowledging Darn's presence with an occasional "hmm".

Darn and Alex sit down with Anna in her quarters for dinner, where Anna asks after her family and gives a derisive snort when Darn reiterates that they're looking for her. He pesters her again about sending them home and tries to get more out of her about Colf. When that fails, he tries to ask her more about her life back on Earth and is swiftly and firmly shut out.

By the time he and Alex get back to the room with the hammocks, Darn is bored out of his mind.

"How much longer are we going to be out here?" he asks Alex, pointing at the ceiling and counting the boards across it—*again*.

"I—I don't k-know. I think Anna said—a couple of days?" His voice is soft and smoother than usual, weighed down by exhaustion. "You know—she m-might tell you something, if you didn't push so hard."

Darn lets out a heavy sigh, and leans over the edge of his hammock to look at Alex. "There's just nothing to *do* out here," *and I can't talk to my parents or Trish, I have no idea where I am, and there are blue horses in the ocean that are only supposed to exist in fairy tales.* "Look, I'm sorry if I've been a little…snappy. I'm not mad at you, or anyone really, except the guy who kidnapped us and dumped us in the ocean."

"S'alright," Alex mumbles, his eyes closed.

"Do you think—" but the other boy's snoring softly, already asleep. Darn flops back into his hammock, staring at the ceiling. He smells. His clothes are dirty, he hasn't been able to wash his hair in days, and his feet are starting to hurt whenever he puts on the black shoes. Would it kill these sailors to stop some time for a bath? Showers are out of the question, but there's plenty of water around. He asked one of the sailors yesterday about another pair of pants, and the man had laughed in his face. Do the people here know nothing about germs? His nose wrinkles in disgust. The other sailors don't seem to smell much, but that's probably because Darn smells so bad he can't smell anyone else over it.

But that's not the only thing bothering him. As pathetic as it sounds, he wants to talk to his mom. He misses being able to call her or his dad up on a whim, even though he hardly ever does. It's just that he *could*, before, if he'd needed to. They're probably calling and calling his cell, and he can't pick up and let them know he's alive and stuck someplace with hippocampuses and certifiably crazy pirates and no toilets or showers. He glances back over at Alex, who's still sleeping peacefully. He wonders if Alex misses his family, or if it was really so bad at home that he's happy to be in some strange world so far away.

He lets out another sigh and tries to settle into the

hammock. After what feels like several hours, his mental exhaustion catches up with him and he drops off to sleep.

The next morning, Darn wakes up a while before Alex does and just stares at the ceiling. *Again.* He's going mad. If he isn't already. What would Trish do in a situation like this? Sit around making wry and sarcastic comments—probably make fun of Darn for being bored on a *pirate ship.* He sighs, heavily—he's lost count of the number of times he's done that on this boat.

When Alex *finally* wakes up, Darn rolls out of his hammock and trails after him like a lost puppy. They end up leaning on the railing, watching the sea, being *quiet.* Again.

"S'cuse me," Anna pushes her way between them.

"What?" asks Darn, careful to keep the snap out of his voice.

"Someone's out there," she says, "But—not that other ship that was chasing us before. As far as I can tell, they aren't following us. But they shouldn't be that close to the cliffs in the middle of the day." She squints, leaning forward over the deck. "It looks—I think it's a Thethrian ship. There's a green flag, up top. Just—be ready to lock yourselves downstairs if I say the word."

"Why?" *Is there some other kind of strange, awful creature out there that wants to eat people?*

"You could say that," mutters Anna, pushing past them

again to go back to the helm.

Darn's head whips after her and then turns back to Alex. "Did she just…?"

Alex quirks his eyebrows at him.

"I can't read your mind, you said that out loud," Anna calls over her shoulder.

"Oh."

Alex looks incredibly amused, so Darn flicks him on the forehead.

"Ow," Alex frowns at him, rubbing the spot.

"Serves you right," Darn grumbles.

"W-what did *I* do?" Alex asks.

"You smell," Darn informs him.

Alex snorts, "Because n-no one else on this sh-ship d-does."

They lapse into silence, which is mercifully broken a few seconds later by Zer.

"We are *go-ag* a save those folk, ya knowe," the kid says, trotting up to the railing and gripping it tightly next to Darn.

"Save who?"

"That other *barviat* Captain *sàbh* over there, by a' cliffs. She dith tell me a say: 'get ready a *dol* 'neath a' deck'"

"Why do we need to go below the deck?" Darn stares out over the endless blue ocean, flicking a fleck of dust off the railing. "We'd have to miss all this *riveting* scenery." Alex barks out a laugh, but covers his mouth to keep more of his mirth from escaping.

Zer glares at him, puzzled. "Ya do not want a' sirens a

eat yar guts out, do ya?"

"I th-think I'd like to k-keep my guts, thanks." Alex says.

All lighthearted humor aside, the kid just said that with a straight face. Darn frowns. "You really mean that, huh?"

Zer nods importantly, his eyes traveling to a point behind Darn's head. "Yorren is *go-ag* a drag ya hence *si* ya do not listen," he adds.

"ZER!" Yorren yells, stomping down the deck toward them, "Why art ya still up here? Get out o' here!" Yorren grabs Darn's sleeve and starts to tug.

"Hey!" Darn plants his feet, trying to yank his sleeve out of Yorren's grasp, "What's going on?"

"Sirens," Yorren snaps, "Ya has't a get in a cellar, now. I do not *ware si* Anna dith say otherwise, it is too tangled f'r ya a be up here."

Darn opens his mouth to say something, but the sound of someone screaming cuts him off.

Yorren lets out a colorful stream of expletives, grabbing Darn by the sleeve again and hauling him off toward the stairway. He grabs the back of Alex's shirt as they go.

But it's too late, because it's just at that moment that Darn hears the most beautiful song he's ever heard before in his life.

Chapter Twenty Seven

ALEX

3rd day of Tivar
Year 1452

Cliffs of Bone
Altibrl Sea

orren's grip slackens, and Darn freezes. Alex wriggles out of Yorren's grasp. The first mate doesn't put up much protest: in fact, he hardly seems to be paying attention to Alex at all. There's a soft noise in the distance, getting louder. The pressure builds behind Alex's eardrums until he can't bear it any longer. His hands clap forcefully to his ears, a scream ripping out of his throat.

He can't move—he can't even think. His ears are throbbing, his hands unable to block out the bloodcurdling screech echoing through the air.

Darn and Yorren don't seem to care about the noise. They're frozen, faces turned to the sky with slack jaws and reverent expressions. That scares him more than the noises. How are they not hearing this?

Alex staggers forward, knocking into Darn and trying to break his concentration. "Wrom!" Anna yells from the wheel, "*Dol* y grab Yorren, bid ya?" At least Anna isn't in whatever trance this is. Alex removes one hand from his ears and grabs Darn's elbow, shaking his arm.

"Darn," he says, "D-darn, wake up. What are y-you doing?"

There's no response. When Alex grabs his elbow and tries to get him to turn away, to look at him, Darn jerks out of his grip and starts walking forward.

The black specks in the distance are getting closer, and if Alex squints hard enough he can make out blurry outlines. They look like birds. The noise still buzzes through his eardrums, but its effect is fading. He lifts his other hand away from his ear.

Darn and Yorren are walking toward the railing.

"ALEX!" Anna yells even louder, "Don't let them jump off the boat!"

Why would they do that? But even as he thinks that, Darn steps up onto the railing. Alex sprints towards him. His fingers close around Darn's elbow just as he gets the other foot up and over. Darn slips forward, off the edge of the boat, and Alex swings his other hand out to grab Darn's other arm.

"What are you *d-doing?*" he yells, trying to haul Darn back onto the ship while his friend struggles against his grip, "Darn," he gasps, "*Stop* it!"

"Sounds…so pretty…" Darn mumbles, craning his neck to look at the bird shapes over his shoulder. Alex uses the distraction to haul him back over the railing.

They collapse in a heap on the ground. Darn writhes around, trying to escape Alex's grip on his waist. It's mostly futile, since Alex is a lot stronger than him, but his limbs are still flailing around and Alex doesn't want to get elbowed in the face. Someone wrenches Darn's wrists back and over his head. Alex looks up and sees one of Anna's crew, Wrom, knotting a length of rope around them.

"There," she says, sitting back on her heels, "Now let's get him up y into a' brig."

"Y-yorren?" Alex hadn't gone after the first mate. Guilt twists through his gut at the thought of Yorren falling off the boat while Alex was trying to control Darn.

Wrom quirks a smile at him. "Don't worry, I did get him. Come on now, he's *go-ag* a get more stubborn."

Darn struggles against the rope. "Why can't I listen to the song?" he whines.

Alex gets up and helps Wrom hoist Darn to his feet. "W-what's going on?"

"Oh, ya knowe, sirens," Wrom explains, "Makes a' men *dol* mad. At least, most men." She winks at Alex. He tries to fight the flush that floods his face, but he can't help it. She can't possibly mean...can she? He's used to being good at hiding everything about himself, so it's pretty disconcerting that she might *know* something. If she can find *that* secret, what about the others? What about the ones that are actually *bad*? He tries to slow his breathing down, to keep his looming panic at bay. "*What?*"

"Oh ya knowe, sirens? *Eundege*-women? Sing seductively at sailors *y* steal *sofolk* hence?"

Oh—she thinks he meant the *sirens*. Alex decides to just go with it. "Th-those *exist*?"

Wrom shrugs. "Do here."

Once Darn is locked safely in the brig—Alex wants to stay and watch him, maybe have a break down while he's at it, but Wrom convinces him to come back. There are only three sane people on the ship right now, and they need any help they can get. They might have been able to count Zer, but Anna wants him locked down with the others just in case.

Alex and Wrom make their way up to the deck, where Anna stands behind the wheel. Even though it's quite a bit taller than her, she has no trouble turning it.

"I'm sorry about that," Anna says, "I thought Zer understood when I told him it was *urgent*. I also didn't think we'd run out of wax. Just—we've never had to go by the Cliffs with refugees before, and I didn't realize our stores had run so low. I suppose we could've stuck cheese in their ears—" Alex wrinkles his nose and she laughs, "No, I guess not. At least the noise is muffled below the deck, and they're locked up so they really can't try anything. We usually go by at night, since the sirens never come out then, but I don't want them taking that ship over there." Anna frowns, "Normally I wouldn't bother, but…"

"It's the right thing to do," Wrom finishes.

Anna twitches, as if bitten by a nasty bug. "I suppose. But I don't like risking the crew like this."

"Why are you d-doing it, th-then?"

Anna glances back at him before returning her attention to the wheel. She grips the spokes so hard her knuckles turn white. "I haven't told you some things that I should have," she murmurs, "I came here with my friends, the other two people Darn saw in that newspaper he's been going on about. Kaylor and Sarah. I…sent for Kaylor, not long before you and Darn showed up. I overheard Colf talking about her, and I pieced together her whereabouts from there.

"It's almost time for her to meet me in Husifi. If I know her at all, she took a ship herself instead of going with… instead of doing what I told her she should do."

"She c-could be on th-that ship," Alex finishes for her.

Anna nods. "And about that…" she pulls a folded piece of paper out of a deep pocket in her coat and hands it to Alex.

It's a letter. The handwriting—and the signature—match the one Alex found in his pocket on the way home from school, a lifetime ago.

"I got one too," he says, "I'd sh-show it t-to you, but it got l-lost in the ocean."

Anna nods, her lips pursed, and snatches the paper back. "I was beginning to suspect as much." She tucks it back into her coat pocket.

"You knew a-about us. About m-me and Darn."

"Not before I found you. Choffson gave me the letter a little too late. We're lucky we were in the area anyway. But this *Mr. Lee*," Anna pauses to frown, "I have a feeling he made certain I'd be going that way anyway, just in case I never got the letter."

Alex doesn't remember everything that was in his letter, but he does remember Mr. Lee saying that he knew Alex's parents. Could they have been sorcerers in hiding? Were they like Alex?

"Captain?" Wrom calls from the deck, "We're getting nigh!"

Anna calls back, "Most ready! *Dol* y get Alex a sword, would ya? Y a' *flurs*, too."

Wrom salutes her and hurries off.

"I-I'll need a sword?"

"Sirens can be vicious. Do you know what they do to the people they take?"

Alex shakes his head.

"Once they've got what they want from them, they kill them and eat them."

He winces. "Th-that's—awful."

"I think I know how to drive them off." Her eyes narrow as she watches the sirens swarming above the other ship, "They owe me something."

"Oh?"

Anna's eyes dart to his for half a second. "Are you up for a fight, Alex?" she asks in a soft voice.

Alex swallows. "M-maybe," he says.

Anna's smirk is positively feral. "Okay, here's the plan…"

Chapter Twenty Eight

TYLER

3rd day of Tivar
Year 1452

Cliffs of Bone
Altibrl Sea

Tyler flattens the page of the book down against his knee, straining to read the words in the inconsistent light from the porthole. The page is worn and stained, creased in the center and taped back together. This is Tyler's favorite part: when Hamlet first talks with the ghost of his father. He mouths along to the words as he reads.

Murder most foul, as in the best it is;
But this most foul, strange and unnatural.

A spray of salty air whips in through the porthole and hits Tyler in the face. He slams the book shut, tucking it away beneath his arm. He can't let it get wet. This isn't going to work—he's going to have to find something else to do. Sighing, he grabs his backpack out from under the bunk he's sitting on and slips the book into it, zipping it closed. The water laps noisily at the sides of the ship. Tyler looks up to watch the brilliant blue waves drift endlessly toward the horizon. *Strange and unnatural indeed.*

He gets up with half a mind to go and find Kaylor. They've been on this ship for a day and a night, and he's starting to think she's avoiding him. She's spent almost every waking moment with Captain Darkin, or else one of the other crewmen—she never seems to be alone. And Tyler doesn't want to bare his—*their*—secret in front of strangers.

But he needs answers. So he slings the backpack on—he never leaves it alone, the contents is too precious—and makes his way up to the deck.

He spies Kaylor and Captain Darkin through an open doorway at the back of the ship, in the room just below the deck with the steering wheel on it—the quarterdeck, if he remembers correctly. He leans against the wall next to the door, straining to catch some of their conversation through the wood. It's too muffled: he can make out their voices, but no words. Darkin laughs at something Kaylor's saying, and then one of them steps across the room toward the door. Tyler snaps his head sideways, towards the ocean, trying to look like he's pondering the movements of the waves instead of eavesdropping. But when Kaylor trails out after the Captain, Tyler inserts himself between them, stopping Kaylor in her tracks.

"There you are," Kaylor startles, taking a step back, "The Captain and I were just—"

"Are you a sorcerer?" Tyler snaps.

Kaylor blinks at him, frowning, "What does that—?"

"Are you?" he asks, struggling to hold her gaze with a

hard one of his own.

She lets out a breath, staring down at her hands. "I—I'm a Sheildmaker. It's how I won....the fights I won in that tournament, and probably why Casteor wanted me to work for him." She swallows. "And you? Don't think I didn't catch that—Darkin said *both* of us."

"It's like the pot and the kettle, then," Tyler mumbles. She gives him an odd look, and he backpedals, "Sorry. I'm a Flamestarter—I guess. Keripen told me not to tell anyone."

She tucks a stray strand of hair behind her ear as she nods. "Okay."

They stand in silence for a couple of seconds. It's uncomfortable.

"Sorry," Tyler blurts, "I mean, I just...I needed to know."

"Look," Kaylor says, "There's something else I should tell you—"

Someone shouts, and several of the crewmen around them look up and point at the sky. Tyler turns to try and see what's going on, and...

A noise—no, a song—drifts down through the air, filling up the space and echoing softly against the sails. Kaylor clamps her hands over her ears and screams. But Tyler doesn't understand why. It's—why, it's *beautiful*. It's the most beautiful thing he's ever heard. He walks—no, he drifts—across the deck.

All around him, the sailors have frozen. Every gaze is directed toward the sky. He wants to know what they're looking at. It must be important.

Someone yells behind him before he can look, cutting through the song in the air. Annoyance prickles through him. Can't this person be quiet, now? He wants to hear. But —the voice sounded vaguely familiar. Vaguely important. Oh, well. He's too busy listening to the song right now. It can wait, whatever it is.

And then he snaps back to his senses with a jolt. The ship rocks below his feet, and he's nowhere near the cabin anymore. He's up just behind the figurehead. How did he get here? A few feet in front of him, a pearly pinkish-orange plane ripples through the air.

"TYLER!" Kaylor yells from somewhere behind him, "Get back here, you need to get inside! I can't do this forever! I'm...I'm running out! Tyler!"

He should listen to her: he doesn't want to go foggy again. But just as he starts to back up, just as he's going to turn around and run, the pink plane in front of him pops like a bubble.

Why did he ever want to go back to that girl? Sure, Kaylor's kind of pretty, but that doesn't matter. *None of it* matters, except that he needs to keep listening to this *wonderful* music. No—wonderful isn't a good enough word. It's *exquisite*. He has to find the source of it.

He looks up. Brightly-colored birds circle above the ship, and that's surely where the song is coming from. But no, they aren't birds. What are they? Girls with wings? At any rate, they have human faces. They glide about through the clear sky, their glossy feathers shimmering in the sunlight as they circle closer. Their skin, which is not

covered in feathers from the waist up, is just as glossy and…
and…Tyler loses his train of thought as one of them
swoops down, separating herself from the others, and lands
on the railing not five feet from him. Tyler blinks. She's still
singing, and it's beautiful. The…the girl-bird…smiles
blindingly at him as he steps closer. Her long, straight, dark
hair flows over her body when she shuffles her wings and
folds them onto her back. Tyler swallows thickly.

"Hello," her voice is almost as musical as the song the
others are still singing, "My name is Narda."

Tyler clears his suddenly dry throat. "Tyler." His voice
still sounds scratchy. Drat.

She laughs. Tyler can't help it: he takes another step
forward. And then another. Narda unfolds her wings again,
settling the wrists—or what would be her wrists if she had
them—on his shoulders, wrapping him in a cocoon of
feathers. Something in the back of his head screams at him
that this is wrong, this is all wrong, but he ignores it. She
leans forward, her chocolate brown eyes staring into his,
until their noses are touching. He closes his eyes.

"Get your filthy hands off him! Or…wings! Get your
filthy wings off him!"

Something clicks in Tyler's brain and he takes a step
back. But then it's squashed down, gone again.

"We're taking this one! He's mine now!" Narda snaps.
She lifts one claw off the railing and grabs Tyler's arm with
it. It hurts. Why is she doing this? Why would she hurt him?
He thought she liked him.

"Let go of him right now or I'll cut your wings off!"

Kaylor yells, swinging her sword at Narda. The siren shrieks. Kaylor's worn out, her breath coming in heavy gasps, but her eyes are narrowed and full of fury. Tyler doesn't like that expression much, especially not when it's directed at Narda.

The bird-girl hisses again and lets him go, flinging him backwards as she takes off. Kaylor drops her sword to catch him by the shoulders, and forces him to sit on the deck before she grabs her weapon again and steps forward, putting herself between Tyler and Narda. He tries to get up, but the ship seems even rockier than normal. Kaylor's standing just fine, though. Why does he feel so disoriented? Narda perches on one of the sail's beams above Kaylor's head, her wings wrapped protectively around herself. A small spot of red is visible on one of Narda's wings. Why did Kaylor do that?

"What did you do?" he asks Kaylor. She ignores him. Someone's coming up behind him, he can hear their footsteps.

"You!" Narda hisses, presumably at the newcomer. Tyler cranes his neck to see who it is.

There's a girl there, in a flowery purple skirt and a trench coat, tight, dark curls tumbling out from beneath her enormous hat. She sneers back at Narda, "Me."

PART 4

INCARNATES

Chapter Twenty Nine

ANNA

3rd day of Tivar
Year 1452

Cliffs of Bone
Altibrl Sea

nna sneers back at the siren. "Me." She takes a step
forward, drawing the sword out of its sheath at her
hip and swinging it around, her eyes never leaving the blade.
She shoots a sideways glance at the siren as the tip of the
sword hits the deck. The siren flinches.

"What, exactly, are you doing on this ship?" Anna asks,
strolling forward, masking her fluttering heart with a facade
of icy calm. The siren fidgets, ruffling her wings and
shifting her weight from one foot to the other.

"This isn't your ocean," she spits. She lets out a small
cry, and the sound of wind rushing through feathers
permeates the air overhead.

"What's wrong, Narda?" a second siren asks, lighting
down next to the first on the beam. A third follows her a
second later, while a fourth lands in a clumsy flurry of
feathers on the deck just in front of Kaylor. Anna hasn't
seen her in a year, but here she is now, facing down the
sirens by Anna's side. Anna's ears are buzzing and her chest

feels too warm. She wants to hug Kaylor, right now, so tightly that she'll never be able to leave her side again. But she can't, because right now they're facing down a group of angry sirens.

"You owe us, Anna," the siren on the deck turns from Kaylor to her, shaking her long blond hair back over her checkered wings.

"I owe you nothing," Anna spits.

The second siren, a pretty brunette, flutters her wings and shifts her weight from one claw to the other. Kaylor's eyes dart back and forth between the siren on the deck and the three on the beam, unsure which is the bigger threat. Anna notices Kaylor's sword arm is shaking. The first siren leans forward, letting out a low hiss. Kaylor lifts her sword up and spreads her feet, staring the siren down.

"I've gutted a manticore with this sword," Kaylor snaps, "So if I were you, I wouldn't come any closer."

A *manticore*? Exactly *what* has Kaylor been doing this whole time? The siren in front of Anna hisses, jerking Anna's attention back to her. "We helped you with your mutiny," she takes a step forward, forcing Anna to scoot back about a foot to stay out of range of her claws, "You owe us."

"You broke that agreement," Anna snarls, "I said you could take the captain, *and* the officers. It's not *my* fault they got away from you. Patrick was never part of that deal."

The siren fluffs her feathers out, lifting her wings above her back. "How are we supposed to tell the difference? You all look *the same* to me."

Anna grinds her teeth. "He. Was not. Part. Of. The deal."

The siren stamps her foot, sending a cloud of feathers sailing through the air around them. Anna tries not to flinch. "We *need* more children," the siren spits, "So we need more human males. Only *one* of these ships is yours, we should be free to take what we want from the other."

"Guess what? I'm claiming this ship. I'm kind of a pirate, haven't you heard?" Anna sneers up at the siren, "Oh, that's right, *you're* the ones who helped me stage a mutiny. So really, *you're* the reason I'm running around claiming ships that aren't mine. So it's *your* fault that you can't have this ship."

"That wasn't part of the agreement." The siren's eyes blaze, her mouth curling into an ugly grimace, "You never said we couldn't go after another ship."

Anna shrugs, dropping the sword a couple of inches and trying to look casual. "Actually, we agreed on some terms before the mutiny, remember? You're never to harm me, my crew, or my possessions." She frowns, letting her eyes rise to the sails, "Of course, you might have already broken those terms."

"They ended after the mutiny."

Anna shrugs again, ignoring her sweaty palms and rapidly beating heart, "How would you like to settle this, then?"

She hopes that all this posturing and ridiculous sword-waving is enough to hold their attention until Alex and Wrom accomplish what she asked them to. Where *are* they?

They should be finished by now.

Anna will have to keep stalling. She takes a step forward and opens her mouth, but she's interrupted by a strangled yell from somewhere to her right.

A Thethrian woman, a hood concealing her face in shadows, leaps down from the quarterdeck.

"I wouldn't threaten them if I were you," she says.

"Why not?" the siren snarls, turning from Anna to her.

"Because we have something of yours," she says. Anna takes another step back, away from the siren.

"What could you possibly have—" A series of shrieks echo through the air, then trail off into soft murmurs. Anna smirks. They did it.

Alex, Wrom, and a few other sailors come into view from behind the cabin, a struggling mass of netted feathers between them.

"Are you forgetting how I tempted you last time?" says Anna, moving to stand between the siren and the Thethrian woman.

"Velvet lilies," the siren murmurs, "Stolen from our valley."

"Very good," says Anna, "Laced with Kohlflower seeds. Now, if you don't want—"

"How *dare* you!" she shrieks, rearing up to her full height and spreading her wings wide. Anna stumbles backwards. "How *dare* you capture one of our sisters with the secrets of our valley! It's blasphemy! It's—" She stops, shakes her head, and snarls. "It cannot be tolerated."

She lunges at Anna.

With a yell, Kaylor runs in front of her and straight at the siren, sword drawn. The siren lets out a screech, flapping her wings in a wild flurry of feathers and lifting her claws up to strike. One of the other sirens lands on the deck with a thud. Anna doesn't have time to think. She lunges across the deck, sword up in the air and ready to plunge into the siren's flesh. But she hits nothing. Claws screech against the wood as the siren scrambles away, pumping her wings and trying to get airborne. That didn't go the way Anna thought it would.

Ear-splitting screeching fills the air around them as the sirens start to sing again. Anna resists the urge to clap her hands over her ears, keeping her sword at the ready and chasing after the blond siren. The others have launched themselves into the air, flying above the crew and scratching at them with enormous talons. Someone screams in agony. Anna blocks it out.

The sirens continue to sing. Anna slashes and runs and cranes her neck to watch the bird-women dance about through the sky. She only manages to hit one—the blood trickles down her sword in a syrupy stain. She slashes at the big blond siren again, and hits the railing instead. The blade cracks and shatters, leaving Anna with only a small shard stuck to the end of the pommel. She pauses to look for something—anything—to help her, or replace it. Her eyes scan the skirmish for a familiar head of tangled blond hair. She doesn't see Kaylor anywhere.

Feathers sweep through the air above her head, and Anna half-falls, half-trips onto the deck. Talons swipe the air mere inches above her back. She gulps, trying to force air down and into her lungs.

"Here!" someone shouts over the commotion. Something cool and metal is pressed into Anna's hand. Her fingers close around the leathery grip of a sword pommel, and she looks up and into the eyes of the Thethrian captain. Blood drips from a gash on her nose. "You're going to need this," she says, covering Anna's fingers with her own. Anna struggles to her feet, gripping the new sword unsteadily. It's a Thethrian cutlass. "Quickly, now," says the other captain, "We need to get back to the battle."

She takes off in a sprint for the other end of the boat, screaming at the sirens as they dart about overhead. Anna follows her.

Something else rises above the screaming: a sort of deep, bellowing growl that reverberates through the deck and Anna's bones. She wipes a soggy bit of hair out of her eyes and looks up.

A glittery, golden creature snakes its way through the sky, roaring to the clouds as smoke trails out of its nostrils. The sirens rush about in a panic, shoving each other and flapping around in a cluster of drifting feathers. There's something astride the creature—the *dragon*, Anna realizes— a tiny dark spot just behind it's shoulders that's growing as the dragon gets closer. Anna feels it in her gut before she even sees that Sarah's come back to them—that they're a trio again.

Chapter Thirty

SARAH

3rd day of Tivar
Year 1452

Altibrl Sea

arah tucks a loose strand of hair out of her face and back into one of her braids. The wind whips around her as she settles herself more comfortably into the saddle on Nellie's back. The dragon huffs and flaps her wings in great arcs, kicking up more wind and tugging more of Sarah's hair out of place. Sarah tucks it angrily back behind her ear. How's she supposed to scan miles and miles of ocean if her hair keeps getting in her eyes?

"*See anything yet?*" she asks Nellie. The dragon's body expands and contracts with a sigh.

"*I haven't. How do you know they're coming by boat?*"

"*I don't, I just…that Cremon guy said Anna was the captain of a ship, right? So it seems logical that they'd show up on a boat.*"

"*How do you know Kaylor's with Anna?*"

"*I don't, okay? But it's all we've got to go on.*"

"*We were out here all of yesterday.*"

The rest of Nellie's sentence hangs in the air between them. Sarah swallows.

"*I know, okay? But I can't just sit around while they could be out there…*"

"*I know, Sarah. But I can't fly around all day, everyday, for weeks on end. I do have a job, you know.*"

"*I know,*" Sarah says absently, running her fingers over the small scales on Nellie's neck, "*They usually give you time off after a trip.*"

Nellie huffs. "*Time off so I can do things like rest and spend time with my family, not so I can fly anxious human girls all over the ocean to look for their friends. Didn't Juanna say this Colf person was going to bring them to Husifi? Why can't you leave it to him?*"

Sarah bites her lip, playing with the straps on the saddle. She still hasn't told Nellie about the letter she received from Mr. Lee. "*I've heard some things about him—not good things. Besides, he's locked up by now. Those soldiers in the street took him away. What if his way of getting them here is just to tell them to get here themselves? Don't you see how dangerous that could be? How many things could go wrong?*"

"*Yes, they could. But if they got here at the same time as you did —and got themselves into so much trouble already—don't you think they'll be able to overcome it? Your friends aren't helpless, Sarah, especially if they really are the way you describe them.*"

Sarah stops fiddling with the hair in her eyes. "*I guess you're right. But I can't just sit around and wait. They should be here soon—it shouldn't take more than a week.*"

Sarah can hear the smile in Nellie's voice as she responds, "*I suppose. But I'm only doing this for one more day. And then we'll have to wait.*"

The rest of the morning drifts by without incident.

Sarah's anxiety grows with every minute, her hair-tugging turning to finger-tapping and then to knuckle-cracking and fingernail-chewing. The sea stays quietly empty.

Off in the distance, something glitters in the light of the setting sun. Sarah squints. *"Do you see that?"*

Nellie grunts in assent, diving down and speeding up.

It's a ship—or, two ships. And a flock of sirens is swarming the air above them. *Cremon said Anna made a deal with sirens.*

"We have to get down there!" Sarah yells, *"They're after the people on those ships!"*

Nellie's already going, wings scrunched up in a diving position, shooting forward like an arrow while the wind whips past Sarah's face. Sarah grabs the handles on the saddle, just in case the straps holding her legs aren't enough to keep her from sliding backwards.

Sirens hurtle past them as they get closer, fleeing the wrath of a dragon or else getting caught in her slipstream. Sarah winces as one tries to grab at Nellie's wing with a pair of enormous, razor-edged claws. Swallowing, she tries not to think about what claws like that could have done to her friends. She has to *do* something, *now*. Sarah leans down and starts to unbuckle the straps around her legs. Nellie twists through the air, throwing her off-balance.

"What are you doing?" Nellie snaps.

"I need the straps off to jump onto the boat."

"Sarah—absolutely not," Nellie thrashes sideways again when Sarah grabs another buckle, *"It's too dangerous. I thought you were the* sensible *one?"*

249

Sarah keeps fiddling with the buckle. Nellie snorts, turns her nose downward, and dives for the crest of a wave. Sarah yelps as water strikes her face, submerging her for almost half a second before she breaks the surface.

"*There,*" Nellie grumbles, "*Now you can finish with that, and then you can swim over to the boat.*"

"*Nellie!*" Sarah coughs, wiping seawater out of her eyes. "*You didn't have to do that.*"

"*I did. You were about to do something stupid, and I had to stop you.*"

A shiver that has nothing to do with the cold water tingles down Sarah's spine. She feels suddenly nervous. But what does she have to be nervous about? She's excited too. Maybe that's why her hands are shaking. "*Was that them? Are they here?*"

Nellie turns her long neck around to gaze at Sarah. "*Only one way to find out.*"

Sarah swallows, nods, and slides down the dragon's side into the water.

Nellie didn't land far from the ship. It only takes Sarah a couple of strokes to make it there, and by then there are several people waiting to pull her up with a couple of ropes. She makes it onto the deck, sopping wet and gasping, a minute later. But she only has a second to collect herself before her breath catches in her throat and she stops breathing altogether.

Standing in front of her, in a trench coat and a pirate hat, and a knight's chain mail and insignia respectively, are Anna and Kaylor.

And then all three of them are grinning and running to each other, throwing arms around shoulders and necks in a clumsy three-way hug.

"Where have you *been*—!?"

"I swear, Anna, you have twice as many freckles—"

"I *can't* believe you're here too—"

"Kaylor, you have a cut on your face—"

"I have worse scars than that—"

"How long has it been?"

"Too long."

"I'm never letting you out of my sight again."

Sarah steps back and grins down at her friends, the tight ball of anxiety in her chest finally starting to loosen.

"So what have *you* been up to?" Anna asks, scrutinizing her with familiar, unsettling green eyes.

"I've been living with the dragons in Husifi. But I heard you made a *deal* with *sirens*. Is that why they were after you?"

Anna rolls her eyes. "No. They were after the ship Kaylor was on, actually, and I had to swoop in and save their asses."

"Did not, Anna," Kaylor says, beaming, "We had it under control."

"*If you'll excuse us,*" a voice breaks into their little bubble, "*I need to be getting to Husifi before the end of the week.*"

Sarah turns to find a tall Thethrian woman watching them, an amused twinkle in her eye. "*I'm sorry,*" Sarah says, slipping into Thethrian, "*Are you the captain of this ship?*"

The woman's eyes widen. "*You're a Speaker,*" she says in Sarenian, "*I haven't met a Speaker since…*" she trails off.

All this scrutiny is making Sarah nervous. She steps back towards her friends, until they're standing in a line.

The Thethrian straightens, sheathing her cutlass. *"Forgive me. But yes, my name is Captain Darkin. It's a pleasure to make your acquaintance…"*

"Sarah."

"Sarah. And, I'm not quite sure I caught your name, what with the fight and all…?" She pauses, looking to Anna.

"Anna. Captain Anna Thomas. And here," Anna says, lifting her own cutlass up and presenting it to Captain Darkin laid out on both palms, *"You let me borrow this."*

The captain smiles down at her, but makes no move to accept the sword. *"You can keep that,"* she says, *"You've earned it. You may have saved my life, and that of my crew."*

Sarah clears her throat. *"How many were wounded?"*

"None of mine," Anna pipes up.

"We have a couple of injuries, but nothing that our Healer shouldn't be able to treat." Captain Darkin says.

"I think…if it's okay with both of you, of course—that Kaylor, Anna, and I should go to Husifi on Anna's ship; Captain Darkin can take herself and her crew and follow us closely. Nellie can give us an escort, just in case. We're not far—it shouldn't take more than a few hours to get to the docks."

Captain Darkin nods, her eyes glittering from under her hood. *"Kaylor—your Ratha can ride with us, but he can't spend the night on the ship. We're going to leave as soon as we can, and I don't yet know when that will be."*

Kaylor nods, *"Of course. I'll retrieve him as soon as we get to the harbor."*

Captain Darkin nods, then turns away to order her crew back to work. They swarm over the ship, getting her ready for departure. Anna twists on her heel, beckoning for Kaylor and Sarah to follow her. A girl—another pirate—falls into step behind them. A dark-haired Asian boy trails after her, his sneakers squeaking across the deck. Sarah frowns. Is he one of the boys mentioned in the letter? Where are the others? They walk across a couple of planks, onto a navy blue ship Sarah assumes is Anna's.

"Oh, crud. Wait a second, Anna, I have to go and get someone. I'll be right there, don't leave without me!" Kaylor darts back over the planks. *Much too quickly, she's going to fall one of these days.*

Anna turns to Sarah and raises her eyebrows. *Do you know where she's going?* Sarah shrugs. Anna purses her lips, but turns to the strange boy. "Alex, this is Sarah. I'm going to let the others out of the brig. Can you fill her in on how you got here? You can trust her with your life—I do."

And with a swirl of her new too-long trench coat and her old purple skirt, Anna heads off in the other direction.

"S-so…you're Anna's f-friend?" The boy gives her a forced smile. His skin is ashen, so much that it looks almost grayish. Sarah wonders if he's sick.

She smiles and tries to sound friendly, "Yeah. So where did Anna find you? I mean, no offense or anything, but she's not really one to pick up strays."

Alex frowns, "I d-don't know, she seems nice t-to me. And I'm not exactly the only s-stray here: she's got a whole sh-ship full of refugees."

Sarah looks away for a second. Never in a million—Now, if it were Kaylor, she would understand. But Anna? Anna doesn't care; if she doesn't see an advantage to helping people, she doesn't do it.

Sarah turns back to Alex, friendly smile plastered on her face. "So, what's your story? How did Anna find you?"

"I—She f-found us out on a p-peninsula—Y-you're from…Colorado, too, right?"

"Yes."

"W-well, there are two of us, m-me and D-darn, and we fell into the ocean, out there," he waves a hand to the south, "and Anna p-picked us up. I—we're b-both from around Denver," he reaches up to scratch the back of his neck, "N-no idea how we g-got here."

"Just one other boy?" The letter had mentioned three, not two.

Alex nods.

Someone taps her on the shoulder. Sarah turns around and ends up face to face with Kaylor, the cut across her cheek still covered in red. A lump rises in Sarah's throat, and she has to swallow hard to keep down a sudden onslaught of tears. Kaylor's *here*, she's actually *here*.

"Hey, Sarah, there's someone you and Anna need to meet." Sarah nods, and blinks, at a loss. She has so many things she wants to tell Kaylor—and she can't think of a single one now that her friend is here in front of her.

"Are you K-kaylor?" Alex asks, stepping around Sarah and holding out a hand.

Kaylor takes it. "Yeah! You're part of Anna's crew,

right? You were helping us fight the sirens! How did you do that? I mean, all the men on our ship went kind of loopy, but you were there with Captain Darkin," Kaylor's all friendly smiles, but Alex looks as if she's smacked him.

"Shut it, Kaylor," Anna snaps, appearing from somewhere behind them. There's another boy with her, a redhead wearing what looks like tights and a long t-shirt. "We'll talk about that later." Her eyes drift up and fasten on something just behind Kaylor. "Who's that?"

Sarah glances in the direction of Anna's gaze and—she can't believe she didn't notice him before—but there's a tall boy with bright blond hair standing behind Kaylor, looking nervous and trying to hide behind the much shorter girl.

"Oh, this is Tyler. He's—"

"From Earth, too, right?" Anna says, "So are Darn and Alex."

Kaylor's forehead screws up in confusion. "Who?"

"So…Kaylor brought—Tyler?—with her, from Tallipeg?" Sarah asks. That's three, everyone mentioned in the letter. No one's hurt, everyone's here.

"Well, I found him at the Inn—the *Chatty Sphinx*, which is right by where I landed. It's in Caimig forest," she adds at Anna's questioning look.

"Okay. And Anna found Alex and Darn—is that your real name?"

"Uh, not really, it's Max. But I've never answered to that. Just call me Darn."

"Oh. So Anna found you on a—peninsula?"

"Not far from Tallipeg, yeah. I thought they were

refugees. Also—" Anna's eyes dart to Tyler, and then back to Sarah, "I received a letter, from someone named Mr. Lee." She reaches into her coat pocket and pulls out a sheet of paper.

"I got one too," Sarah says. She should have thought to bring it with her. "From the same person—Mr. Lee. He told me he wants to meet with us? That he gave you a time and place?"

Kaylor bites her lip nervously, "I got a letter, too. But it wasn't signed with a name."

"Alex and I got them too," says the other boy— Sarah thinks his name is Darn, "From that Mr. Lee guy. Do you think he's the one that kidnapped us?"

Anna shakes her head and starts to open her letter A strange man comes up behind her and clears his throat. "*Captain?*" He must be one of Anna's crew. Anna turns to him, her features pinched in annoyance.

"*Yes, Yorren?*"

"*Just straight to Husifi? There's no wind. Did you want us to paddle there?*" His tone is harsh, almost biting.

"Anna, we can talk when we get to my house. If you need to direct the ship…" says Sarah.

Anna sighs and presses the bit of paper into Sarah's hand. "I suppose I should. We should compare the letters. There's a table in my cabin, Alex knows where it is. I'll be back."

The redheaded boy—Darn—whistles. "*That* was a little crazy." He turns to Sarah, "I recognize you. They had your picture in the paper. You too," he says to Kaylor, "There are people back home, looking for you."

Sarah's hit with an image of her mother and father, printing out signs and calling the police and doing all the things parents of lost kids do. Her brother might have stopped going to soccer practice. Her sister might have cried. Guilt twists through her gut. Sarah takes the images and pushes them away. She doesn't want to think about that.

Kaylor swallows, her eyes bright. "I—" she starts, and her voice cracks, "Do you know them? My family, I mean? The Williams?"

Darn puts a hand on her shoulder. "I don't. I'm sorry," Kaylor nods, wiping at her nose. Darn swallows, "But they're looking for you."

Kaylor pulls the boy into a hug. "Thank you," she whispers, "I know that's next to nothing, but it just…it's good to hear they still *exist*."

"Kaylor," Sarah says, feeling the lump rising in her throat again, "I missed you."

Kaylor gives a watery laugh, and then lets go of Darn to hug Sarah instead. "I missed you, too," she says softly, "But now we're all together again."

Chapter Thirty One

ANNA

3rd day of Tivar
Year 1452

Cliffs of Bone
Altibrl Sea

Anna watches from next to Choffson at the wheel while Kaylor and Sarah hug, and something deep in her gut twists. It's always been Kaylor, Sarah, *and* Anna. Always.

She turns away to watch the brilliant cerulean waves of the Altibrl Sea as they leave it behind. The *Zephyr* follows the *Annihilator* closely, it's sails a dull yellow against the bone-white of the cliffs.

Yorren shouldn't have snapped at her like that in front of her friends. *She's* the captain, not him, she gets to order everyone around. She would have noticed the lack of wind eventually. She'd be yelling at him about it right now if he hadn't disappeared off under the deck. If she didn't know him better, she'd think he ran off to hide. But her first mate has a bigger backbone than that: it's part of why she gave him the position in the first place.

She should go back down to them—her friends. She's coaxed the air into a steady wind, gotten the rest of the crew in order, she can take a break now. And yet—

They haven't gone inside her cabin to look at the letters, like she told them to. Sarah keeps glancing up at the quarterdeck, as if to make sure Anna doesn't go up in smoke while she isn't looking. Anna can't help but grin a little at that. Just like old times, Sarah's looking out for them.

Anna runs her hands along the wood of the railing. This is her ship. *Her* ship. What if Colf, or her friends, want her to leave it? She's never even considered that before this moment, but she knows she'd do it—she'd have to. No matter how much hard work she's put into her ship and her crew, her mother and her friends come first. Always.

So Anna descends from her post and goes back to them. Sarah, Kaylor, and Darn seem to be getting along okay: they're standing near each other, talking. Alex and Kaylor's new friend—Tyler?—are standing to the side, staring off in opposite directions. Anna saunters up and stands directly between the two boys.

"Hi," she says, and smirks when Tyler jumps about a foot in the air. Alex greets her with a warm smile.

"H-hey, Anna," he says.

"No more seasickness?"

Alex shakes his head.

"What about you?" she asks, turning to Tyler, "I hope you don't get seasick, too."

Tyler stares at her, his eyes wide, then coughs. "Uh—no. I don't, as far as I know."

Kaylor glances over at them, and Anna smiles at her.

She grabs Sarah's hand and pulls her over.

"I think it's about time you told us how you're captain of a ship, Anna," she says with a watery smile.

Anna nods. It is about time for that. She wants to hear what's happened to them, too.

She stalks over to her cabin and motions them inside. Kaylor sits cross-legged on the floor and Sarah perches on the desk. Darn turns the chair around and straddles it, Alex drops into a boneless heap on her bed and leans back against the wall, and Tyler hovers uneasily in the corner until Kaylor grabs his hand and tugs him down next to her.

Anna hops onto the desk next to Sarah and launches into her story.

She tells them how she fell into the ocean, about the ship that floated by and picked her up, about the horrible former Captain and his officers who treated their crew like dirt, and the sorcerers working for them worse. She talks about finding the Velvet Lilies in a locked chest hidden in the storeroom and how Yorren knew exactly what they were and how to lure the sirens with them. Then she tells them how she made her deal to overthrow the Captain, then about going back and warning the crew away before the sirens could take them, and then about the wild goose chase she sent the sirens on trying to find them. She gives them a heavily edited story about her meetings with Colf and her agreement with him to ferry refugees to Denadia. But she doesn't say a word about Patrick.

Sarah tells her story next. Anna's fascinated by the intricacies of Gaentuki culture and impressed with Sarah's courage: is this really the same timid, cautious girl that Anna remembers from so long ago? Part of her always thought Sarah was hiding an adventurous streak, that she only pretended to be reluctant when Anna or Kaylor came up with another crazy idea. Anna catches her eye, raises an eyebrow at Sarah and smirks. Sarah flushes and hides her face behind the loose strands of hair escaping from her braids, but she grins and laughs when Anna nudges her with an elbow.

Kaylor talks about the knights—and isn't that fitting, Kaylor as a knight. It's almost like Sarah stole some of Kaylor's courage: Kaylor stumbles through her story, bashful and reluctant to divulge the details, her usual vigor absent. Anna watches her closely, trying to meet her eyes, but Kaylor turns away, laughing uneasily or biting her lip. She's lying—she's hiding something. For a second, Anna's terrified that Kaylor's year in Sarenia has drained her old reckless bravado right out of her. But that *can't* be; it's almost too horrible to contemplate.

But then she flashes Anna a cheeky grin and makes a snide comment about the Prince, and Anna's so relieved her limbs feel a little shaky.

Alex and Darn take turns describing their landing in the ocean and their struggle for the shore. Darn almost makes Anna laugh when he tells them about the hippocampus.

Kaylor has to prod Tyler a few times and whisper something in his ear before he'll talk. He stammers out a few nearly inaudible sentences about a nightmare in the forest, his posture rigid and his eyes fixed on a point above

Anna's head.

And then they get to the letters. Anna gets down from the table and spreads hers out on the floor, followed by Kaylor. Tyler hesitantly produces another letter out of his sleeve.

Anna skims through the letters in front of her, and looks up sharply when she's done with Tyler's. "You're looking for your parents, too. And you know this Mr. Lee."

Tyler nods and swallows. "I did. It—was a long time ago, when I was very young."

"Do you trust him?"

"I don't know."

"He seems to know a lot about us," Sarah says.

"He does," says Anna, "He doesn't seem to want to hurt us, but there's still a chance it could be a trap."

"We should go anyway," says Kaylor, "We just need to make sure we're ready for any problems."

"Wait—hang on a second," says Darn, rubbing at his temple, "We're going to go and *meet* the guy who kidnapped us?"

"It s-said in my l-letter he didn't want to d-do what he did."

"Yes," Anna snaps, getting impatient, "Because Colf would have brought you here himself if Mr. Lee didn't do it. I think Mr. Lee is a Vanisher. He must have been working with a Cursemaker to make those letters transport you. Colf has another Vanisher working for him, it's how he brought me, Sarah, and Kaylor over," she lets out a harsh laugh, "Whoever Colf's Vanisher is did a pretty shoddy job of it.

At least you three landed where you were supposed to."

"That's settled then," says Sarah, "We'll go home—well, to my house in Husifi, anyway—get a good night's sleep, and we'll meet this Mr. Lee tomorrow," Anna scowls at her, and Sarah gives her a half-smile, "*But* we'll be careful. I'll ask Nellie to go with us."

An hour or so later, Anna guides Kaylor, Sarah, and the boys to the edge of the ship, then watches them climb down the ladder onto the docks. Sarah's the last to go.

"Are you coming?" she asks, waiting at the top of the ladder and watching Anna with eyes narrowed in concern.

Anna pats her hand, "I will in a minute. Where's Kaylor going to leave her pegasus? I can meet you there."

Sarah furrows her eyebrows and opens her mouth, but Anna cuts her off before she can say anything. "I need to talk to my crew. I'll be fine, Sarah, I promise. I'll find you."

Sarah bites her lip and nods. "Okay. We'll wait for you at the stables—it's about a block straight ahead, to the east, there's a big sign, you'll see it. Just—hurry up?" She waits for Anna's nod before slipping down onto the dock where the others are waiting for her.

Anna turns around to find her crew watching her, Yorren at the front.

"I'm mad at you," she tells him, "so I'm not happy about leaving the ship in your hands."

He folds his arms in front of his chest, frowning, but he doesn't say anything.

Anna glares at him for a few seconds, then continues, "I need to go, though. Choffson has the list of Colf's contacts: there are two in Husifi. I'm going to leave it to you, Yorren, to get those refugees to safety. Can I trust you to do that without my assistance?"

Yorren returns her glare. "Yes, Captain," he snaps.

Anna fights to keep her face impassive. "Good. I'll be back tomorrow night." She turns sharply on her heel so that her coat swirls out behind her, then climbs over the railing, down the ladder, and onto the docks.

The city doesn't loom through the darkness the way the castles and walls do in the south—most of the buildings are tucked into crevices dug deep into the cliffs, or behind the greenery of the trees at the bottom of the valley. A lone dragon, probably Sarah's, soars overhead, a dark silhouette against the fading light.

Anna finds Sarah and the boys waiting out on the cobblestone street in front of the stables. Sarah holds out a hand as she approaches. Anna grabs it, lacing her fingers through Sarah's, and they wait.

Kaylor emerges moments later and takes Sarah's other hand.

They make their way up an enormous staircase and into one of the crevices. The buildings remind Anna a little of the Pueblo structures she saw once on a family trip, except these are circular or curved, and often have heavy curtains drawn in front of enormous windows or doorways. They're smooth to the touch, probably covered in Jewel Paint, but it's hard to tell in the low light.

They wind through the shadowy buildings, talking only softly or not at all. Sarah ducks into a narrow cave set into the back wall, motioning for them to follow her.

"It's not much, but it's where I've been living for the past year." Sarah trails the tips of her fingers over the rock as they're plunged into darkness. Anna copies her. "You guys can pick anywhere you want to sleep, my...um... roommates are out on a hunting trip. They won't be back for a few days. Except Nellie, but you've met her." Her voice echoes around them.

Eventually the narrow tunnel opens up into a wider space, lit with a crude chandelier and several large oil lamps. There are five more tunnels in the opposite wall: four are on ground level, one of these much smaller than the others. The last tunnel is about eight feet off the ground.

"That's my room," Sarah says, gesturing to the smaller one on the ground floor, "Nellie's is next to mine. She got here just before us, but she's probably asleep already. You can bug her if you want, she won't mind. But if you need anything," she glances over at the boys, "just come and get me. Nellie can be a little...clueless about humans, sometimes."

Darn agrees and Alex nods, but Tyler's too busy gaping around at the inside of the cave to say anything. Anna grins.

"Never been in a cave before?"

Tyler starts, "I uh...No, not really."

Alex chuckles, and Tyler shoots him a glare.

"Um, well, maybe we should get some sleep? It's late, and there are some things I think I should show you guys tomorrow." Sarah says, wringing her hands.

Kaylor grabs her arm and then reaches for Anna's hand. "I think we'll stay in Sarah's room? Maybe the boys can take the others?" she says.

Darn shrugs. "Sounds like a plan," he says, "But does anyone have some clothes I could borrow? Morph suits aren't the best thing to be running around in for days on end…"

"Oh!" says Kaylor, "Is that what you're wearing? I thought it was pajamas or something. Tyler, you still have your old clothes in the backpack, don't you? Is it okay if he borrows them?"

Tyler swings the backpack off his back and fiddles with the zipper for a good thirty seconds before he finally gets it undone. He pulls a wad of clothes out and tosses them to Darn. "They might be a little big," he mumbles.

Darn nods back at him, "Thanks, man."

"Does anyone need anything else? I forgot to mention —if you need a bathroom, there's a public one just outside, it's the little orange building. We don't have one in the house —er, cave. Is anyone hungry? I keep some water in my room, but there really isn't anywhere to get food this late—"

"Sarah," Kaylor says with a laugh, "We're fine. Let's just get some sleep."

Anna grabs Sarah's hand and walks to her room. Kaylor, still latched onto Sarah's arm, follows.

A few minutes later, the three of them are stretched out on their backs on Sarah's bed, elbows touching. "Have you changed clothes even *once* since you got here, Anna?" Kaylor asks from Sarah's other side.

Anna laughs. She has washed them—a few times. And she *does* have more than one set of clothes. But she hasn't been able to joke around with her friends for a whole year, and she can't help herself. "Maybe once or twice. There just isn't really time for it when you're sailing on a ship."

"What about you, Kaylor?" Sarah says, and Anna can hear the grin in her voice, "When was the last time you had a bath? There's dirt all over your face, and probably blood still from that cut—"

Kaylor snorts. "I don't know. Maybe when I fell in the river last week?"

"You guys are disgusting," says Sarah, wrinkling her nose, "I'm going to make you go to the bathhouse tomorrow. And buy you some new clothes."

Anna laughs. Kaylor snorts again, and soon Sarah's laughing too. This feels right, good. "I missed you guys."

"Missed you too, Anna," Kaylor's hand reaches over Sarah to grasp Anna's, and Sarah wraps both of their hands in her own. There's silence for a moment. "It's like one of those sleepovers, you know? The ones we used to have when we were eleven. Except now there aren't any parents to tell us off about not going to bed."

They all start to laugh again. There's a hysterical edge to it, sure, but Anna's too happy right now to think about why.

Anna waits for them to fall asleep before she disentangles her hands from theirs and gets to her feet. She drifts out the door, through the streets, and back to the stairs on the side of the canyon. She sits on the top step and waits.

A minute or so later, a figure detaches itself from the shadows and starts up the staircase toward her. Anna stands up, her grin threatening to split her face.

Patrick grins back at her, taking the steps two at a time. She throws her arms around his neck when he reaches her, burying her face in his shoulder. "How did it go? I half expected you to show up with Kaylor, but she didn't say anything."

He steps back, grabbing her hands and holding them between his. He shrugs. *It went alright.*

"Nothing too bad? I mean, you don't look like they *maimed* you, but…"

Patrick smirks, teeth flashing in the low light, and shakes his head. *Nothing too bad. I'm fine.*

"I really should introduce you to Sarah. Maybe she can teach us both sign language, and then I won't have to guess what you're thinking all the time."

Patrick's grin widens. He grabs her hand and leads her back into the streets, between the buildings, until they reach one that's a pale blue color. He brings her hand up to his face and kisses it, and Anna can't stop the blush that spreads across her cheeks. He leads her into the building, which doesn't have any doors or locks to impede them, and up a set of spiraling stairs. They reach the roof, and Patrick leads her over to the edge, where they sit with their feet dangling out over the city. He fishes a ballpoint pen and some paper out of a pocket in his coat. Anna has to squint and lean forward until her nose almost touches the paper, and she still can't make out the writing in the dim light. Patrick grins and snaps his fingers. A small, glowing ball of light appears in the air between them. Sometimes Anna forgets he can do that. She gives him a look and turns back to the paper.

You found them?

"Yeah, I did. I take it the necklace worked?"

Patrick grabs the chain, pulling the charm out from inside of his shirt. He rubs the ridges of Anna's carving between his finger and thumb, then pulls it up over his head and hands it to her. Anna takes it and fastens it around her own neck.

Kaylor did not want me to go with her. She said she had something she needed to do.

"Yes—she got a letter. I did too, while you were gone. From someone named Mr. Lee. He told her there was a boy lost in the forest, so *of course*, she had to go and save him." Patrick nods, his brow furrowed in mock-seriousness. *Of course.*

Anna grabs his hand, tangling his fingers with her own.

Patrick squeezes her hand and scrawls out another message with his free one.

What will you do now?

She sighs. "I'm not sure. I might not be able to go back to the ship. Yorren's getting tetchy again."

Patrick raises an eyebrow, leaning a little away from her.

Anna rolls her eyes, trying not to laugh. "I'm *kidding*. He's nothing I can't handle. He's not the reason I'd leave, no matter how annoying he gets. There are other people who are from where I'm from—Earth, America. Colf has a hand in it, I'm sure. And I have a feeling he's not going to want me ferrying refugees anymore."

You know I will follow you anywhere.

Something twists in Anna's gut when she meets his eyes. "I—I really don't know if you should. It's going to be dangerous, whatever it is, and you'd be safer staying with the crew on the *Annihilator*. It's not that I don't want you with me—" Anna stops. Patrick's staring at her, one corner of his mouth quirked, his eyes dark and drilling into hers. *I'm coming with you, whether you want me to or not.*

Anna swallows, her heart pounding in her chest. "You don't have to," she whispers.

But I want to.

Anna scoots closer, and lets her head fall onto his shoulder. "Just...do me a favor and stay hidden for now. I couldn't live with myself if something happened to you because of Colf—or me." Which is why she hasn't told anyone about him yet. Well, that *and* the uncomfortable questions Kaylor and Sarah would subject her to. But mostly because she doesn't want him getting hurt.

Patrick wraps an arm around her waist and pulls her close. Anna closes her eyes, and when she opens them next the sun is rising, brilliant and gold, over the far edge of the canyon.

Chapter Thirty Two

KAYLOR

4th day of Tivar
Year 1452

Sarah's House
Husifi

The siren sneers at Kaylor from above her, teeth white and sharp. Her wings shimmer in the bright sunlight. There's blood on her feathers, coating the primaries on her wings and the fluffy down around her feet.

She takes off and flies through the air. There's a body hanging from her talons, an arm dangling lifelessly from it. Four other sirens fly on either side of her, bodies clutched in their talons, too. One of them has two long black braids. A pirate's hat falls off the head of another, zig-zagging down through the air to fall in the ocean.

Kaylor stares at them helplessly from the deck, her sword clutched loosely in her hand. She can't move. She tries to scream, but she can't do that either.

She gasps and sits up, her heart pounding. It's dark, almost pitch black, the cave walls around her rough and solid. She takes another gasping breath and tries to calm down. It was just a dream.

Her hand is on the hilt of her sword where she left it on the floor next to the bed, grasping it tightly—she doesn't remember reaching for it. She lets go and runs her hands over the bedding on either side of her, looking for her friends. She finds Sarah's warm arm and lets her fingers trail over it. She reaches over Sarah to feel for Anna, but she's not there. The bedding's still warm, though—she must have gotten up to go to the bathroom.

Kaylor can barely see well enough to make it to the tunnel leading out of Sarah's room. There were some candles in the big room: she can light one and use that when she gets there. She needs to go check on the boys.

When she makes it through the tunnel into the first room, she finds Tyler curled up into a tight ball, *Hamlet* clutched to his chest, his pale blond hair falling into his eyes. He shivers and curls tighter, his face turning in to the puddle of straw he's using as a pillow. Kaylor bites her lip, then moves forward and grabs the blanket, tugging it up to cover his shoulders. She's tempted to run her fingers through his hair, to pat it into place and then stroke his cheek, but she doesn't. She doesn't know how he would react; if he'd be upset with her for touching him. She lets out a breath and turns away to go check on the others.

She finds them in the next cave over. They must have fallen asleep before they meant to: they're both sitting propped up against the wall, Darn's head on Alex's shoulder and Alex's face buried in Darn's hair. Relief floods her veins as she backs out of the cave. They're all here: they're all safe. Except for Anna.

Sarah sits up and rubs sleep out of her eyes when Kaylor gets back. "I'm sorry," Kaylor says, grimacing, "I didn't mean to wake you up."

"Do you know where Anna went? I woke up and both of you were gone."

Kaylor winces. "I'm sorry."

"No, no. It's fine. You went to go check on the boys, didn't you?"

Kaylor lets out a quiet laugh. "How did you know?"

Sarah grins. "I've known you for six years. You're not exactly unpredictable."

Kaylor flops down onto the bed, puts an arm around Sarah's waist and rests her head on her friend's shoulder. "No," she says, "Anna's always been the unpredictable one."

For a minute, they both stare mutely at the edge of the bed. "She's changed," says Kaylor, at the same moment as Sarah says, "I wonder where she is?"

Sarah grins and Kaylor laughs. "She probably just went to the bathroom, or something. I don't think she's been gone for very long."

It's quiet. Too quiet. It's uncomfortable now, in a way it never has been before. Sarah sighs and gently nudges Kaylor away. "We should really get some sleep."

Kaylor swallows. She doesn't want to go back to sleep yet. "Um…are you tired, or…"

Sarah puts her head in one hand, looking at Kaylor sideways. "A little. But we can talk if you want."

"I…She made a deal with sirens. Sarah, *she made a deal with sirens.*"

Sarah looks down at the floor, drawing circles in her blanket with a finger. "I know," she says softly, "And you were a knight. You were living right under the Mad King's nose."

Kaylor tugs at a strand of her own hair and starts to braid it. "I know. It…I didn't think it was dangerous. I was registered, so…" she stops, not sure what else to say about that. It obviously bothers Sarah, but Kaylor doesn't know why. "I was *safe*, Sarah. You know I can take care of myself."

Sarah nods, "I know. I just…I worry. I know it's not always rational, but I do."

"I promise not to leave your field of vision for as long as I possibly can."

Sarah smiles slowly at her. "Thanks. But you wanted to talk about *something else*, didn't you?"

Kaylor sighs. "Yeah. I—how could she *do* that? Sirens are vicious, everyone knows that. They don't listen to reason. She almost got the old captain killed—she could have got *all of them* killed, including herself. I just—she's just not the same person I knew before."

"But she got them out of it. In the end, she didn't let anyone get hurt."

Kaylor scowls. "But they *could* have. She put her crew in danger."

"And it saved your life just now, didn't it?" Sarah won't look at her. Kaylor knows it's really just because Sarah hates it when they fight with each other and this is how she distances herself from it, but it feels almost like a snub.

"I know," says Kaylor in a small voice, "but…what if she does that to *us*? She's going to be with us now, whether we want her or not. She never tells us about these schemes of hers until they're already in place, she was *always* getting us into trouble, and now that trouble could actually get us *killed*."

"Kaylor," Sarah says, an edge to her voice, "She's your *best friend*. She's *my* best friend. Besides, *you* used to get into just as much trouble as she did."

Kaylor deflates, suddenly feeling incredibly small. "I just...I left her behind. I saw her, once, in Morento, and..." she chews on her lip, not really wanting to talk about this but knowing it'll eat her alive if she doesn't, "And I just left. I didn't try to seek her out, or talk to her, to get her side of the story, I just...she was working against the crown, and I was working for it, so I left," her eyes are starting to sting, so she rubs at them before going on, "I just...I *gave up on her*, Sarah, and I don't know if I can ever forgive myself for that."

Sarah nods, biting her lower lip, then reaches forward and pulls Kaylor into a hug. "I could forgive you, if it were me. Anna though," Kaylor can feel her frown against her neck, "I don't know what Anna will think. Just...promise me you'll try not to fight about it?"

"I promise."

"Good." Sarah smiles—her sweet, genuine, loving smile she reserves just for Anna and Kaylor—and Kaylor's heart melts a little bit.

"I'm sorry I woke you up. And...I know you were worried about me. About both of us. If I'd known where you were, I would have sent you something, or come to see you."

"I know. I don't mind, not really. I'm just glad to have you both back."

"I am, too."

Chapter Thirty Three

ALEX

4th day of Tivar
Year 1452

Sarah's House
Husifi

𝒜lex wakes up leaning against something very warm. The remains of his dream drift from his mental grasp like mist: he was down at the river with Lilly and her friends, and Cassandra had been there too, her tiny arms wrapped around his neck and her toes kicking the small of his back. The feeling of contentment fades with the details, the rock against his back and the straw under his legs drawing him slowly awake. He breaths in deeply, but doesn't open his eyes. Mm…what's that smell? It's a bit like apple pie, but not quite; it's spicier and deeper, somehow. He buries his nose in the hair next to it, still half asleep.

Muffled voices drift into the room through the tunnel entrance. The warm thing he's leaning on shifts. Crap.

Alex propels himself away from Darn, jerking fully awake. His heart stutters in panic, his breath getting shallower and shallower. He wraps his arms around himself as his eyes dart around the room, seeing no movement. He glances at the open entrance, but he doesn't see anyone. The room is still as dim as it was the night before. No one saw him.

He forces his eyes closed and counts back from twenty, taking a deep breath between each number. No one's going to find him out—no one's going to dig out his secrets. A dry chuckle escapes his throat. It's not like no one's ever fallen asleep on someone else's shoulder before. It's not like anyone would think anything of it.

But he needs to be more careful: if they find out any of his secrets, they might turn on him. Like his mother and his sister. He doesn't want to get thrown out, cast aside, told to fend for himself. Back home, he'd had his father to look after him, but here he can't trust that anyone will have his back. He glances over at the boy still sleeping, slumped against the wall next to him. His mouth is hanging open, his neck craned back against the cold stone of the cave. No, not even Darn.

Though he has to assume Anna knows. It's going to eat at him, wondering what she'll say—if she'll say anything. She doesn't seem to care, but he could be wrong. She knows one secret—but that one's harmless, compared to the others. What would she think of the ghosts? His baby sister? What he almost did to himself? He can't tell her any of that.

Alex lets out a breath and digs his palms into his eyes. He'll just have to watch it, that's all. Just be careful not to give anything else away.

Something scrapes against the rough stone of the tunnel, and Alex looks up and sees Anna standing in the doorway. *Speak of the devil.* "If you two are awake," she says, her face blank, "Sarah wants to take us out into the city. Everyone else is up. She brought breakfast—I hope you're not a vegetarian."

Alex forces a smile and nods. "I-I'm up. I'll w-wake Darn, we'll be out in a m-minute."

He shakes Darn awake and they stumble down the short tunnel to the main room, Darn trying to smooth down his hair and straighten the clothes Tyler let him borrow.

"I wonder what they're going to feed us," Darn asks through a yawn.

"Probably s-some kind of meat," Alex offers, "Anna s-said she hopes we're not v-vegetarians."

Darn grimaces. "I hope it's not some sort of fantasy animal, you know? I don't want to be eating unicorn, or anything," he leans over to whisper in Alex's ear, "Could be poisonous, or something."

Alex snorts, hoping like hell his cheeks aren't flaming.

"Don't be ridiculous," Anna interjects from where she's sitting, cross-legged on the floor with a plate in her lap, "Unicorns aren't poisonous."

Kaylor elbows her. "But you shouldn't eat them anyway."

Sarah looks up from her own plate, setting it down and sliding off the ledge she's sitting on. "Here," she says, grabbing a couple more plates off another ledge, "These are yours. And don't worry, it's not unicorn. It's antelope. We eat it all the time, and no one's died from it yet."

It definitely looks like meat, in some sort of red sauce.

Alex lifts the plate up to his nose. At least it smells appetizing.

"Are there—do you h-have any forks?"

Sarah shakes her head. "I'm sorry. We don't really use those, here. Just eat with your hands, I have soap and water to wash the sauce off when you're done."

Alex nods and sits down on the floor next to Anna, picking up a piece of the meat and popping it into his mouth.

Darn's still standing, grimacing down at his plate. "And…what's on it?"

"Oh, just Gernaise sauce. It's made out of a fruit that's kind of like a tomato, and spices, and—"

"Human blood," Anna announces, chewing thoughtfully on another piece. Tyler coughs violently from across the room.

"Anna," Kaylor smacks her friend lightly on the arm. Anna grins back at her.

Sarah glares at Anna, "Antelope blood," she corrects, waving a sauce-covered finger in halfhearted reproach.

Alex doesn't feel quite so hungry anymore. He swallows the last bit in his mouth and sets the plate aside. Darn makes a face at the food and mutters, "Like that makes it any better."

"Anyway," Sarah says, as if nothing just happened, "We have a while before we're supposed to meet Mr. Lee, so I can show you all around the city if you'd like." She eyes Darn's untouched plate, "We can stop for something else to eat, too."

Bright sunlight streaks in through the cave entrance, and Alex has to shield his eyes. The light shows what he couldn't see the night before: the buildings are stucco, clay, and brick, but in all colors of the rainbow, from light pastel greens to deep fire-engine reds. The cobbles beneath their feet glisten with the polish of over-use. People streak past them in many directions, down side streets and between buildings.

Sarah sighs, "And this is one of the less crowded streets."

She leads them down the widest side street, bustling with shops and people, until they reach a sort of circular courtyard with a tree in the middle. Shadows flit across the sun above them: Alex looks up and sees a dragon—no, two —flap lazily through the air, drifting above the city. In fact, the longer Alex looks, the more he sees: dragons fill the sky around them, flapping and gliding from one place to the next.

"Wow," Darn says from somewhere near Alex's elbow.

"Yeah," Sarah mutters, "You get used to it after a while."

"What's that building, over there?" Kaylor asks, pointing to a huge round hemisphere that rises above the other buildings.

"That's the Scholar's Library," Sarah says, "If you want, we can stop there after we eat. We have four hours before we have to meet Mr. Lee." She leads them to the left of the courtyard, to a cafe with no front wall. Alex assumes it's to accommodate the dragons. Wooden chairs sit in clusters around heavy stone tables, and patrons chat and eat over brightly-dyed tablecloths. Sarah picks a table in the back corner, and leaves to order food at the counter once Alex and the others are seated.

She brings back a bowl full of what looks like spinach and red-colored corn kernels. Anna grabs a leaf and starts to nibble on it. Alex follows her lead. "It's just spinach and corn, no sauce. They'll bring the rest in a minute," Sarah says. Alex doesn't particularly like spinach, but it's better than nothing, so he'll eat it.

"So something's been bugging me," says Darn around a mouthful of the spinach, "From the letters. If this Mr. Lee is from here, if he's here *now*, how did he get the letters to us? And why would he know my parents? Or Tyler, for that matter?"

"If he's a powerful enough Vanisher," says Kaylor, "He might be able to move between worlds."

Sarah's forehead furrows. "When I met with her, Juanna said Colf recognized me because he knew me—knew us—when we were children."

"How is that possible?" Kaylor says, at the same time as Darn blurts, "But that's just you three, right?"

They're quiet for a second as the waiter comes over and sets a steaming bowl of stew, thankfully along with six wooden spoons, in front of them. "It's just chicken and potatoes," Sarah explains, "I thought you might like that better than the antelope. But Darn—" Sarah shakes her head. "I don't know. Juanna only mentioned us girls, but that doesn't mean you're not a part of this. Most of the letters mentioned you in them, too."

Something lump-like works its way into Alex's chest. "So w-what you're saying is…it's—it's possible we're…" he stops, swallowing, but he can't force the words out.

"From here," Anna says, smiling softly to herself, "It's possible that we're all sorcerers, and for that to make sense —"

"Well," Darn snaps, "Are you? Cause I'm sure as hell not."

Kaylor sighs and puts her hand up, "I'm a Shieldmaker."

Sarah swallows a mouthful of food and adds, "Speaker."

"Stormbringer," says Anna.

Kaylor nudges Tyler, and he clears his throat, "'M a Flamestarter."

Ghostspeaker. Alex mouths the word, but doesn't dare say it aloud. He feels eyes on him, and looks over to see Anna watching him thoughtfully. He swallows, heart hammering, and hopes like hell she didn't catch that.

Darn throws his hands up in the air. "And I'm nothing," he says, "So much for that."

"Look, I don't believe all of this either," Kaylor says, "But there has to be *some* explanation, and there has to be a reason you're here too," she picks halfheartedly at her food, "Maybe you *are* a sorcerer, and you just don't know it yet."

Darn looks at Alex. "What about you?" he asks, "You're not a—you don't have some freakish kind of powers too, do you?"

Alex swallows hard, and looks down at his plate. He shouldn't say anything, can't say anything, no one can know. And yet—maybe he should just get it over with. Spill everything in front of them, right now, and let them kick him out and push him away.

"Right then!" Sarah says, smacking her hands on the table, "It looks like we're done with the food. I think we wanted to go see the library, why don't we do that?"

Relief floods Alex as Sarah leaps out of her seat and hustles them out the door.

The light and color of the city is almost overwhelming as they make their way to the library. Dragons perch on rooftops, in alleys, and even behind enlarged market stalls. A particularly large green one even nudges Alex aside as it lumbers down the street. The people wear bright or pastel colors, sometimes white but never black, their clothes contrasting with their dark skin and hair. The few outsiders Alex sees stand out painfully amongst the crowd.

They reach the library a little while later—Alex is having a hard time keeping track of anything, including the time, in this sea of bright light and color—and Sarah pushes through the doors. They file through behind her.

The vast interior of the library is just as amazing as the city's exterior. There are several levels, all with shelves upon shelves lining the circular walls and continuing in spirals toward the open center. Titles gleam gold and silver on multicolored bindings, all in languages Alex doesn't recognize. Sarah leads them through the shelves, past desks where people sit and pour over piles of books, to a small section at the back that's secluded from the rest with other shelves.

Darn runs his hands along a row of titles, "I would have loved this place when I was little," he mumbles, and Alex thinks he's the only one who hears it. Alex has never been much of a reader. His family's never really been big on books, and none of his friends really have either. He thinks he remembers his mother reading to him and Lilly when they were younger, but that was so long ago he isn't sure. He had to read things for school, but most of the literature had been complicated and hard to follow. He'd liked reading some of his textbooks, the history ones in particular, which some people think is a little odd. But Alex is odd already, so he doesn't mind that. He isn't about to add something so trivial to his vault of secrets.

He reaches a hand up to copy Darn, running a finger down the edge of a cover. The gold letters spiral out: *A Griffinwatch: First Account* and below that in smaller print *General Icterod: 36th Tivar Year 1213*. Alex gently pries it off the shelf, letting it fall open in his hands. Large, blocky letters stare back at him out of the page.

"What's that?" Darn asks, and Alex nearly jumps. Instead, he forces a smile and tells Darn the title.

Darn's nose wrinkles. "Griffinwatch? Are you telling me there are griffins here too?"

Alex shrugs. "Why not?"

Darn's mouth twitches at the corners, like he's trying not to smile. "Yeah, I guess. Might as well just assume everything exists here, right?"

"Right."

"See anything interesting?" Sarah's voice hisses from behind them.

"Oh, n-no, not really." Alex says, closing the book and shoving it back into place.

"This is probably the largest collection of books that exists outside of Gorthrofen, and they have plenty in Sarenian in this section," Sarah grins at Alex, "It's fairly similar to English, it shouldn't be too hard to puzzle out. It might take a little longer, but," she shrugs, "Tyler picked out a whole pile of things that look useful; about travel between worlds and things like that. We've stacked them on that table over there," she motions behind her towards one of the tables, where Tyler is sorting through a stack of books and glaring at anyone who so much as looks at them, "If you wanted to look. Oh, and if you find anything you want to look at later, we can make note of it and go to a scribe. They'll make us a copy we can keep, as long as it isn't something too obscure."

"O-okay," says Alex. Once Sarah wanders off, out of hearing range, Darn turns to him.

"You don't actually believe any of this, do you?"

Alex drops his gaze, good mood gone. "I—I d-don't know."

"I mean, I have *parents* back home. Mr. Lee—whoever he is—has to be lying."

"I th-think I'll just go see what th-they found," Alex says.

But Darn grabs his arm before he can wander off. "Hey," he whispers, "I'm sorry, I didn't mean…Are you doing okay? I mean, there's kind of a lot going on now, and you look a little green around the gills, you have since that thing with the—" he frowns, "—sirens."

Alex is torn between feeling touched that someone's noticed and irritated that Darn doesn't think he can take care of himself. "I'm f-fine, thanks."

Darn shakes his head. "Look—you can talk to me, you know. If you ever feel like—look, I know—" Darn clenches his teeth, looking uncomfortable, "I *know* why I found you in those bushes under your apartment, okay? Just—if you ever need to talk to someone—"

Alex fights the urge to gape, panic, then run and hide. Instead, he chokes out "Yeah, I know. But I don't r-right now."

Darn lets out a long breath. "Okay."

Chapter Thirty Four

DARN

4th day of Tivar
Year 1452

Scholar's Library
Husifi

Something prickles across the back of Darn's neck. He reaches around to scratch it, then looks up at the second level of the library. A pair of bright yellow, slitted eyes stare down at him out of a draconian face covered in horns and feathers. The dragon's eyes blink, showing a translucent inner eyelid. Even weirder, though, is the giant pair of spectacles perched on its nose and the book clutched in it's enormous talons inches away from it's face. Darn tears his eyes away from its face—no matter how friendly Sarah says the dragons are, he still doesn't want it to catch him staring—and notices one of it's legs several yards away. His gaze follows the snake-like curve of it's body all the way to the tail. It's at least twenty feet long.

There are dragons everywhere in this city, and for the most part that's freaking Darn out. He's been trying not to show it, because the others don't seem to mind much, but all of this is just so *strange* and *weird*. Everything—falling in the ocean out of nowhere, the hippocampus, the ship, the sirens, and now the dragons. How is he supposed to wrap his head around all this?

He doesn't even remember much about the sirens, which is actually what freaks him out the most. One moment he'd been standing on the ship joking around with Alex, and then next he'd been sitting in the brig, behind bars, with his hands tied behind his back. Alex had to tell him what had happened later. He could have fallen off the side of the ship—in fact he almost did—and he wouldn't have been able to stop himself. He doesn't want to be anywhere near any of these strange creatures that aren't supposed to exist, and he doesn't want to be here. He wants to go *home*.

Darn swallows and slaps the book he's holding against his palm. *ATLAS* is printed in large, capital letters across the front. He was looking for something to do with travel, because he thought there might be a book on travel between worlds, but he couldn't find anything. So the atlas will have to do.

He wanders back to the table, where Tyler is sorting through books and Alex has his nose buried in one, and sets the atlas down in front of another chair. Alex looks up and gives him a dimpled half-smile, but Tyler doesn't acknowledge his presence, choosing instead to shift some more books over and continue mumbling nonsense under his breath.

Darn sighs and collapses into a chair. "See anything useful?" he asks.

Alex shakes his head. "N-not much."

Tyler glances up at them and then back to the book he's skimming through.

"What about you?" Darn asks. Tyler ignores him. Darn clears his throat. "Tyler?"

"Oh—what?" Tyler looks up at him with wide eyes, and then coughs. "I—um, there's some stuff in here—this one's particularly interesting, it's about an English monk—"

Darn sits up straighter in his chair. "There was an English monk *here*?"

"Well, not here exactly, but in Sarenia, yes. His name was Merrick—here, do you want to look?" Tyler holds out the book, a worn brown thing with silvery writing on the spine, "Of course, it's been translated several times over, so the text might not be exactly as it was when it was written…"

Darn pulls the book out of his hand and lets it flop open to a random page on the table.

Y a' Priest Merrick dith say unto King Gaflen, Yar worship is worthy, ach yar gods art not true: there is a sole…

Darn frowns down at the text. That doesn't help. He flips through the pages, looking for any useful tidbits of information, until he gets almost to the end.

A' Priest dith live a' rest of his long life at King Gaflen's side, assisting in commanding a' slag y asserting a' true claims of a' King's faith

Darn slams the book shut, closing his eyes and resisting the urge to punch something. So this priest was here, but he never went back. He sets the book down on the table and reaches for another. Tyler grabs the monk book and sets it back on top of the stack in front of him.

Raised whispers cut through the stillness around them, and Darn lifts his head to see several Gaentuki women sitting at another table, staring at them. One of them narrows her eyes while the others look timidly away. Blood rushes to his face. If he were in a better mood, or if he knew the language, he'd go over there and talk to them to try and figure out what the glaring is about, and probably ask some questions about the library. As it is though, he resists the urge to glare back at her, instead staring pointedly down at his book.

Sarah comes back a few minutes later, empty handed. "I found a few things that weren't in Sarenian," she says, "But I looked through them and I didn't see anything, really." She takes a seat at the table and grabs one of the books from Tyler's stack. The nervous boy looks up from what he's reading for a second, watching her take the book. Darn bets he's noting its title and which pile it was in so he can put it back when she's finished. He smirks a little, turning back to the book in his hands.

Darn's deeply engrossed in a passage about some famous wandering traveler by the name of Zandra Kahrin when someone slams a book down on the table next to him. He starts and looks up at Kaylor, who waits until she has everyone's attention before she says, "I think I found something," she points at the book on the table, "Apparently, a couple of ships just showed up one day, in the ocean somewhere between here and Telegarath. There were a lot of people on them, and lots of gold, too. They ended up in Tallipeg."

"I found some of those, too. I mean, stories about strange ships drifting into harbors, or out at sea," Tyler mumbles from behind his book, "That might be why Sarenian is so similar to English, and why the ships look so similar to the ones back home."

"And why sirens, dragons, and all these other creatures are mentioned in ancient mythology," Sarah adds, drumming her fingers on the table, "Maybe there's… something out there that can take people back and forth? Like, a portal of some kind?"

Which is good news. "So, there's got to be one of those out at sea, right? We've got to go and find it," Darn says.

Kaylor claps a hand over her mouth. "The Forgotten Wood!" she slides into her seat, "We're warned not to go there, not even to poke around. People disappear, never to be seen again. I can't *believe* I didn't think to look *there*."

"Maybe we should wait until after we talk to Mr. Lee before we go looking for one of these portals," Sarah says, "He might even know where *exactly* we can find one. Or better yet, he might be able to send us back—I mean home —himself."

"Wait," Darn says, "Can he just, like, snap his fingers and send us back?"

"If he's a Vanisher, maybe. But it's not that simple," says

Anna from somewhere behind Darn. He scoots around in his chair so he can see her. She looks grave, like no one's going to like what she's going to say. "That's possible if you're traveling from one place to another on the *same* world, but it's a bit more complicated going between them. But speaking of Vanishers, I found something interesting."

She holds another book out, and Darn takes it from her. *A Mad King of a' South: Rise y Fall of a Rebellion* is printed in fancy gold letters on its ornately decorated cover.

"I looked through it," she says, "and guess who's name comes up, several times?"

"Colf?" Sarah asks.

Anna nods. "This isn't the first time he's tried to overthrow the King."

Darn frowns. "So...he wants us to help him go after this King? But—why on Earth would he want *us*?" It doesn't make any sense. If these books are to be believed, Sarenia is *full* of sorcerers. So why would Colf go to such lengths just to get a few kids to help him?

"I don't know," says Anna, frowning, "There was a Vanisher named Leam who was working for Colf, but he disappeared," she taps the top of the book, "This book's claiming Leam was an Incarnate."

"A what now?"

"An Incarnate," Kaylor says, "It's like—" she pauses, tapping her fingers against her chin. Tyler nudges her with his elbow and hands her an open book, pointing to one of the paragraphs. She furrows her brow, mouthing along as she reads through it.

"Each god selects people that match their goals or personalities, so certain characteristics are shared between certain types of sorcerers," she says slowly in English. Darn realizes that she's translating it for them. "Incarnates, however, do not...only possess those um...*certain* shared qualities with their patron god: they are near-perfect copies of that god's personality, shaped by their patron god even before their birth. Incarnates are very...no, *exceptionally*— powerful, able to accomplish feats that the *slag*...I mean, the rest of us—could only dream of. The accepted theory is that Incarnates are direct creations of the gods themselves." She frowns, "So...it doesn't quite mean the same thing here as it does back home?"

"Right," Tyler says with a nod.

"There's a Gaentuki legend that says the human founder of Husifi was an Incarnate," Sarah says, "We know Incarnates aren't the gods themselves, since the gods like to show up and talk to their Incarnates or give them advice. They're supposed to just be like...conduits, like someone who channels the god's power and works towards that god's goals. The Elder-sages at the temple said that the gods can sort of—*possess* them, sometimes. They apparently show up during great times of crisis or turmoil, and they've identified several over the years."

"I think I remember reading something at the castle— the six children of the three founding princes of Sarenia were supposed to be Incarnates," Kaylor adds, "Each prince had a son and a daughter, and those kids started the lines of the Dukes and Duchesses, which is supposed to be why there are two noble houses in each province," she frowns, "They sure seem to like threes, twos, and sixes."

"The Imperial Six are supposed to be in charge, to keep all the other gods in line," says Sarah, "It's three gods and three goddesses, and sometimes they're divided into three sort of…sub-groups. The goddesses are the Triplets; they're not really triplets, I don't think gods really have siblings, but they're always seen together so people started to call them that. Then the Old Ones, the gods of life and death, they're supposed to be the oldest. The Elder-sages say they created the other gods. And then the Lone God, who shows up by himself," says Sarah.

"Wow, Sarah," says Anna, grinning, "I didn't know you were *that* religious."

Sarah shrugs, a dark blush creeping up her face, "I'm not…I mean, I've gone to temple with Nellie a few times, and…" Kaylor and Anna stare at her, eyebrows raised and arms crossed over their chests. Their expressions are eerily identical.

"I was *just* curious," Sarah grumbles.

Which is great and all, but how is that going to help them get home? "Yeah—cool. So the guy working with Colf is one of these—Incarnates—and how does that help us?" asks Darn.

"If anyone's going to be able to send us home," says Anna, "It's going to be an Incarnate."

"Mr. Lee," Tyler says. He's frozen, hand half-way across the table, hovering over another book.

Anna inclines her head. "That's what I think."

"So, hang on," Darn says, "The guy who kidnapped us is working for the dangerous rebel, and we're going to waltz right into his trap tonight? Great," He throws up his hands, done with them all. Does anyone here have *any* common sense?

"We *need* more information," Anna hisses.

"I don't think he'll want to send us back," Kaylor says in a small voice, "If he brought us here in the first place."

Darn slumps back in his seat, letting the back of his head hit the top of his chair. Isn't that what he's been trying to tell them this whole time?

Chapter Thirty Five

SARAH

4th day of Tivar
Year 1452

Ellata's Paint Shop
Husifi

Of course he won't want to send us back!" Anna snaps. Kaylor winces. "That's not why we're going to see him."

"Anna…" They shouldn't be fighting, Anna doesn't need to be yelling. Especially not at Kaylor.

"Don't start, Sarah," Anna snarls.

"Then *why* are we going to see him?" Darn asks. Sarah closes her eyes and pinches the bridge of her nose. Boy, is he in for it now.

"What do *you* want to do, then?" Anna spits, stalking around the table and drawing herself up to her full height so she can glare down into Darn's face, "If you're so smart, tell me, why don't you enlighten us all? What's the plan? You want to get home: how are we going to do that without Mr. Lee? *How?*"

Darn leans back in his seat, away from her, but his eyes still glitter with anger. He opens his mouth, "Look here—"

Sarah's had enough of this. "*Shut up!*" Darn's mouth

snaps shut, and so does Anna's. Kaylor, Alex, and Tyler stare at Sarah, faces blank and startled. It makes her uneasy. "Right. If you keep carrying on like this we're going to get kicked out of the library." She takes a deep breath. "This is what we're going to do. We'll go back to my house, and anyone who wants to stay behind, can," she looks between Darn and Kaylor, trying to make her expression seem open and friendly, "And anyone who wants to meet Mr. Lee can come with me and Nellie." Anna relaxes, but shoots Darn a parting glare before she slinks back to her seat. Darn stares down at the table, angry lines etched into his face. Kaylor swallows, her eyes darting between Anna and Sarah.

Tyler looks up, his eyes drilling into Sarah's. "I'm going. I need to talk to him."

Kaylor sighs. "I'm going too. I know this isn't what you want to talk about," she says to Anna, "But I want to ask if he can send us home."

"You know I'm not going with you if he can," says Anna. Kaylor's face falls, her gaze dropping to the table.

"I'll c-come too," Alex says, shrugging, "I w-want to know what's g-going on."

Darn sends Alex a sharp glance, "Fine. I'll go."

The walk back to Sarah's cave is shrouded in stony silence. Sarah retrieves Nellie, telling her only that they intend to meet someone in the city. She doesn't mention the letters, but she doesn't need to: Nellie is instantly suspicious, narrowing her eyes and insisting that Sarah let her go with them.

They arrive at the *Four-Eyed Griffin* half an hour after

they're supposed to meet Mr. Lee. Jash waves at Sarah through the window as they pass by. Sarah forces herself to smile and wave back. They don't enter the inn; instead, Sarah leads them down an alley a few buildings away that loops around behind, to a small area used as a drainage ditch and a back exit. Nellie clacks along across the rooftops above them, keeping Sarah and the others in her sight at all times.

No one's there. Sarah's muscles relax in relief. She leans against the wall, watching the others as they stop behind her. Kaylor's left hand falls from where it's been clutching the pommel of her sword. Maybe they're too late. Maybe he's gone already. Maybe that's for the best: this way, there's no chance they'll be ambushed. Anna's letter said he'd be here for a few days. Maybe they can come back tomorrow, when they're better prepared. *This way, I won't have to go back: at least not yet.*

"Mr. Lee?" Tyler's breathless whisper drags Sarah out of her thoughts.

"Tyler?" A dark shape steps into the light from the doorway. It's a tall, Gorthrofenese man in a dark brown cloak.

"Why did you leave?" Tyler's voice shakes, and so do his hands. "Where did you *go?*"

Mr. Lee takes a step forward, and Tyler steps back, shaking his head. Sarah pushes herself off the wall and stands in front of the group, clenching her fists to stop her own hands from shaking. "What do you want with us?" she asks.

Mr. Lee's voice is soft and devoid of emotion. "I think it would be best if we were to discuss this somewhere less —" he glances up at Nellie on the rooftop beside them, "— crowded."

Sarah tilts her head, copying Anna's 'innocent' look. "As long as Nellie can come with us," she gestures at the dragon.

Mr. Lee inclines his head, a smile twitching at the corner of his mouth. "Of course. I only mean to get out of the heat. It's almost time for the city to close."

Sarah looks over her shoulder at the others. Anna's face is an emotionless mask, just as Sarah expected. Kaylor's eyes shift from Sarah to Mr. Lee, her hand resting on the pommel of her sword. Darn is irritated, Alex is curious, and Tyler is stricken, but none of them look hesitant to follow her. She turns back to Mr. Lee and nods.

He leads them to a crumbling, cheap structure toward the front of the crevice and closer to the sweltering heat of the canyon's sun. Sarah represses a sigh of relief when he opens a trap door, revealing a deep basement. He motions for them to descend ahead of him. The trap door isn't big enough for Nellie to fit her body through, but is big enough for her head. She waits until the last person has descended into the basement, then winds her long neck down the stairs and rests her chin on the bottom step.

The basement is an open, square room with a set of benches around an old table. Three doors line the wall to the right. Sarah picks a bench and sits cross-legged on it. The others sit next to her, except for Mr. Lee, who sits across from them. Kaylor grabs one of Sarah's hands and gives it a squeeze.

Mr. Lee leans forward, resting his elbows on his knees. "I take it you got my letters?"

Sarah nods. Nellie makes a small noise in the back of her throat, but no one says a word.

"I'm sure you have questions."

Darn clears his throat. "Yeah, actually—why? Why did you bring us here? And what was with those *creepy* letters?"

"I didn't want to, believe me. But Colf—" he swallows, "If I hadn't brought you over for him, Colf would have had his Vanisher, Vupcin, do it. Colf and Vupcin don't realize how grave the consequences can be if a Vanishing— especially between two worlds—is done incorrectly. Sarah, Anna, and Kaylor are incredibly lucky. They could have *died*."

"So," Kaylor bites her lip, fiddling with a bit of her chain mail shirt in her lap, "You can't send us back?"

Mr. Lee shakes his head. "I'm afraid that if I do, Colf will try to bring you here again. It might be possible to Curse you so that he can't find you, but he has a Cursemaker too—a strong one. It's within his power to break all but the most powerful Curses we could put on you."

"Does that mean our only choice is to go through with Colf's plans for us?" Anna's expression is still impassive.

Mr. Lee nods. "For now. But *only* for now. It will ultimately be up to you. It's in Colf's interest to train you, teach you how to control your magic. And once the six of you realize your full potential, I doubt anyone could stand in your way."

Sarah opens her mouth to ask what he means by that, but Alex talks before she can.

"Y-you said you knew m-my parents? In—in the letter?"

Mr. Lee's expression softens. "I did. And I'm sorry I can't tell you where they are now. I don't know."

"And what about my mother?" Anna asks, her voice a little too high.

Mr. Lee sighs. "I should have known you would ask about her. But I can't tell you anything—she made me swear not to. Just know that she's alive, and she'll come looking for you when the time is right."

Anna nods, but her eyes are far away. If Sarah knows her at all, she's far from satisfied with that answer.

It's quiet again, so Sarah decides to ask her question. "What do you mean, 'realize our full potential'? I mean, I know we're sorcerers," Darn opens his mouth, but Alex elbows him and he closes it again, "but it seems like you mean more than that."

Mr. Lee nods. "I think it's about time you knew why Colf wants you specifically. Is everyone familiar with the Sarenian gods?"

Sarah nods, and so do Anna and Kaylor. Alex gives an odd jerk of his head. Tyler shakes his head, and Darn remains motionless.

Mr. Lee fixes his eyes on Tyler as he speaks, "There are seventeen gods, each associated with a certain kind of sorcerer. Out of these, there are six gods who control the others and attempt to maintain order on the mortal plane. These are the Imperial Six." Sarah has a feeling she knows where this is going. From the look on Anna's face, she does too. "Do you know what Incarnates are?" asks Mr. Lee.

"We went to the library earlier," says Kaylor, "We found a book on them there."

"Good. You know that their powers are rumored to be so immense that any sorcerer—even an expert—would be hard-pressed to defeat them, even if they've had little to no training?" Sarah nods, and Mr. Lee continues, "The reason Colf brought you back—the reason he wants you to be a part of his rebellion so badly—he believes you're the Incarnates of the Imperial Six."

Sarah was expecting him to say that, but it still sends her mind reeling when she hears it out loud. It's quiet: no one else knows what to say, either.

"It will take time, training, and practice, of course. You're not there yet; most sorcerers your age have been using their powers for years already. But once you get started, I think you will learn quickly. That is what Colf used to do at the castle, before he became a rebel: he used to teach sorcery. He'll want to train you."

"You mean…how? Why?" Tyler's quiet voice cuts the silence like a knife, "I—I don't understand."

Mr Lee closes his eyes, swallows, and then motions to Anna, Kaylor, and Sarah, "The Triplets," then just to Anna, "Larosri, goddess of storms and chaos," then to Kaylor, "Sheolida, goddess of defenders and reclaimers," Sarah swallows as he looks straight into her eyes, "Gweligen, goddess of languages and leaders."

He motions to Alex and Darn, who are sitting together a little apart from the others, "The Old Ones: Lefyrin, god of life," he says to Darn, "and Theoloden, god of death," he says to Alex.

Last of all he turns to Tyler, his voice falling to a whisper, "And the Lone God, Reygreon; god of fire and of victory."

"You're all from this world—yes, *all* of you—you're an integral part of it. No matter what you want, or what I want —no matter what you do—you're stuck here. Until Colf's rebellion succeeds or fails."

Chapter Thirty Six

ANNA

4th day of Tivar
Year 1452

Mr. Lee's House
Husifi

Anna blinks, trying to quiet her scrambling thoughts. Is he lying? He could be lying. But *why*? What reason would he have to lie to them?

He said he *knows* Anna's mother. He's talked to her. She made him swear not to tell Anna anything. She's too elated with the knowledge that her mother is alive to care that she's shutting Anna out of her plans. That's going to change later, but for now Anna can ignore it.

Anna is from this place, from *Sarenia*, and that means it's okay that her step-mother and step-siblings mean nothing to her at all, and that means Anna's life can finally start to fall into place, that *Anna* can finally find her place. Here, in this world.

She's been right all along. There has always been a small, cynical part of her mind that thinks her mother is really dead and that Anna is from Earth. That her father and her step-family is all she has left. That small part of her is squashed, done, *annihilated* as Kaylor says something to Mr.

306

Lee—her tone hurt and indignant the way it always is after someone's lied to or manipulated her. Anna knows, she's brought it out herself once or twice. But only ever for Kaylor's benefit. Anna doesn't hurt her friends. At least, not on purpose.

Kaylor pulls Anna through one of the doors into an empty room. She turns to them—she's brought Sarah too, of course she has, both of them would be hopeless without Sarah, who's the only one that looks calm right now. Anyway, Kaylor's gearing up to say something so Anna forces herself to try and pay attention.

"He's lying to us."

Anna's face scrunches up until she can't hold it in any longer. Her mouth bursts open as the first giggle comes out, and then she can't stop laughing.

Chapter Thirty Seven

KAYLOR

4th day of Tivar
Year 1452

Mr. Lee's House
Husifi

*A*nna *laughs* at her. This isn't funny. Mr. Lee *can't* be telling them the truth. Kaylor is *not* an Incarnate. She's not that important. She's just a girl from another world who's trying to help, trying to do the right thing.

Didn't Anna try to warn them about this? Didn't she say this might be a trap? Mr. Lee could be lying to them. *Just like Prince Casteor lied to me.*

And yet…a small part in the back of Kaylor's mind, no bigger than a pebble but all the more irritating for it, is screaming that he's right. That Anna, Kaylor, Sarah, and the boys are from here, that the reason Anna and Sarah befriended Kaylor when they were eleven is because they're *the Triplets*, and the Triplets *always* find their way to each other, as soon as possible. It's written in all those stupid stories and children's fairy tales in the library at Shaltac Castle.

But what's even worse is the reason that Kaylor's a knight. She came in thirty-sixth place. *Thirty-sixth.* The King and the Prince pick knights almost exclusively from the top ten. Kaylor made a shield that day at the tournament, and Casteor *knew* what she was, why she was able to block the sword and then the fist and then the rain. The Prince wanted her close because he wanted her on his side when the time came for war. He wanted her close because he thinks she's an Incarnate.

Kaylor is adopted. Sarah isn't, as far as anyone knows, but maybe she is and her parents didn't tell her. Anna's mother might be here, in this world, instead of dead and in the ground at Morrington Cemetery. What about Kaylor's real parents? She hasn't thought about it—hasn't wanted to think about it: she's happy with her mother and her father and her brothers and she doesn't want to do *anything* to damage that. But now she has to. She can't go home, *not now*. Not until she knows the truth about Casteor, not until she corrects her mistakes.

But Kaylor's *not* an Incarnate.

Chapter Thirty Eight

SARAH

4th day of Tivar
Year 1452

Mr. Lee's House
Husifi

arah looks between her friends. Anna's in shock, but Kaylor can't see that. As Sarah watches, Kaylor's fists clench into tight balls as her face gets redder and redder. Part of her is relieved that Kaylor's back to behaving like herself, but the rest of her wants everyone to just *stop yelling*, calm down, and talk it out.

"Kaylor," Sarah looks at her friend, trying to pin her in place with her eyes.

Kaylor rounds on Sarah. "You can't honestly believe he's telling us the truth, can you?"

Sarah swallows. She *wants* Mr. Lee to be telling the truth. She doesn't want to go home. But does that mean she's betraying her family? They've always been good to her, she's always been a good daughter, she's always loved them. Granted, she's never loved them quite as much as she loves Anna and Kaylor. Could that be because they aren't her real family?

She's had suspicions for a few years now: how could she

not, when she looks nothing like her parents? Sure, she has the dark skin and the brown eyes and height, but now that she really thinks about it, she looks a good deal more Gaentuki than African American.

And Anna fits in here perfectly–her bronze skin, dark freckles, even her bright green eyes more common in the population here than they ever were in Colorado. And Kaylor, too: her hair, face, and stature not unlike that of the Normathy pirates Sarah's seen down at the docks.

But even if Sarah doesn't belong to her family, even if they weren't her birth parents, they've never wronged her. So why does she want this so badly—this other reality, so far from home? *Because you want to be important,* says a small voice in the back of her head, *You want to be something more than just pretty, boring, perfect little Sarah. You want to be a hero.*

It's funny, because Kaylor's usually the one who wants to stay and fight, while Sarah wants to head home and curl up in the safety of her bed with one of her favorite books. She swallows again, briefly gathering her courage before she looks Kaylor straight in the eye.

"I believe him," she says, "I want to stay."

Chapter Thirty Nine

DARN

4th day of Tivar
Year 1452

Mr. Lee's House
Husifi

hat a load of crap. Since the first time Darn saw his letter, he knew Mr. Lee was lying to them. Darn wasn't born here—he has a mother and a father back home on Earth. He's not a sorcerer, and he's not an Incarnate either. He's never been able to do anything special, anything out of the ordinary. Sure, maybe the others are from here—Anna, Kaylor, Sarah, Tyler, maybe even Alex—but not Darn. Darn doesn't belong here, he belongs at home, and he intends to get back there as soon as he can. He's going to open his mouth and tell Mr. Lee all of this when Kaylor interrupts him.

"Do you mind if we talk alone for a minute?" she asks, grabbing Anna's right hand and Sarah's left.

Mr. Lee nods, and motions to one of the doors. The girls disappear through it. Darn bets she can't stand to be in the room with Mr. Lee anymore, and he doesn't blame her. He turns to Alex, intending to ask his friend if he actually believes any of this hogwash. But Alex looks like he's going to be sick.

Thinking that maybe they should get out of there too, get away from Mr. Lee, maybe go outside and get some fresh air, Darn tugs on Alex's arm and shoots Mr. Lee another glare. The man still looks infuriatingly calm. Darn resists the urge to stick out his tongue, instead turning back to Alex.

"Come on," he says, "Let's get out of here for a second." Alex follows him to the stairs. He's a little hesitant to approach Sarah's dragon, but Nellie blinks at them and retreats, snaking her head back up through the stairway and letting them by. She grumbles something out in a series of low hisses and clicks, which Darn assumes is what she sounds like when she talks, then retreats from the house and lumbers off down the street.

It's *hot* upstairs, but still somehow easier to breath. Darn leans against a wall. Alex crosses his legs and drops down to sit on the floor. Darn slides down the wall until he's sitting, too.

"So that was a load of crap," he says.

Alex stares off into the middle distance, clearly deep in thought.

"What's on your mind?"

"It wasn't a load of crap," he murmurs. He doesn't stutter.

"Well, why not?"

"Because...b-because it makes sense." And that's when Darn notices how bright Alex's eyes are, bright with tears that are starting to collect in the corners, "B-because it

313

means I'm not a freak."

Chapter Forty

ALEX

4th day of Tivar
Year 1452

Mr. Lee's House
Husifi

Darn just stares at him, mouth open, and suddenly Alex doesn't want to have secrets anymore. So he tells him. He tells him everything: how he took his baby sister, Cassandra, to the park one day. About the ghost he saw, a haunting image of a woman in a tattered silk dress, how he couldn't tear his eyes away even when his sister started screaming. How he didn't even hear—couldn't even recognize her screams for what they were until it was too late, she was gone. How he chased the car down the street, yelling at the top of his lungs, but he was still too late to save her. How she floated in through his window a few days later to tell Alex that she loved him then and always would, even though he wouldn't get to see her again for a long, long time.

He tells Darn about his father who loves him and his older sister who believed him (for a while, anyway) and why his mother finally got fed up and left. He tells him why and how Alex shut out the ghosts, stopped seeing them altogether through sheer force of will, how hard Alex tried to just be *normal*. And finally, even though Darn already knows, he tells him why he found Alex in the bushes under his father's apartment that night so long ago. How Alex thought he'd lost everything, and how the only thing he'd wanted in that moment was to end it and be with his dead little sister. And he cries. Tears stream down his face and it's embarrassing and he can't help it, but Darn shifts over and sits next to him and he buries his face in his friend's shoulder, and it's been years since Alex felt better or more at peace than he does in this moment right now.

Chapter Forty One

TYLER

4th day of Tivar
Year 1452

Mr. Lee's House
Husifi

He's numb. His thoughts swim in sluggish circles through all this new information, all these overwhelming feelings. His parents. Mr. Lee. The Incarnates. He has to come up with a plan of action, but he can't until he's processed everything he's just learned. So he sits on the bench and he stares at the ground. Almost absently, he lifts his hand up and curls his fingers. A tiny flame jumps to life just above his palm.

When he first saw Mr. Lee, just minutes ago, it felt like he'd taken a bullet to the chest. All the breath went out of him. And now it's coming back. He can't be friends with Mr. Lee—he can't trust him, never again. But it's going to be hard to remember that. Mr. Lee puts a hand on his shoulder, in the same comforting way he always used to before he left.

"Tyler—your father is dead. The Prince killed him, a long time ago." And isn't that just fantastic? An icy claw of fear and a shadow of grief tumble in with the chaos in his mind. He never knew his father, and now whatever chance there might have been is gone. The flame atop his palm flickers. "But I have reason to believe that your mother is still alive. There's a prison—a cave system in the Nedlim mountains that's heavily guarded, where Shirot keeps the sorcerers he thinks are dangerous but doesn't want to kill. Tyler—your mother is Duchess Jia Jisund of Normath. As her firstborn child, you are her rightful heir."

So Tyler's literally nobility. He wonders what those bullies would think of him now. Actually, they probably wouldn't care. They'd probably call him crazy. But they don't matter now.

"What was my father's name?" He wants to know more than that—so much more—but he has to start somewhere.

"Licolm. Licolm Jisund. He was Licolm Ariet before he married your mother."

Tyler whispers the name, feeling it roll across his tongue and past his lips. *Licolm Jisund.* And then his mother's: *Jia Jisund.* He swallows. His own name—his *real* name—isn't Tyler Martin.

"What is it?" he clears his throat, "What's my name?"

Mr. Lee lets out a soft sigh, "Jameol. Your name was Jameol Jisund."

Tears start to prick at the corners of Tyler's eyes. *I have a family. I have a real, actual family and my mother—she could still be alive.*

So that's what he's going to do. He can't go back. He'll help with this rebellion, make this place safe for his people again, have his revenge on the Prince who killed his father and stole his family and his life away from him—

> *Haste me to know't, that I, with wings as swift*
> *As meditation or the thoughts of love,*
> *May sweep to my revenge*

—and he'll find his mother and rebuild it. He's going to kill the Prince, the King too, and Mr. Lee was right: he can't do it alone.

ACKNOWLEDGMENTS

I started writing The Triplets when I was sixteen years old. The characters came before Sarenia: Sarah, Anna, and Kaylor first, then Tyler, then Darn and Alex. They were each based on a fragment of my own personality, and built on from there. Sarenia and the world around it was created just for them to run around in and wreak havoc on. It took years, lots of hard work, and the support of many amazing people to turn this book from the errant pipe-dream of a sixteen-year-old kid into something actually worth reading.

First, I'd like to thank my parents, for teaching me to read and write, encouraging me to pursue my passions, supporting me whenever I fell short, and trying to proofread drafts while I kept nit-picking and changing things. Also my extended family, particularly my Grandpa Al and my Aunt Jenny, for believing in me no matter what. And my cat, Onyx, for keeping me company and inspiring the personality of his fictional counterpart (Tiffany).

I'd also like to thank my teachers, particularly Mrs. Parson, Mrs. Jozdani, and Mr. Watson, for being incredible, encouraging mentors and pushing me to make my writing the best it can be. And my classmates, though I don't remember most of your names: without any of your nerve-wracking criticism, I wouldn't have improved nearly as much.

And last but not least, because friendships are such an important part of this story, I'd like to thank: Maia, who encouraged me from the very beginning to the very end; Shauna, who helped edit several of the first chapters, and provided some valuable advice; McKenna, who planted the seeds for some very interesting side plots; Katie, for all those wonderful book recommendations; Elli, who published her own book with her friends (it's called Rogue and it's by Tayllor Bailey, Savannah Gagnon, and Elizabeth Wallace, you should read it), and proved to me that it could be done; Beth, for encouraging my insane sense of humor by letting me help her dig through piles of bird guts; Tyler Berry, who is nothing like Tyler Martin; Adam, who said he wouldn't read the book unless I included a map (there are two, I hope you're happy); Harley, who probably isn't going to read the book even with the maps; Greg, to whom I give express permission to find another writer to finish the sequels in the unlikely event that I die before I'm done; and TJ, Melissa, Gabriella, Velma, Katie A, and Stephanie, just because they're such amazing friends and wonderful people.

I couldn't have done it without you.

APPENDIX

CAST OF CHARACTERS

The Incarnates

Tyler Martin (aka Jamoel Jisund)—seventeen-year-old boy who was
    dragged into Sarenia by Mr. Lee. A Flamestarter.
Alex Scott (aka Zaryc Wredsa)—seventeen-year-old boy who was
    dragged into Sarenia by Mr. Lee. A Ghostspeaker.
Darn (Max) Harrison (aka Darion Ariet)—seventeen-year-old boy
    who was dragged into Sarenia by Mr. Lee. A Lifebringer.
Sarah Miller (aka Ennia Auna)—seventeen-year-old girl who was
    dragged into Sarenia by Vupcin a year ago. One of the missing
    girls. A Speaker.
Kaylor Williams (aka Tersa Runret)—seventeen-year-old girl who was
    dragged into Sarenia by Vupcin a year ago. One of the missing
    girls. A Shieldmaker.
Anna Thomas (aka Conrina Banir)—seventeen-year-old girl who was
    dragged into Sarenia by Vupcin a year ago. One of the missing
    girls. A Stormbringer.

Valliseg Court

King Shirot Tybold—the current King of Sarenia. Imprisoned
    sorcerers, attacked the Gaentuki, has dubious claims to power.
Prince Casteor Tybold—the current Prince of Sarenia. Kaylor's boss.
Sir Martic—Kaylor's superior. Member of the King's Guard who
    mentors new recruits for up to two years after their enlistment.
Sir Redbrak—Kaylor's friend: was knighted at the same time as she
    was.
Lady Faria—One of the first Sarenian people Kaylor met: Kaylor
    was mistaken for her at the tournament. Was knighted at the
    same time as Kaylor.
Sir Vonor—a friend of Kaylor's.
Ratha—Kaylor's assigned pegasus.

Colf's Rebels

Colf Ariet—the leader of the rebels. A Powersenser.
Mr. Lee—found Tyler wandering the streets when he was three and later gave him the set of Shakespeare books. Was once Tyler's only friend. Sent a letter to each of the six Incarnates; might be an Incarnate himself. An exceptionally powerful Vanisher.
Juanna Ariet—Colf's daughter. A Speaker.
Cremon—Vupcin's younger brother. A Cursemaker.
Vupcin—Cremon's older brother. A Vanisher.

The *Annihilator*'s Crew

Yorren—the first mate, assisted in Anna's mutiny.
Wrom—a refugee turned crew member. A Cursemaker.
Hisef—a refugee turned crew member. An Earthmover.
Choffson—the helmsman, assisted in Anna's mutiny.
Zer—a 10-year-old refugee turned crew member. A Healer.
Patrick—one of Anna's most trusted companions. Once was a stowaway, assisted in Anna's mutiny. An Illusionist.

Gaentuki of Husifi

Nellie—a dragon who took Sarah in. A diplomat trying to negotiate with the wild dragons in the North.
Jash—a bartender at the *Four-Eyed Griffin*. Sarah's friend.
Ellata—the owner of a paint shop. Juanna's girlfriend.
Tiffany—a stray cat who has adopted Sarah.

The Chatty Sphinx

Keripen—the innkeeper at the *Chatty Sphinx*. Helped Kaylor when she first showed up in Sarenia.
Agred—Keripen's nephew who helps him run the inn.

Other People

Gretta Thomas—Anna's mother: left Anna shortly after she turned seven. A Cursemaker.

Captain Darkin—Keripen's friend: helps Kaylor and Tyler. Captain of the *Zephyr*, a Thethrian trade ship. A Powersenser.

Characters from Earth

Evan Thomas—Anna's father.

Rick Andrews—a bully who goes to Tyler's school.

Brian Johnson—Tyler's foster father.

Emily Johnson—Tyler's foster mother.

Lilly Scott—Alex's older sister.

Cassandra Scott (Sandra)—Alex's younger sister. She was kidnapped while Alex was supposed to be watching her.

Trish Harrison—Darn's cousin.

Sarenian Magic and Gods

Cursemaker

Powers: Can curse or bless objects or people.

God: Orsoastath, goddess of justice

Oracle

Powers: Can see versions of future events and what actions will lead to them, or present events as they take place.

God: Eondronor, god of foresight

Healer

Powers: Can heal physical wounds without any outside help.

God: Adwuldon, god of compassion

Earthmover

Powers: Control of the earth and of plants. Can cause earthquakes, make trees move, etc.

God: Crefolon, god of earth

Flamestarter

Powers: Control of fire, ability to produce fire and walk through fire unharmed.

God: Reygreon, god of fire

Windmaker

Powers: Control of air and the wind.

God: Dhaelgin, god of wind

Watermover

Powers: Control of water.

God: Boasheilia, goddess of water

Stormbringer

Powers: Control of weather. Shares some powers with Windmakers and Watermovers.

God: Larosri, goddess of storms

Shieldmaker

Powers: Can produce shields or strengthen already present ones

God: Sheolida, goddess of defenders

Speaker

Powers: Can speak and understand any and all languages.

God: Gweligen, goddess of languages

Illusionist
   Powers: Can create visual (sometimes auditory) illusions
   God: Osthrosain, goddess of deception
Vanisher
   Powers: Can "vanish" from one place and appear in another.
   Vanishers can "vanish" other people too.
   God: Stoltana, goddess of travel
Ghostspeaker
   Powers: Can speak to ghosts and control the undead.
   God: Theoloden, god of death
Shapeshifter
   Powers: Can change their shape for a limited amount of time.
   God: Enudillian, goddess of change
Mindinvader
   Powers: Can enter people's minds and read them or give them
   visions.
   God: Marcori, god of discovery
Powersenser
   Powers: Can detect the power type and the power strength of the
   sorcerers around them.
   God: Noanotia, goddess of intuition
Lifebringer
   Powers: Can move, reshape, or bring objects to "life".
   God: Lefyrin, god of life

Sarenian Calendar

There are six seasons that each consist of 45-70 days, making 374 days in a Sarenian year. There are 17 festival days, one for each of the Gods, and there are around 22 days between each of these festivals. The turning point for each season is a festival day for one god of the Imperial Six.

Season of Wind (Vern)
Festival of Dhaelgin—22nd day of Vern
Festival of Orsoastath—43rd day of Vern
Festival of Gweligen—68th day of Vern - 1st day of Spring
Season of Growth (Spring)
Festival of Crefolon—21st day of Spring
Festival of Noanotia—47th day of Spring
Festival of Sheolida—65th day of Spring - 1st day of Summer
Season of Sun (Summer)
Festival of Osthrosain—24th day of Summer
Festival of Marcori—42nd day of Summer
Festival of Larosri—67th day of Summer - 1st day of Tivar
Season of Storms (Tivar)
Festival of Boasheilia—22nd day of Tivar
Festival of Theoloden—45th day of Tivar - 1st day of Fall
Season of Loss (Fall)
Festival of Stoltana—23rd day of Fall
Festival of Enudillian—41st day of Fall
Festival of Reygreon—67th day of Fall - 1st day of Winter
Season of Snow (Winter)
Festival of Eondronor—20th day of Winter
Festival of Adwuldon—46th day of Winter
Festival of Lefyrin—62nd day of Winter - 1st day of Vern

MAPS AND PLACES

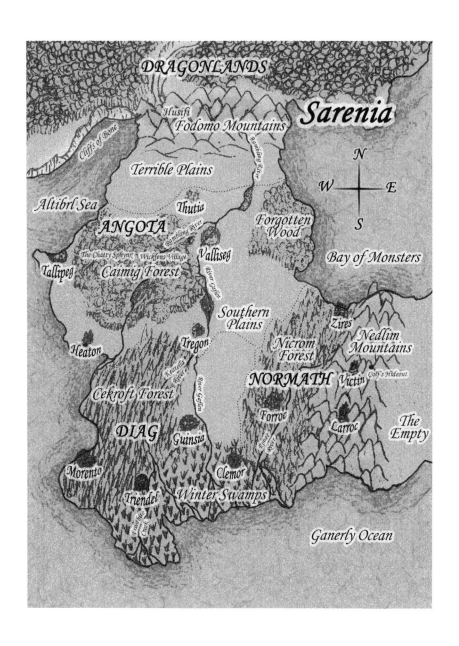

DRAGONLANDS

Sarenia

Husifi

Fodomo Mountains

Cliffs of Bone

Rambling River

Terrible Plains

N

W — E

S

Altibrl Sea

Thutia

ANGOTA

Forgotten Wood

Rambling River

The Chatty Sphynx   Wickfens Village   *Valliseg*

Bay of Monsters

Tallipeg

Caimig Forest

River Gaffen

Heaton

Southern Plains

Tregon

Zires

Nicrom Forest

Nedlim Mountains

Krattella River

River Gaffen

NORMATH

Victin

Colf's Hideout

Cekroft Forest

Forroc

Roora River

DIAG

Guinsia

Larroc

The Empty

Morento

Clemor

Triendel

Winter Swamps

Frawtell Creek

Ganerly Ocean

Angota

The northernmost province of Sarenia: the warmest and most fertile. Made up of dry plains and deciduous forests.

Diag

The southernmost province of Sarenia: the coldest and wettest. Made up of wet plains, swamps, and coniferous forests.

Normath

The easternmost province of Sarenia: the smallest and harshest. Made up of mountains and coniferous forests.

Valliseg

The capital city of Sarenia, where the King and his court live.

Tallipeg

Valliseg's "twin city": the main port city in Angota. Most of Sarenia's trade with other countries goes through this city.

Caimig Forest

A very dangerous forest in Angota, filled with fairies, Gaeukos, vampires, and manticores.

Cliffs of Bone

A section of cliffs on the southern coast of the Dragonlands, so named because of their bone-white color. A notable roost for sirens.

Altibrl Sea

A sea between Tallipeg, the Dragonlands, and Husifi with unusually brilliant blue water.

Derkor Canyon

A canyon in the Fodomo Mountains: Husifi is built along the bottom and sides of this canyon.

Husifi

An enormous city that runs almost the entire length of Derkor Canyon. Home of the Gaentuki.

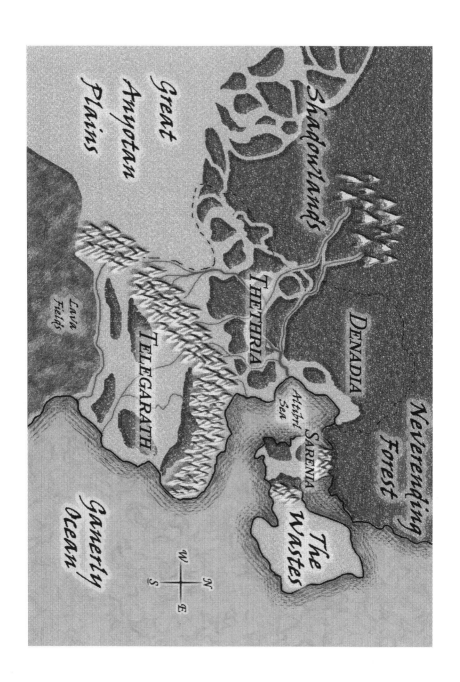

ABOUT THE AUTHOR

Nicole M Davis was born in Sunnyvale, California (one letter away from the vampire capital of the world), but she grew up in Boulder County in Colorado. She has a bachelor's degree in Zoology with a minor in Creative Writing, which she got in the beautiful town of Laramie, Wyoming. At the moment she's back in Boulder County living with her family and a small army of scaly pets. She probably started writing when she was about five years old, and hasn't been able to stop since.

Visit her website:
nicole-m-davis.com

Made in the USA
Monee, IL
22 February 2020

22152407R00201